THE TRIAL OF GWEN FOLEY

JANE O'CONNOR

Print ISBN 978-1-913942-98-4

For Billy and Toby

'There are, in every age, new errors to be rectified, and new prejudices to be opposed.'
— **Samuel Johnson, 1751**

LICHFIELD, STAFFORDSHIRE

1723

1

EARTH

The gallows went up in Shorbutts Lane late Sunday afternoon and cast a dark shadow over the road into town.

Nobody wanted poor Joanna to hang. He had been a brutal man, her William. We had all borne witness to her hobbling up Rotten Row, a scarf hiding her swollen face. Who among us could blame her for rubbing arsenic on her husband's eyelids as he slept, until one morning he never awoke? Where she got the toxin, I don't know, but Dr Crouch said it was the cause of death because of the stripes on William's fingernails and the pallor of his skin. So it was deemed murder, with his wife and bedfellow the only suspect.

Matthew had gone to speak to Joanna hoping he could find a way to exonerate her, but she had confessed all to him even as her children plucked at her clothes and beseeched her to stop. He'd had no choice then but to take her to the Guildhall Gaol to wait for the assizes court to make its way down from the north and decide on her punishment.

No more than three or four minutes did Joanna's trial last in the end, despite Matthew urging the judge to consider the mitigations put forward by her sister Agnes about William's cruelty, and to take into account the dire situation of her children. The judge wasn't disposed to listen – it didn't help matters that Matthew was only the acting magistrate in his brother's absence, nor that it was coming towards luncheon.

'He put his stomach before compassion.' That's how Amber put it in her usual direct manner as it seemed to us the judge passed his dreadful sentence in haste, clearly aggrieved that he'd had his feeding delayed.

'Murder is murder,' he'd said, interrupting Matthew's carefully prepared speech in Joanna's defence and striking his anvil on the splintered table that was as old as the Guildhall itself.

'The woman has confessed, therefore she will hang and let her demise be of instruction to any other disobedient wives in this city who take it into their heads to dispatch of a displeasing husband. That is my final decision in adherence with the laws of this country and the dictates of the King.'

The judge had pulled his tricorn on over his wig and bustled out the door before the booing of the gathered crowd could reach him, and that was the end of the matter. It had broken my heart to see Agnes run after him down the street sobbing and begging him to reconsider his verdict, but it had done no good and the judge had threatened to have her swinging beside her sister if she didn't desist from her petition.

Matthew had presided over Joanna's execution, the first under his jurisdiction, the following Monday. My husband had no stomach for such affairs, gentle soul that he was, and spent the nights in between sleepless with angst over her fate.

It was at least fortunate, if it can be called such, that the nature of Matthew's impediment meant that he needed an arm to steady him as well as his stick so I had reason to accompany him on his official duties and it gave him courage and strength to have me by his side. That bitter Monday morning, though, I would have paid the devil himself to stay safe at home with Liberty and close my mind altogether to the miserable happenings on Shorbutts Hill. It was with the greatest reluctance that I put aside my embroidered dresses and red cloak and clothed myself in black, my auburn hair hidden under a cowl. Matthew wore his full regimental uniform and looked almost his old self tidied up so, despite his wooden leg.

I held Matthew's elbow firmly as we made our way up to the raised area of the gallows, and felt him tremble as the guards led the pitiful woman from the cart to the wooden platform where the single noose awaited her.

Joanna tripped and stumbled along the muddy path, her legs barely able to carry her and I had to avert my eyes for fear I would cry out at the cruelty of her treatment and cause an embarrassment to Matthew in front of the city's dignitaries.

Joanna had been in the gaol for weeks awaiting trial and her clothes and face were streaked with grime. Amber and I had gone to see her several times, bringing food and reading matter as we always do for those poor souls who find themselves in such a situation. Joanna had tried hard to keep her spirits up for the sake of her children, although she knew the fate that awaited her, as did we all.

'Perhaps there will be a pardon for me from King George?' she had said on our final visit the day before her hanging. She grabbed on to my wrist as I made to leave, her red-rimmed eyes beseeching me to agree. I had nodded, sharing her hope of a last-minute reprieve, but not truly believing such a miracle to be possible.

As Joanna climbed up the steps of the scaffold I found myself staring out at St John's, the road that led to London, willing a lone horseman to appear on the horizon wearing the colours of the Crown and clutching a scroll with the King's seal.

What jubilation there would have been had that occurred! But alas no such pardon came and Joanna's life drew to its unnatural end.

Matthew had barely voice enough to read the indictment. He had to state the judge's verdict twice. A clutch of starlings rose noisily from the copse behind us during his first attempt, as if the birds themselves were protesting at the injustice of Joanna's fate.

His accountabilities finally completed, Matthew bowed his head and the Reverend Mr Brown moved forward to preach to the condemned woman from his prayer book. He stood close and spoke directly into her ear. She inclined towards him and it seemed that his holy words were a comfort to her, if only for a brief amount of time. The hangman stepped up behind them onto the gallows before any one of us was ready for it and Joanna gasped at the sight of him.

The vicar reached out then and took a hold of Joanna's hand and continued with his ministrations until Sheriff Michael Johnson lumbered up from his seat at the side of the gallows and with a panicked wave of his arm shouted, 'No contact with the deceased permitted.'

Samuel, his son, who was sitting next to him, lowered his face in shame, and I felt it a pity that the sheriff had required the company of the boy on such an occasion.

The Reverend Mr Brown dropped Joanna's hand and she let out a cry as the last human contact she was to have on this earth was taken from her. The vicar glanced towards the spires of the great cathedral which overlooked the city and shook his head as if in disappointment that God himself would allow such a thing. I wondered if he had lost his faith somewhere on life's journey as I had myself.

Joanna didn't speak a word as the noose was placed around her neck. Her gaze was fixed on the front row of the crowd where stood her three oldest children along with her sister Agnes. The biggest boy and girl were in much distress as the trapdoor was released and Joanna's head jerked upwards. But Joanna's other boy who couldn't have been more than eleven, was silent and still, frozen in fury as he watched his mother choke and die. I was flooded with pity but I knew the trouble it would cause Matthew if I was to interfere in the proceedings or speak my mind aloud. It cost me much effort, though, to bite my tongue and keep the expression on my face a passive one.

Most in the crowd had the decency to lower their heads as young Samuel Johnson had done, but a few empty-headed lobcocks jeered and shouted 'Witch', throwing turnips and clods of earth as Joanna jerked and swung. They should have been ashamed of themselves adding cruel acts and wicked slurs to the indignities already wrought upon her.

Matthew stood firm until the deed was done and the townsfolk began to make their way back up the hill in a melancholy silence broken only by the occasional mutter of 'Shame', and 'God's mercy on her'. When the last of them had turned the corner Matthew bent over, leaning hard on his stick and retched onto the stony ground.

'Take me home, Hettie,' he whispered as I helped him right himself.

Sheriff Johnson was overseeing the loading of Joanna's body onto the gravedigger's cart, Samuel standing awkwardly beside him, so we slipped away to the other side of the common ground where we were grateful to see George waiting for us with a carriage, ready to take us home.

I was helping Matthew up onto the bench when I sensed someone standing behind me. I turned and saw that it was Agnes, the hanged woman's sister, fixing me with a stare so piercing that I was rooted to the spot. 'My dear, how sorry we are...' I began as I reached out my hand to take hers.

'Don't touch me,' she said, snatching her arm away.

I was confused, quite taken aback by the scornful cast of her eyes.

'You should be ashamed of yourself, Hester Albright. You pride yourself on being a good woman of this city, always ready to help those in need, but for my defenceless sister you did nothing. You stood there with your lips pressed tightly together and a pious expression on your face and you watched my Joanna hang from a gibbet and for what? For the crime of defending herself and her children against her brute of a husband.'

I put my hand to my heart, stunned at her anger towards me. 'Agnes, please,' I beseeched her. 'I share your distress and condemnation of what has taken place, but you must understand there was nothing I could have done to prevent Joanna's death.'

She shook her head and, as she pushed her dark hair from her face, I saw how much she looked like her sister. 'You have his ear,' Agnes pointed up at Matthew who was watching the scene aghast from his seat in the open carriage. 'You could have acted or spoken in Joanna's favour. You could have tried; you could have at least added your voice to mine. I'd wager you would have spoken up if it had been your sister.'

I flinched at that, but stopped my mind turning towards Nell. I thought instead of how Agnes had had the courage to beg the judge to reconsider his verdict on Joanna and of my own silence both at the trial and today.

'Let me try to explain,' I began, wanting to make Agnes understand how it had been impossible for me to help because of my loyalty to Matthew and my deep fear of bringing difficulties to our own family, but she was in no humour to listen.

'Shame on you,' she said, and my soul withered at her words.

She spat on the ground at my feet and walked back to where Joanna's children were huddled together waiting for her.

I climbed into the carriage and sat flushed and speechless on the bench next to Matthew as George urged the mare up the hill.

'My dear,' he said, reaching for my hand. 'Don't let Agnes upset you. She is not in her right mind; who would be at such a time?'

I stared ahead as the familiar buildings of the city rose up before us and the disgrace of Agnes's accusations seeped into my bones. 'Perhaps she is right,' I said slowly as the great cathedral came into view. 'How can I call myself a good woman and stay quiet in the face of such injustice as we witnessed today?'

Matthew furrowed his brow. 'Because you know as well as I that women who forget their place and speak out against the customs and laws of the land bring trouble to themselves and their families. We want no trouble brought to our door. Think of our own daughters.'

'I am thinking of them,' I said anxiously, pulling my shawl tighter against the chill morning air. 'What if one day Esme or Liberty or even Amber found themselves in a deathly predicament and there was no one to protect them or act on their behalf?'

'I understand that you are upset by what we had to witness today. God knows we both are,' Matthew said, lowering his head at the memory. 'But I have been burdened with an official role in this city and, until Philip returns, I am duty-bound to fulfil it.'

'I feel ashamed, Matthew,' I said in a hollow voice. 'I can't do that again.'

'Then next time – as unfortunately there will undoubtedly be a next time – you will stay safely at home with Liberty,' Matthew said kindly, as George rode us past the market square and up into Dam Street. 'I am sorry if it was too much to ask of you to accompany me today but you know how much I needed you there, my dear, and I thank you for that.'

'No,' I said, realising that he had misunderstood me. 'I mean that I can't stand by and do nothing the next time a woman is punished so unjustly. I must at least try and find a way to prevent such a thing.' My voice wavered as I spoke but I nodded at the conviction I felt.

Matthew looked at me with concern and patted my hand as if I had fallen into a sort of madness. I'm certain he expected me to forget my intention as time moved us on and away from the dreadful spectacle of Joanna's death, but it stayed with me like a tiny burning ember hidden deep inside, fuelled by my dismay and guilt at Agnes's indictment against me.

2

COINS

On my way to market several days later I made a visit to the Johnsons' bookshop on Breadmarket Street to see my friend Sarah, and to return to her some volumes she had lent me. I was not to know it then but an unusual visitor to the shop that day would set in motion events that would change all of our lives forever and ignite the ember of shame inside me into a flame of action.

Michael was out front when I arrived, berating the postboy for being late with his letters. I watched him finish his tirade and storm back up the steps into the shop, cross as ever with the world and everyone in it. His body and features matched his temperament well I always thought, he being a large, gloomy man with a fleshy face and lips, bushy eyebrows and bulging eyes. He rarely smiled and seemed to find all aspects of his bookshop business a burden, even though he had the enviable honour of publishing books as well as selling them. And Michael Johnson seemed to find little satisfaction in his role as Sheriff of Lichfield. I often wondered why he had chosen to take on such a position of responsibility. I could only imagine it fulfilled in him some deeply held desire to be a figure of importance in the city, borne from the hidden complexities of his character.

Sarah was a quiet mouse of a woman with a good heart fortified by her strong faith. She suited Michael well and he was lucky to have her in my opinion. She worried constantly about their oldest boy Samuel, whom she didn't bear until she was forty having almost given up hope of ever becoming a mother. Samuel was fourteen by then and, unlike his younger brother Nathaniel who was a cheerful, even-tempered lad, Sam was beginning to show signs of the melancholic like his father, although it has to be said that he was altogether more genial. Sam's skin was ugly though, blighted with scrofula he was, poor soul.

Sarah and Michael were so perturbed by it that when Sam was small they had taken him to London to receive the Royal Touch from Queen Anne, but despite their high hopes the condition had remained much the same so far as I could tell. It was a shame as his affliction made Samuel reluctant to be in company and he tended towards hiding at home with his books rather than skylarking around the town with Nathaniel and the other boys his age.

'Good morning, Sarah,' I said as I came through the door, setting the bell tinkling. 'How goes you this fine day?'

Sarah gave me a watery smile, but I could see her eyes were troubled. 'I am well enough, Hester, although I have not been able to find solace since Joanna Baker met her end. Those poor children, orphans all. How many did she have, six was it?'

I reached over the counter and took her thin hand in mine, rubbing it gently. 'She leaves seven children,' I said quietly. 'Amber is collecting money and clothes for them as she makes her rounds today, I will ask her to visit your shop so you can add to the offerings.'

Sarah nodded. 'And we must pray for them,' she said.

'Yes, that too,' I agreed mildly, although to my mind Amber's plan had more use to it. 'How is Samuel?' I asked, laying aside the talk of Joanna's children that saddened us both. 'I saw him at Shorbutts Lane at the hanging.'

'He was most upset by having to accompany his father. Michael insisted though, said the sooner youngsters face up to the harsh realities of breaking the law the better. Sam has been suffering again with his skin since then, God relieve him. He has been itching at it at night and it is inflamed and causing him grief.' Sarah creased her brow in angst.

'Have you tried using a poultice of figwort?' I asked her, pulling a package of dark green leaves from my basket. 'I picked this from the thicket by Minster Pool. I read about its uses in here.' I placed a book of herbal remedies on the counter along with the other volumes I was returning.

Sarah took the figwort from me gingerly and put it to her nose. 'It smells foetid,' she said, recoiling in disgust.

'Take no heed of the odour of it, it is said to be balm to enraged skin. Amber says it will do your Samuel no harm if it is not effective.'

Sarah's face brightened. 'Thank you, I will try it on him this evening. He is reading now and will not be disturbed.' She leant forward and told me quietly, 'If he would spend more time outside in the fresh air and the sunshine I think it would do his skin more good than sitting in reading always just like his father, but he takes no heed of my advice. Young people of today lack the obedience that we adhered to, don't you think?'

I nodded in sympathy, although I couldn't in truth agree with her, not after the mighty defiance my sister and I had showed our father when we were of a similar age. 'They find their own way. You couldn't be a more dedicated mother,' I told her.

Sarah wiped her nose with a handkerchief and gave me a

small smile of gratitude. 'I do my best with the grace of God. And how fare your children, Hester? Is little Liberty being good? Have you heard from John? And how is Esme? She must be nearing her time, is she not?'

My stomach clenched as she asked after Esme, but I made efforts to answer her enquiries in the same pleasant spirit in which they were asked. 'Liberty seems to be settling into Dame Oliver's school and we are thankful for that. We received a letter from our John only yesterday saying he and Ruth and the little ones have taken a cottage next to her father's farm. The Welsh air suits him he says and he feels at home there, but he wishes it would stop raining!'

'The rain is God's blessing,' said Sarah.

'I do believe it is easier to be of that opinion from inside a warm bookshop in Lichfield than it is on the side of a Welsh mountain,' I said playfully, and Sarah let out a rare, surprisingly loud laugh that she hid behind her hand.

Michael's grey curly head appeared from the top of the cellar steps at the sound. 'Hush up,' he admonished us. 'I must have silence as I take stock of the newly arrived books.'

'And Esme?' Sarah whispered as her husband's head disappeared again from view.

'Esme fares well,' I said nodding. 'As well as can be expected,' I conceded with a worried sigh. 'She is such a slight girl, though, her belly sticks out from her like a pumpkin and her back bothers her greatly with the weight. I hope constantly that she has a safe delivery. She seems too young still to become a mother herself.'

'You must have been younger than Esme when you had Amber,' Sarah reminded me, 'and all was well.'

I went to speak but decided against it, not wanting to lie to my friend.

'You will be there with her when her time for childbed

comes, along with the midwife and Amber too I'm sure, if she can be spared by Dr Crouch. I will pray for dear Esme and her child.'

I thanked her and pulled my red cloak around me. 'I nearly forgot,' I said, pulling a couple of coins from my dress pocket, 'could I have a small bottle of ink and a few sheets of writing paper? There is a letter I have been meaning to write for some time.'

Sarah nodded and placed the items in my basket. 'You will be writing back to your John, no doubt,' she said. 'Do remember me to him and pass on my best wishes.'

As I turned to leave, the door from the street burst open causing the bell to jangle loudly. A short, handsomely dressed gentlewoman strode confidently into the shop and up to the counter. 'Do you have any books on science?' she asked as she pulled off her green silk gloves, the bell still tingling behind her.

Sarah stared at the woman in bewilderment and couldn't find her voice so I stepped forward to help. 'What in particular interests you, my lady?' I asked, taking in her rich velvet jacket and the large purse of coins which hung at her belt.

She tutted in irritation. 'I want books about science. Did you not hear me?' She had such an abrupt, unpleasant manner, so unlike most visitors to the bookshop who tended to be meek, polite types, that I had to subdue a smile.

'My daughter and I, we hear my husband and his associates talking about Copernicus and the planets and Isaac Newton and these laws that govern the natural world and we are fascinated,' she said emphasising the final word as her eyes wandered over the shelves. 'I'm tired of superstition and balderdash about witchcraft, magic and the like. There is dangerous nonsense being talked in our village even now about a woman they call the White and claim is a witch. I will tolerate none of it and have warned my household that if I hear anyone spreading such rumours they will be dismissed. I want to learn the truth behind the mysteries of the world and the planets and so does my daughter. My husband won't tell us what he knows: he says it's not for women to concern themselves with such things.'

She looked at me imploringly and I could see sorrow in her sharp brown eyes. 'But we simply must know. Claudia is deeply curious and she has a quick mind, far quicker than her brothers. She desperately wants a telescope but I have no idea how to procure such an item, so I promised her I would get books instead so we can teach ourselves. I cannot bear for her to spend her life sewing and simpering, unaware of the scientific elucidations and revelations which are becoming common knowledge to the educated men in our circles.'

She reached into her purse and drew out a pair of delicate silver-framed spectacles which she placed over her eyes, magnifying them greatly. She clipped the centre piece tightly onto her nose to keep them in place and pursed her lips in anticipation of our response.

'Well, you have come to the right place,' I said, admiring her courage to go against her husband's wishes. 'Michael Johnson has the finest bookshop in Staffordshire.' I wanted to ask her more about the rumblings about witchcraft in her village, but missed my chance as Michael arrived noiselessly by the lady's side and she turned to give him her attention.

'Can I be of service, madam?' he asked with a bow, drawn up from his stocktaking once again, this time by the amount of coin he sensed this illustrious customer intended to spend in his shop.

I gave Sarah a friendly wink and made my way out and down the stairs into the street where quite a commotion was being caused by the lady's grand carriage and four blocking the way into the marketplace.

I glanced up at the shop and noticed Samuel standing at one

of the top windows gazing out over the chaotic scene with interest, but he withdrew back into the room, out of sight when he saw me waving at him.

~

I returned to our little black and white house at the end of the row on Dam Street around noon and found Matthew huddled over his books by the unlit hearth in the parlour.

'Do you not feel the chill, my love?' I asked him as I placed kindling and coal in the grate. 'You should have asked Sal to set the fire for you. That's what we pay her for and she's more than willing if you instruct her clearly.'

'Hettie,' he said as if surprised to see me there in our own house. 'I was quite lost in Homer. I am teaching Sir Dalston's sons this afternoon and thought to try and introduce some appreciation of poetic language into their lesson.'

I smiled at his optimism and tied my apron around me. I pulled a bundle of lavender stems wrapped in a linen cloth out of my bag and held them to my nose, before pulling off the flower heads and dropping them into an earthenware bowl.

'You make lavender essence when someone is hurt,' Matthew said, concerned. 'Are you thinking of Esme?'

I began working the pestle and nodded. 'She may need it after childbed. To help with the healing.'

Matthew watched me as I worked. 'You are a caring woman,' he said. 'That is your essence. You look after us all.'

I nodded, although I had been perturbed by what the lady in the bookshop had said about witchcraft rumours starting up in her village. I was about to tell Matthew once again of my desire to act against injustices meted out to women in the locality but was interrupted before I began by the front door scraping open across the flagstones. A clear fresh light entered the room, along with some cheery street noise as Amber strode across the parlour and grabbed a piece of bread from the table.

Matthew's face lit up and I could see that his spirits were raised by the presence of our oldest daughter, as people's often were.

'I am in need of this,' she said, taking a bite of the crust. 'I haven't had a morsel to eat since dawn. I've sewn up a grog-soused fellow who thought it a lark to jump from the clock tower, treated a farrier's burnt hands and made a poultice for Mrs Evesham's carbuncles and it's not yet noon.'

Matthew and I looked at her fondly, familiar as we were with the enthusiasm and dedication Amber had for her work as apprentice to the city's surgeon.

'By the way, Liberty is outside playing with a mange-ridden cat,' she said, reaching for the jam. 'I think she means to bring it inside and make a pet of it.'

Matthew struggled to his feet and grabbed his stick. 'No more stray animals in this house!' he said. 'That ferret she kept hidden in her room ate through one of my best boots before it disappeared up the chimney. Help me up the step, please, Amber.'

For all his bluster about no more creatures in the house, it was a surprise to neither me nor Amber that Matthew, with his soft heart and love for Liberty, returned several minutes later holding the grubby white cat to his chest. Liberty grinned triumphantly behind his back holding her pinafore dress out at the sides with glee.

'It's cut its paw, Hettie,' Matthew said, stroking its ears. 'Can you help the poor thing?'

I took the animal off him and held it up to the light of the window. It squirmed when I touched the soft pad of its feet and it was bleeding between two of its claws.

I passed it to Amber and she put down her bread and

examined it carefully. Liberty watched the proceedings with solemn concern.

'It'll heal,' she said. 'Give it a clean with some of that lavender oil you're making.'

The cat patted Amber's nose with its paw and she laughed.

'I think she likes you,' I said, drawing a smile in the air for Liberty so she would understand.

'We're not keeping it,' repeated Matthew weakly, but I could see his resolve fading as he watched Liberty dance round the table with joy.

It was balm to us to see our youngest daughter happy as she was lonely much of the time and seemed to have no knack for making friends with other children. Matthew and I would have let her have the cat as a pet, but as soon as I had cleaned its paw and it had had a saucer of milk it slipped out the window, and into the freedom of the street. Amber went to look for it but it was nowhere about. She had to take her leave to attend afternoon surgery so could spend no longer searching. Liberty's face fell when she realised the cat wasn't coming back. She cried and cried and I held her close while Matthew retreated upstairs, not being able to bear the sound of her tears.

3

VINEGAR

'She dresses as a man,' whispered a plump tradesman's daughter, rather too fond of finery from the look of her. Her friend replied behind her hand and they both dissolved into giggles as Amber and I walked past them into town the next day.

I paid them no heed, so used to that manner of comment had I become. I loved Amber dearly but I could see that she was a curious sort of woman, especially to those who didn't know her. She was twenty-seven then, never been interested in getting wed and her dark hair was cropped short round her ears like a boy. She wore brown serge trousers and a leather doublet and boots and paid not the least attention to her appearance or to frivolities such as the lace and ribbons that seemed to fascinate so many of the young women in the town. She had the handsomest face though, the colour of honey with twinkling brown eyes and appled cheeks. There had been many a suitor over the years who came to our door, especially when she still wore frocks, but since she'd been taken on as the surgeon's apprentice when she was fifteen she had eschewed all signs of femininity in favour of practicality. I could see she felt all the better for it and that it was her truest way of being herself so I was happy for her.

Those who knew Amber regarded her in the highest of terms both for her skill in her profession, and for her wise counsel and courage to stand up for those who were weaker than her or in need. Those who didn't know her saw nothing more than a slightly built woman in a doublet and britches and found her an oddity, but their opinions didn't bother Amber so they didn't bother me.

We were on our way to visit Esme and George at their rooms above the inn at the carriage stop on St Michael Road. My son-in-law George was a groom and carriage driver. He spent his days rubbing down the horses which came flying in pulling coaches full of mail or important folk from London, before they carried on their journey up to Chester or back the way they came. We spotted George as we made our way through the arched gate into the yard where he was holding the reins of a large skittish grey who needed calming down before she could rest.

'Stand back from her, she is keyed up,' he warned as we approached. 'I tell the coachmen not to whip them so hard. "Faster," they urge but the horses can only go so quickly. Her heart's beating like a bird's.' He stroked her neck. 'She's out again in an hour,' he said shaking his head.

'You do a fine job here, George,' said Amber, filling a sack with water from the butt and bringing it over for the grey. 'You can only do what you can.'

'That's true enough,' said George, taking off his cap and greeting us properly. 'Esme is lying down indoors,' he said, running a hand through his sandy hair. 'She will be pleased to see you. She is cross because she is bored. You know how much she hates to be idle.' He smiled at us showing the gaps where his front teeth should have been had they not been kicked out by a grumpy mare when he was a lad. 'It won't be long now, will it?' he asked apprehensively.

'No not long. You will have your bonny babe in your arms soon enough,' I said brightly, although my stomach tightened at the prospect of Esme's labouring.

We made our way through the alley between the stables and the coach house and up the outside stairs at the back of the building. Esme and George had two rooms on the top floor and Esme had done much to make them homely and warm. She was struggling to crouch over her pot when we came in after a gentle rap on the door, and Amber stepped forward to hold her under the arms so she could pull up her shift and balance without falling sideways due to her size and her swollen ankles.

'Only have I got back on my bed than I need to go again,' Esme complained, blowing her brown curls out of her eyes with an upwards puff. 'I woke poor George a half dozen times last night to assist me.'

'It'll be good practice for him for when the babe arrives,' I told her as I helped Amber get her back on the bed.

I placed my basket next to the hearth and began unpacking the contents.

Esme watched me in amusement. 'What have you brought me, Mama? All but the scullery pan it seems,' she said with a giggle. She strained to see over the other side of the room as I placed two loaves of bread, a chyne of mutton, a Cheshire cheese, a turnip, several wraps of herbs and a bottle of vinegar on the rough wooden table.

'A little food for you, my sweet, and vinegar to wash the boards and bedstead to keep the bugs away.' I placed next to them a large book and two smaller volumes.

'And some poetry for you to read to keep your spirits high – Marvel and Milton,' I told her, holding them up for her to see, 'and Culpeper's directory for midwives so you will know what to expect when your childbed begins.'

Amber picked the bigger book up and leafed through it shaking her head. 'No, Mama, this is not for Esme,' she said with a frown. 'Sometimes it is better not to know too much.' She turned to Esme whose mouth had opened in alarm. 'We will be here and guide you through it.' Amber told her. 'All you need to do is stay calm, little sister. I want you to learn a handful of these poems off by heart and when the pains start, you recite them to Mama, word perfect, and all will be well.'

Amber handed the Culpeper back to me and I placed it in the basket, reluctant even though I could see the good sense in her point of view.

'I know a poem already, well a song, I heard some children in the yard singing it yesterday. It made me think of you,' Esme said to me mischievously as she hoisted herself up on her elbows and began to sing:

'A ring on her finger
A bonnet of straw
The kindest old woman
That ever you saw.'

I laughed at that and so did Amber. 'She wears a straw bonnet in the summer that's for certain and she's kind, but it's not nice to call her old. A true song for Mama would have to include her red cloak as well; she wears it every time she is out of doors.'

'And sometimes indoors too if there is a chill in the room,' I added.

'I suppose you are quite old, Mama,' Esme said. She peered at me in the faint daylight that came through the small window by the hearth. 'Light a candle and come nearer so I can see you properly.'

I did as she asked and sat on the side of her bed holding the flame as near to my face as I could without feeling the prick of a burn.

Esme moved her fingers over the coarse skin on my face and traced the wrinkles round my eyes. She gently stroked my long copper plait and touched the white streaks that ran through it. 'Yes, you are getting old, but happy old,' she declared.

'I'm only forty-three,' I told her with a laugh. 'And I have the strength for many more years to come.'

'Have things changed much since you were a girl?' asked Esme.

'Much has changed since then,' I said with a nod.

'Like?' asked Amber.

'Like in those days lots of folk still believed in witchcraft and that manner of thing. Especially in the east country, in Suffolk, where I come from. The old ways of thinking died hard there and may thrive still among some older people, those who hold on to their memories and fears. It was women who suffered, those who were outside the ordinary, who didn't want to live like everyone else, or who couldn't, the ones who had no husband or children, those kind.'

Amber swallowed and shifted on the bed next to me, and I wished I hadn't spoken.

'What happened to them?' Esme asked.

I closed my eyes. 'Terrible things that are best left forgotten,' I said. 'And all in the name of a God who I will never bow down to.'

'Ma,' Amber rebuked me. 'You mustn't say that.'

Esme had her hand across her mouth and stared at me wide-eyed. 'Don't you believe in God?' she whispered.

I glanced at Amber and then at the floor, not wanting to answer.

'But you always go to church, every Sunday.' Esme was confused. 'If there is no God who will look after us when we die? Where will we go?' She swivelled her head to see if Amber had the answer. 'You believe don't you, Amber?'

Amber sighed and nodded. 'Yes, Esme, of course I do,' she said dutifully. 'Our heavenly Father.'

Esme relaxed back onto her pillow, her version of the world back in order in her mind. If Amber said it was so, then it was so.

'Don't take heed of me,' I said, getting up. 'My ideas have been skewed by what I've seen and lived through, but it doesn't mean there isn't a God. It's just that I prefer to put my trust in the things I can see and touch and do myself.'

'Maybe God helps you by guiding you in that?' Esme said hopefully.

'Yes, perhaps he does,' I conceded with a squeeze of her hand.

I made Esme a mint and clary sage infusion to keep her water clear and prepared her a platter of bread and cheese to keep by her bed and pick at when she was hungry.

'Don't forget to learn the poems,' Amber said as we were leaving, pointing at the books on her bedstand. 'Off by heart, you hear me?'

Esme nodded through a mouth full of cheese and we waved our goodbyes.

'A gentlewoman came into the Johnson's bookshop yesterday, demanding to know about science,' I told Amber as we were walking home. I knew she would be interested in such an unusual event, although given our conversation at Esme's I decided not to tell her what the lady had said about the woman in her village they called the White.

'It was the most curious thing,' I continued, 'she said she was tired of hearing about the mysterious workings of a divine being and she wanted to know how the world worked from a different perspective. Her husband wouldn't share his knowledge with her, thought it not befitting of a woman, so she wanted to read books to find out herself and share them with her daughter.'

'I wonder what Michael Johnson made of that?' said Amber. 'He seems the old-fashioned type, he likes Sarah to do as she's told, that's clear enough to all who know them. I don't think he'd take kindly if it was his own wife challenging the teachings of the church.'

I nodded. 'That's as maybe but all I can say is that Michael had a gleam of avarice in his eye as I left. Thinking of all the volumes he could sell her, I shouldn't wonder, and the prices he could get from a woman in such desperate need of what they have written inside.'

'The length and the breadth of people's beliefs and it all comes down to money in the end, doesn't it?' Amber said with a shake of her head. 'I admire the lady's sentiments though. Certainly when Dr Crouch and I are removing a limb or a hulk of blackened flesh it is the anatomical learnings we have on the physic that are most useful to us, rather than the teachings of the Bible.'

'You would do best to keep those thoughts to yourself,' I said as we started up Dam Street, although I heartily agreed with Amber's point of view. 'As women it is safer for us to keep our counsel. It is all too easy for us to be made into scapegoats and put ourselves and those we love in danger, so I suppose we must let the learned men work it out amongst themselves.' I was trying to convince myself of this as much as Amber, and I could hear that my argument lacked the strength of true belief.

Amber stopped in the road and mimed locking her mouth with a key which made me laugh despite the serious turn our conversation had taken. She pulled on her cap and turned off left towards Dr Crouch's apothecary and surgical rooms.

I watched her go with the usual mixed sentiments of pride and apprehension. I longed to tell Amber all she should know about herself and her beginnings, things she was still not ready to hear but which were of great significance to me, and I thought of the letter I had started writing in the fervent hope that one day she would be disposed to read it.

As I walked the short distance home I wondered if there was anything I wouldn't do to keep my daughters safe, and by the time I turned the key in our front door I had come to the conclusion that there was not.

4

SPLINTERS OF WOOD

W e were enjoying a supper of mutton pie one evening several weeks later when there was such a loud rapping on the front door that Matthew spilt the water he was pouring into Liberty's mug.

'I'll go,' I said, standing up and brushing the crumbs off my lap. I half expected it to be George come to tell me that Esme's labour pains had started, but it was the Reverend Mr Brown, his white collar and pale face standing out against the dark of the evening street behind him.

'Whatever's the matter?' I asked, ushering him inside and closing the door against the wind.

He took off his hat and looked around the room, taking in the child present and Matthew's anxious gaze.

'Perhaps we could speak somewhere private?' he suggested. The vicar had a natural air of authority and gravitas about him and I noticed he was older than I had thought when I had first seen him at Joanna's hanging.

'Please sit,' said Matthew, indicating the empty chair which used to be Esme's place at the table.

'But, the child,' said Mr Brown, indicating Liberty who sat

spooning pie into her mouth as she watched the stranger with interest.

'You needn't worry, she can't hear you,' said Matthew, smiling sadly at his youngest daughter.

Reverend Brown nodded and sat down. He took off his hat and cleared his throat. 'Master Albright, you are needed at Little Aston Hall near Sutton Coldfield. The estate falls within the Diocese of Lichfield and I believe you are the acting magistrate in your brother Philip's absence?'

Matthew clasped his hands together in his lap and I put my hand on them to steady his nerves. 'What's happened?' he asked.

'The lady of the house has been found dead. She appears to have been murdered,' the vicar said, pushing his hand through his thick hair so roughly white flakes from his scalp fell onto the table in front of him.

Liberty started to laugh and I shushed her with a finger to my lips.

'Tell us what you know, vicar,' I said, hoping that the matter, however dreadful, would be straightforward and would not require Matthew to travel to Sutton at this late hour.

'Lady Aston was found by one of the housemaids this afternoon lying dead on the floor of the drawing room. The maid, Lena, went in to clear the grate before the fire was lit for the evening and found her lady prostrate behind the settle. She was bleeding from the head, a massive wound having been inflicted upon her, and quite dead. I happened to be in the house visiting Lord Aston to discuss a private matter when there was an enormous commotion from downstairs as the body was discovered. Lord Aston is in a fearful state, as are his sons and daughter. It seemed the best course of action that I should ride into town to alert the magistrate and the coroner.'

The vicar lifted the tankard of beer I had placed before him with a steady hand, despite his trials, and took a long draught.

Matthew pulled himself up from the table in a fluster knocking his chair back onto the flagstones. 'I must go there at once,' he said, reaching for his stick. 'Fetch me my coat, Hettie, and send word to George to bring a carriage.'

I stepped outside and shouted for a message boy. A cheerful lad appeared from the gloom and I gave him his instructions and pressed a coin into his hand. 'There will be another one of those when George arrives with the horses,' I said, in case he thought to disappear into the night with the money.

'I must now disturb Dr Crouch's evening and ready him for a journey to Little Aston Hall that I expect he will be reluctant to take,' said Mr Brown, picking up his hat. 'He is the only registered coroner in this city, though, old that he is, and the only man with knowledge enough to expound on how the poor woman died.'

'We will collect him on the way,' said Matthew. 'Tell him to be ready in a half hour.'

'We?' said the vicar with a frown.

'My wife needs to come to assist me,' he said, indicating his leg and the vicar nodded.

'Of course,' he said, clearly relieved that Matthew had not meant that he himself was to accompany him back to the miseries at Little Aston Hall. 'Then I will bid you goodnight and make my way to The King's Head for a nightcap. My apologies again for disturbing your dinner.'

We sat in silence for a minute or two after Brown had left. Liberty leaned against me and I stroked her hair as I mulled over what we were to find at the Hall and how best I could help my dear husband in his duties.

When George arrived, I instructed Sal to put Liberty to bed and stay indoors with her until our return, then I wrapped myself in my scarlet cloak and helped Matthew up into the carriage before clambering in after him. 'Don't you think it odd?' I said as we turned the corner towards Dr Crouch's house.

'Yes, it is an extraordinary event,' Matthew agreed heartily, adjusting his wooden leg so as to make room for the coroner.

'No not that, although an act of such violence among the gentry is of course extraordinary. No, I mean it's odd that Mr Brown didn't mention God at all, not once. For all his talk of death he never once spoke of heaven or gave a blessing for Lady Aston's soul. And he, a man of the cloth.'

Matthew gave me a searching look. 'What are you implying, my dear, that the good vicar is not devout?'

I shrugged. 'I just find it peculiar that's all,' I said as we pulled up outside the apothecary-surgery wherein lived and worked Dr Crouch and most days, our Amber too. 'A man devotes his life to leading others in the worship of God and yet, when a sin of the utmost magnitude is likely to have happened he talks of everything but.'

Matthew sighed. 'We have more important matters to attend to, my dear, than the Reverend Mr Brown's choice of words,' he said. 'Perhaps he saves talk of God for church.'

'Perhaps,' I agreed as the door to the apothecary opened and the diminutive figure of Dr Crouch appeared, swamped in a black cloak.

He climbed into the carriage and threw back his hood with unexpected vigour. I gasped as Amber's face came into focus in the dim light and Matthew uttered her name in surprise.

'Dr Crouch is fast asleep: he took a sleeping draught not an hour ago as his bones were aching. I was in the back studying anatomy books when the Reverend Mr Brown knocked. I said I would wake the doctor and tell him to await your carriage but I couldn't. He is dead to the world and will be for hours. So I decided to come in his place.' She said the last sentence with finality and neither Matthew nor I could find reason to argue with her.

'If Lord Aston is not agreeable, then Amber can wait outside and Crouch can attend to the body tomorrow,' I murmured to Matthew.

The journey to Little Aston was no more than six or seven miles, but bumping down the stony roads in the dark with Matthew feeling every jolt as a flame in the stump of his leg, it felt like fifty. We arrived a little after ten and George halted the carriage next to the fountain in the turning circle at the front of the grand house. Most of the downstairs rooms were lit, as were the lamps around the porch and we could see the size of the Hall outlined in grey behind it – a central domed structure flanked by two wings, each several floors high. We hesitated in discomfort as we wondered whether it was correct for us to enter such a place by the main door or if it would be more becoming to find a trade entrance at the back. In the end our choice was taken from us as a tall man wearing a gold waistcoat, woolly grey hair covering either side of his face, flung open the huge door and strode down the steps towards us.

'You're the magistrate, I presume? About bloody time,' he shouted as he peered in through the carriage window. 'There's been a murder here. My wife has been butchered to death. The work of the devil it is. Whoever is responsible will hang for it, I'll see to that.' He held up his lantern and peered in at us as we gathered our cloaks and made to alight, quite alarmed by his bellowing.

'What are these women doing here?' he said to Matthew, his red face creased in anger.

Matthew limped forward and held out his hand. 'How do you do, Lord Aston?' he said, his formal politeness overtaking his nervousness as I'd hoped it would. 'I am sorry for your loss and regret the shocking events that have brought us here this evening. I am Matthew Albright the acting magistrate for the Diocese of Lichfield. This is my wife Hester who must attend me due to the physical incapacity inflicted on me from my war wounds.' Lord Aston's eyes flicked down to Matthew's stick and my support of his arm. 'And this is Dr Crouch's assistant who will be examining your wife's body to ascertain the cause of a death occurring in suspicious circumstances in adherence with the laws of this country.'

Lord Aston opened his mouth to object as he squinted at Amber's female face but Matthew cut him off. 'I'm sure you will see the benefit of having a female physician undertake this role in respect of the body of Lady Aston, my Lord, but if you so wish we can return on the morrow with Dr Crouch who is, at this time, unable to attend.'

Matthew held the man's gaze and Lord Aston took a step back in deference to my husband's display of calm authority, unaware of the effort it cost him to keep his nerves under control.

'Yes, I suppose it is more proper that a woman examines my Loella,' he said, pulling absently on the wiry hair next to his left ear.

'Please lead us now to your demised wife,' said Matthew, 'and tell us what you know about the circumstances of her death.'

Lord Aston's eyes were rheumy and the fire of anger seemed to have gone out of him. He nodded.

'Shall we?' Matthew said, indicating the door, and we followed Lord Aston as he made his way up the stairs and into the marble entrance hall. I held my breath as we walked through the house towards the drawing room where the body lay, so hard was I concentrating on keeping Matthew upright so he wouldn't fall and break one of the fine porcelain vases that lined the corridor on plinths. Amber walked behind us with her head down and her hood up, not wanting to attract any further attention from the rest of the Aston family or the domestic staff at being a woman in a man's role.

The ornate drawing room was dark except for a circle of candlesticks which had been placed around Lady Aston's prostrate body. She was lying on her back on a Turkish rug between the grand fireplace and a heavily embroidered settle. Her eyes had been closed but her mouth was open in a circle of shock, showing a set of strong yellow teeth. She was wearing a cream satin dress and black stockings, one of which had fallen down around her ankle. Her neck was twisted at an unnatural angle and her dark hair was matted with blood which had also seeped onto the rug around her. One arm was flung out towards the centre of the room, the hand wide open, and the other was closed in a tight fist against her chest.

I recognised her immediately as the forthright woman who had visited Sarah and Michael's bookshop seeking out books on science, but held my tongue not wishing to complicate the matter in hand.

I could sense that the sight had shocked Matthew and feared that he was about to lose his composure.

'Could we have a seat for my husband, please, my Lord?' I said. 'He cannot stand for long.'

Lord Aston rang a bell above the hearth and a flushed young girl came rushing to attendance, making me suspect the entire household staff were waiting, and probably listening, on the other side of the drawing room door.

'A chair for the magistrate, Lena,' Lord Aston boomed and the girl began dragging a solid wooden seat from under the window. The screeching noise on the floor made Lord Aston wince. Amber leapt forward to help her with the weight of it and Matthew sat down heavily, his leg and my arm not able to hold him a moment longer.

'Who found the body?' he asked, after taking a moment to catch his breath.

'My son Herbert arrived back from visiting friends and came into the drawing room to rest a while after his ride. He didn't notice his mother was there until he stood to ring the servant's bell. He ran directly to my study to fetch me. I was in conference with the Reverend Mr Brown, and by the time I arrived down here the servants were all gathered around her. I sent Lena to fetch my other son Gabriel and daughter Claudia and we stood in desolation at the sight of their mother deceased on the floor.'

'It must have been a most distressing sight for your children, Lord Aston, and for you,' Matthew said as he averted his own eyes from the body.

'Yes and still she lies there.'

'I thought it was your maid Lena who found her body,' I said in confusion, thinking back to the vicar's account of events at the Hall, 'and yet you say it was your son.'

Lord Aston turned towards me, his previous anger reignited. 'How dare you question me?' he raged. 'Magistrate, I suggest you tell your wife to know her place in this house.'

'My apologies, Lord Aston,' said Matthew. 'My wife oversteps her role on occasion. She thinks she is being helpful as she has a quick mind and a good memory.'

'Does she now?' said Lord Aston as he narrowed his eyes at me. 'Women who are too clever are an abomination of nature in my book. Being demure and obedient that's all they should concern themselves with. And looking after their menfolk. That's what the Bible teaches and so it will be in my house.' He reached for a decanter on the side table and poured himself a large brandy.

I looked at Amber for silent support, but she wasn't paying any attention to Lord Aston's outburst. Instead, she was staring intently at the hand clenched on Lady Aston's chest.

She knelt down and opened the stiff fingers one by one. In the palm of Lady Aston's hand lay a small glass bottle. Amber picked it up and held it to the light of the flickering candle nearest to her. It was filled with liquid and small cuttings of plants. There were other oddments inside too, but I couldn't make them out in the dimness of the room.

Amber turned the object in her hand and then looked up at me, puzzled. I took it from her and a tingle of fear ran up my arm. I identified it with a haste which I came to deeply regret.

'It's a witch's bottle, that's what it is,' I said, squinting at the murky contents. Lord Aston let out a low growl as my identification confirmed what he had clearly suspected from the outset.

'I knew it,' he shouted. As if possessed by a demon, Lord Aston threw his glass at the wall so it shattered into a thousand fragments. 'It is clear as day now who murdered my wife. That witch will hang tonight or I will kill her with my bare hands.'

Lord Aston stormed out of the room and Matthew struggled upright, intent on going after him but he failed to find the strength.

'Stay with the body,' Amber said to him, placing a firm hand on Matthew's shoulder. 'Mama and I will try to stop him before someone else dies tonight.'

We hastened into the corridor to see Lord Aston careering across the main hall towards the front door clutching a huge cutlass.

He was followed by a sallow young man calling, 'Father, wait for me.' A teenage boy and girl stood together bewildered on the bottom step of the grand staircase.

A handful of servants holding lanterns had joined us by the time we had reached the fountain in front of the house and we made a group of half a dozen or so as we followed Lord Aston and his son Herbert across the lawn and through the adjoining churchyard down into the village of Little Aston.

Lord Aston and his band of followers marched past the squalid dwellings along Forge Road, across the green and along the gravelly lane that turned into a dirt track as it petered out on the far side of the village. They were joined by a small crowd of men and women drawn from their hearths by the commotion and seeking diversion on that most dull of November eves.

'Where are they headed?' I asked the plump woman who was puffing along next to me clutching a blazing torch, her eyes shining with excitement.

'To get the witch,' she shrieked, and the crowd began to cheer and jeer in agreement.

I clasped Amber's hand and we fell back from the group. 'What can we do?' I asked her urgently as another door opened and more villagers joined the throng.

Amber shook her head. 'We can't stop them all,' she said, looking around in shock. 'Let's at least try and reason with Lord Aston. If we can make him wait and follow the due process of the law then we may be able to save her, whoever she is.'

We ran ahead and reached level with Lord Aston as he came to a halt at a slatted gate set in a tall hedge of holly. He took a step back and I thought with relief that he was hesitating.

'Lord Aston, please,' I beseeched him, but I realised with dismay that he had paused only to get into the position he needed to lift his heavily booted foot and smash the gate to pieces.

He ploughed down the pathway, his cutlass aloft, towards the small stone cottage which was all in darkness. As he banged on the wooden door the rest of the crowd surged through the gate and arranged themselves behind him, their faces twisted in the flickering lantern light.

Lord Aston put one hand on Herbert's shoulder to steady

himself and kicked the door so hard his foot went straight through it. Splinters of wood covered the floor and he pulled the rest of the planks away with his bare hands, crossing the threshold with the menace of a beast. Herbert stood to his right, Amber and I to his left, as he surveyed the room, illuminated as it now was by the light from Herbert's lantern. It was bare and chill inside and the whitewashed walls were decorated in places with queer mosaics of stones and pebbles, quite unlike anything I had seen before. There were several rough-cut wooden shelves holding cups and bowls and other household items and a large closed chest at the foot of a small truckle bed in the corner. There was no other furniture in the room other than a table and chair next to the cold hearth at which sat a completely still figure draped in a grey blanket, their gaze cast down towards the floor. Beside the figure stood a tall, long-haired dog baring its teeth – a wolfhound it was, of the type the Irish use for fighting – and before we knew what was happening it had leapt at Lord Aston with a ferocious snarl. Lord Aston swiped his cutlass across its chest with a furious shout as it came at him and the animal fell to the floor with a whimper. The figure at the table let out a screech so high-pitched it almost didn't sound human, and Lord Aston stamped three times on the floor to protect himself from bad spirits.

'We are here for you, Gwen Foley,' he said, brandishing his bloodied cutlass towards the ceiling. 'Your evil work in this village ends tonight.'

The crowd shouted their agreement and the figure slowly lifted her head to look at Lord Aston. The blanket fell backwards revealing long hair of the purest white and a delicate pale face pinched with cold. Lord Aston stumbled backwards as the woman's gaze moved slowly from the dog crumpled on the floor to him. He pointed at her in terror before making the sign of the cross in the air in front of him.

'See her eyes, her red eyes. This is not a woman. She is not of human form. This is a demon from another world and she has brought death and destruction to this village.'

Herbert moved towards her and she made no movement to resist, frozen in fear she was, as anyone would be. He pulled her up, put his hands under her arms and dragged her backwards out the cottage and up to the dirt road, her feet limp and trailing in the mud along with the hem of her black woollen dress. She knelt on the ground with her face on her lap as the group of villagers made a circle around her and began baying for her to be hanged there and then from the oak tree standing outside her cottage.

A lone voice started to shout 'No!' and I realised it was my own. The ember of shame that I had carried within since Joanna's death, sparked by Agnes' words, ignited into a flame of anger at the woman's mistreatment that made it impossible for me not to act in her defence. 'For mercy's sake, Lord Aston,' I said, pulling at his sleeve as he made towards the woman. 'I beg you not to do this.'

'Get away from me,' he said as he pushed me roughly aside. 'Get a rope,' he ordered and several boys ran back to the village to find what was needed to complete the lynching.

'I am the official proxy of the coroner of Lichfield as appointed by the court of King George,' Amber announced loudly, having jumped up onto a tree stump so as to have the height of authority even if she did lack the gender. 'I order you to back away from this woman and allow her a fair trial. Any person who continues collaborating in this lawless act will face the direst of consequences.'

Her words made an impact that mine hadn't and gave the gathering pause to reflect on the repercussions of their actions given that a person of an official nature appeared to be present. From their mutterings it seemed that in the moonlight it was not clear to many of them if Amber was a man or a woman given her boyish clothes, and this was also in her favour. Not a one of them was willing to bring any trouble to their own doors, however much they might have wanted this woman dead.

Amber's interjection had snapped the madness out of the crowd and many began backing away.

'Return to your homes,' Amber shouted. 'This woman will be taken to the Guildhall Gaol in Lichfield where she will be questioned by the magistrate and, if necessary, tried by the assizes court in accordance with the laws of this country.'

Lord Aston stood fuming as Amber spoke and the villagers and servants drifted back towards their homes, the excitement of the night clearly at an end.

'Sir, please return to Aston Hall,' Amber said firmly. 'Matthew Albright awaits you there and you can recount to him your grievance against this woman.'

'My grievance?' spat Lord Aston. 'My grievance is that she murdered my wife.' He went to kick Gwen Foley as she hunched on the floor, hardly bigger than a dog herself in that position, and I pushed him with all my strength so that he fell sideways onto the ground, his cutlass clattering onto the gravel a little distance away.

Herbert ran to help him up and addressed me with fury. 'You will pay for that. I don't care who you are.'

Amber picked up the cutlass and held it behind her back as Lord Aston and Herbert righted themselves.

'Where's my cutlass?' Lord Aston demanded, looking confused and tired.

'One of your servants has taken it back for you,' Amber said. 'It is time for you to make your way back to the house.'

'This creature will go directly to the Guildhall Gaol in Lichfield, Father,' said Herbert. 'She will be hung in due course and in accordance with the law, there is no doubt about that. Tis only a pity this proxy was here tonight or it would have been done already.'

I crouched down next to the white woman and touched her gently on the back. She shied away and let out a sob.

'They've gone now. You come with us,' I said in my most soothing tone. I held her hand tightly as she stood up and led her through the village and down past the church to the carriage waiting outside Aston Hall. Amber followed carrying the slain dog which she had wrapped in the grey blanket. I wanted to tell Gwen that she was safe now, but it would have been cruel of me to make her believe such a lie.

By the time we got home Matthew and I were too disturbed from the evening's events to sleep. Amber and Herbert had taken Gwen to the Guildhall Gaol, and then Amber had gone back with Herbert to collect the body of Lady Aston so Dr Crouch could undertake the full post-mortem examination the next day. Poor George, it must have been near dawn by the time he finally got home to Esme, but he knew we were all grateful for his service and constant cheerful nature despite the oddment of passengers living and dead that he was asked to carry that night.

Sal had kept the fire alight for us, and we sat by our hearth sipping hot toddies as we tried to make sense of Lord Aston's and the villager's actions towards Gwen Foley.

'He seems utterly convinced this strange woman is to blame for his wife's death,' said Matthew, shaking his head. 'From what you say the villagers were ready to help him hang her there and then.'

'It was dreadful,' I said, bringing my hand to my mouth. 'The menace of that crowd, whipped up into a frenzy they were by that man and his son. It brought to mind the dark times of the witch finders in Suffolk that happened when my mother was a girl. The things she told me and Nell. All those poor women dragged from their homes like Gwen was tonight, and then tried and hanged in Bury St Edmunds. It's brutal that's what it is, and we must not allow this.' I had no idea then that there was a thread connecting the unsettling events in Little Aston that night to the very trials my mother had seen in Bury as a child, but the alarm I felt for Gwen's predicament was acute.

'I won't see another woman hanged in this city,' I said, my voice rising. 'We must try to protect Gwen.'

'I agree with you, Hettie. I have no stomach for ruthless punishments, especially for the fairer sex, you know that,' Matthew replied, making my spirits lift briefly in hope that he would help. 'But my powers are bounded. Under English law any English man may prosecute any crime. Moreover, Lord Aston is a man of considerable authority not only in Lichfield but with family links to the highest London gentry too. If he wants Gwen Foley tried for witchcraft and murder by the assizes judges then she will be and if they find her guilty of either or both then she will hang. That is the law.'

'But where is the evidence? What is she supposed to have done and how? Are you not going to explore the circumstances further, throw doubt on Lord Aston's accusations?'

'That is not my role. I am the magistrate, I assist the sheriff in administrating the law in this diocese, I am not the judge or the jury or indeed a lawyer. Indeed, I am not even the nominated magistrate, that is Philip's job, and I am tired of having to take responsibility for these wretched criminal cases in my brother's absence.'

Matthew put his head in his hands and cursed under his breath, the burden of his duties weighing heavily upon him. 'As is customary in such situations,' he said, 'Lord Aston has paid me to take statements from his family and servants at the Hall in order to add credence to his accusations. He fully expects me to find in accordance with his version of events, even though I am in agreement with you that much is unclear and needs further illumination at this stage.'

'Surely you can use the opportunity to ask questions of those at the Hall to uncover the truth of the matter?' I asked him, seeing a chance for Gwen Foley. 'A woman's life depends on it.'

'Fetch me my rum,' Matthew said faintly. He was steadier after a draft but his face was drawn and his expression deeply troubled.

'I don't have enough force in me to battle with Lord Aston over this,' he said, handing me back the bottle to put away, along with the temptation to drink more.

'No, I don't suppose you do,' I said with sympathy, regarding the broken body and spirits of my dear husband. 'But I do.'

Matthew lifted his head to look at me and our eyes met in a moment of unspoken understanding.

'Do I have your permission to do what I can for Gwen Foley?' I asked.

Matthew sighed several times as he contemplated his answer, knowing how much pursuing such a course of action meant to me, but also knowing the dangers that it would bring. 'I know you better than to stop you, Hettie,' he said at last. 'And I will help you all I can within the boundaries of my duties. But we had better hope that Philip doesn't return until the matter is resolved. He is not the type of man who would sanction the ruffling of gentry feathers. Especially by a woman.'

5

TEETH

I went to visit Gwen in the Guildhall Gaol at first light the next morning. I wanted to hear her side of the story with regards to Loella Aston and to give her some comfort and hope besides. I packed a loaf and some cheese in my basket along with a flagon of beer and two large apples from the tree in our garden. I had made an infusion of St John's wort for her to drink to keep her from despair, and Liberty had picked a little posy of Michaelmas daisies for me to give to her so as she'd have something agreeable to look at in that barren cell.

I knocked at the studded wooden door which opened onto Bore Street and waited for Gregory, the ancient turnkey, to rouse himself from his sleep and let me in. I was a familiar, if not particularly welcome, visitor to the gaol and often took it upon myself to take provisions to prisoners, especially if they had no kin to help them.

'What do you want?' he asked me. His chin, covered in dirty white stubble, was the only part of him I could see so far down had he pulled his cowl.

'Gregory, it's me, Hester Albright,' I told him. 'I am here to visit Gwen Foley, the woman they brought in last night from Little Aston. Stand aside, please, and let me in.'

Gregory tutted and shuffled sideways as I entered. I passed him a coin and he muttered his thanks and reached for the set of keys hanging on his belt. 'She's down 'ere,' he said. 'She's been quiet as a mouse all night and she didn't spit nor fight neither when they brought her in. I wish they was all as well behaved. Witchcraft she's been charged with by that Lord of Little Aston Hall – long time since we've 'ad one of those in this city – as well as the murder of his wife.'

I followed Gregory down the dank stone corridor to the two cells at the end. He unlocked the door of the one on the left and it creaked open revealing the damp, foul smelling room. Gwen lay motionless on the wooden boarded shelf which straddled the width of the walls opposite the door, some hay and an untouched stone pot underneath. Her head rested on the wooden block which served as a pillow and she was covered with dirty hessian sacking. Even though I could see her eyes were open I couldn't rightly tell if she was awake or not.

Gregory grunted and disappeared back to the comfort of his chair as I took a few steps into the dank room. 'Mistress Gwen Foley,' I called out gently. 'I am Mistress Hester Albright, the magistrate's wife. I have come to see you.'

She sat bolt upright immediately I spoke and curled herself up against the wall, her head tucked under her arm like a swan.

'Don't be frightened,' I said. 'I want to help you if I can. I have brought you some food and my little daughter Liberty, she picked some flowers for you.'

I held out the daisies and Gwen slowly lifted her head. She reached out for them and I put them in her trembling hand.

'They are pretty,' she said in the same high-pitched reedy voice I had heard let out that terrible scream the night before. 'Please thank Liberty for me.'

She looked at me with eyes which I could now see were a light pink rather than red. She squinted in the weak light and tilted her head to one side, trying to make out my face. 'You were there, when they took me,' she said with surprise.

'Yes, I was there. I tried to stop them, I–'

She leaned forward from the bed and reached out to touch the cloth of my cloak. 'Please help me. I need my Tam,' she said. 'Is he dead? Did they kill him?'

'Tam?' I said in confusion, thinking for one dreadful moment that there might have been a child at the cottage who had been left behind or worse, fallen into the vengeful hands of Lord Aston.

'Tamworth, my dog,' said Gwen. 'My sight is poor. Tam is my eyes. I tried to send him into the woods when I heard them coming for me, but he wouldn't go. He knew I was in danger and he wouldn't leave me. Please tell me he isn't dead.' A single tear ran down her colourless cheek as she pulled a small leather pouch from her skirt pocket and shook two small pointed teeth out onto her palm. 'These are his,' she said, 'they are all I have of Tam with me here in this bleak place. I found them on the floor of my cottage one day when he had been gnawing on a bone.' She picked up one of the teeth and pressed its sharp end onto the tip of her finger. 'He has a soft mouth with me,' she said, 'but Tam can use his bite viciously on those he dislikes, like those brutes who broke down my door last night. Did they kill him, Mistress Albright?' she asked again. 'Please tell me they didn't kill him.'

She quite threw me with her concerns, as I have to confess I hadn't given a thought to her dog since Amber carried it from the cottage, preoccupied as I was about what was to happen to its owner. Was it dead? I wouldn't know until I had a chance to speak to Amber.

'I can't tell you if Tam is dead or alive,' I said, and she let out a bitter cry. 'But I will find out for you,' I assured her, 'and I will return later and tell you. I promise.'

She put her arms around herself and rocked back and forth on the bed. Without her dog she was lost. She seemed to have no kith or kin to care for her, but I needed to be certain of that.

'Gwen, do you have a family?' I asked her gently. She shook her head and I tried to ken her age. She was slight of build like a maiden but her face, although translucent white like the petals of a winter rose, was dry and lined like my own.

I didn't think she was going to speak but after a few moments she began, falteringly at first and then with more courage, to tell me her tale.

'I came to Little Aston to live with my grandmother – it is her cottage you found me at. My father died. He had protected me all my life. He was a good man but he was a gambler. He lost our little house in Nuneaton, our home, with the throw of a dice and we were destitute. He found work as a labourer on a pig farm down near Hinckley but they had no work that I could do and they didn't want me there after the fever took him: said I was bad luck. I had nowhere to live so I started walking towards Lichfield to find my father's mother, who was my only living relative. I found Tam by the river in Tamworth,' she said with the glimmer of a smile. 'That's why I named him so. I shared my last piece of bread with him and he started to follow me and we have been together ever since. That was three years ago.'

'And where is your grandmother now?' I asked her.

'She fell ill and died a few weeks after I arrived,' Gwen said, her voice breaking at the memory. 'That's when it started, the wicked stories they told each other about me.'

'Who told stories?'

'A group of women in the village. They said I caused my grandmother's death so I could have the cottage to myself. They say I ruined their harvest by making the wheat go rusty with brown spots and that I caused their cows to stagger around and die. They say I curse the pregnant women in the village and do the work of the devil because there were two babies born sleeping last Christmas Eve. Every sad thing that happens in that village they point the finger at me. It was quiet gossip at first, but it has got louder and angrier these last few months. The children throw clods of mud at me and the women and men spit and hiss as I walk past. I took to staying in the cottage with Tam and gathering food from the woods and from what I could grow in my grandmother's garden. I kept myself to myself but I feared they would come for me one day when something very bad happened – and they did.' She turned towards me, her face full of angst.

'I didn't kill Lady Aston,' she said. 'I never even met her. But I don't suppose anyone will believe me.'

'Why do they think these things about you, Gwen?' I asked her, although I was certain I knew the answer.

She gave an unhappy laugh and pointed to her eyes and hair. 'Because I'm different from them. They have never seen anyone like me and they fear that difference. That is why. And because I don't have a man, or anyone, to protect me.'

I nodded, recognising the truth that she spoke.

'I am sorry for your troubles,' I said. 'Rest assured there are those of us who don't share such wicked beliefs about those who happen to be different from the rest, and we will do our best to help you.'

I laid out the contents of my basket next to Gwen on the hessian sacking and assured her again that I would return later in the day with news about Tam.

'I can't promise it will be good news,' I cautioned her as I left, not wanting to get her hopes up. 'Please be prepared for the worst.'

'I always am,' she said softly as I closed the door behind me.

~

I went directly from the gaol to the surgery to find out from Amber what had happened to Tamworth, but I found the shutters closed and the 'out on visits' sign pinned to the door. There was no telling what time Amber would return or where she had gone so I decided not to wait and instead made my way across town to look in on Esme and see if George would take me to Little Aston. I was in luck, he was taking a clockmaker all the way into Birmingham later that morning and would be able to drop me off in the village on the way and collect me on his return journey.

I arrived a little before noon with the intention of talking to some of the villagers about their opinions on Gwen Foley. As most of the women were busy preparing the midday meal and their men were working in the fields or on Lord Aston's farm, I went to Gwen's cottage first to have a look around.

The garden which circled the house was carefully kept, despite the trampling by heavy boots from the previous night's intrusion. There were all manner of vegetables and herbs planted in orderly rows and not a weed in sight. And the flowers! My goodness, Gwen loved her flowers, great clusters of them, many types of which I'd never seen before and fragranced like honey, lined the paths and walls even at that late time of the year. I stepped across the threshold of the splintered remains of the front door and saw that the cottage had a cosiness and a simple beauty to it that I had not noticed yesterday amidst the cold and the dark and the fury. Gwen kept her home neat as a pin and with the sunlight dappling through the mullioned windows a yellow warmth filled the space. I saw now that the pebbles and stones on the wall were cleverly arranged into delicate patterns representing pretty blooms and climbing plants. As I stood marvelling at them, I wondered how Gwen, with her poor eyes, could have managed such a feat. I imagined her picking the stones by touch and holding them to the light to make out their colour before adding them to the design she held in her head and I admired her greatly for striving so hard to make her humble home a place of beauty.

Her bed was covered with a crocheted blanket and on the floor next to it was a thick pile of sacks where Tam must have slept, his presence providing her only comfort in the unfriendliness that surrounded her in the village. I saw the large blood stain in middle of the floor from where Lord Aston had cut the dog down and felt with sore regret that there was but the smallest of chances that Tam still had life in his body.

I opened the wooden chest at the foot of Gwen's bed and carefully brought out the few dresses and undergarments that she kept there. Most of them looked more to suit a much older woman, a widow at that, so most probably had belonged to her grandmother before her. There was a thick, coarse blanket lining the bottom of the chest and I was about to replace the clothes on top of it when I saw a flash of green silk poking out from underneath.

My curiosity was prodded by the presence of such a fine fabric among the poor contents of the box and I lifted the rough woollen material to explore further. I gasped at what was concealed there; a green silk glove, a lock of chestnut hair steaked with grey and a small pair of silver spectacles with a C shaped grip at the centre. I recognised the personal items as belonging to Loella Aston from when she visited the Johnson's bookshop, and the hair matched her colour precisely. I sat for a moment in a state of some mental disarray as I contemplated my discovery and what it might indicate regarding Gwen's involvement in the death of Lady Aston and the wild accusations of witchcraft that were being levelled at her. Hearing footsteps coming up the path I had to rush to a decision and hastily stuffed the items into my cloth bag beside the provisions I had brought with me to keep myself fed on my travels. It was safer, I thought, to keep this to myself for now.

The rugged face of an outdoor labourer was peering through the doorway. 'Is she gone?' he asked.

'Yes,' I said uneasily, standing up from the bed. 'She is in the Lichfield Gaol.'

The man leaned back against the door post in relief and took off his hat. 'Thanks be to God,' he said, gazing upwards.

'And who might you be?' I asked him sharply – a little piqued by his dramatics.

'I'm Tom Hardwick,' he told me. 'I work on Lord Aston's land and I live in the village with my wife, Mary.'

'And what do you have against Gwen Foley, young man? What did she ever do to you?'

'What did she do to me?' Tom laughed bitterly and took a step towards me, pulling up the sleeve of his shirt. I winced at the lines of rough red skin wedded together in ugly scars which reached from his wrist to his elbow.

'I near lost my arm in the wheels of the seed drill,' he said. 'She put a curse on my family, she did. My Mary has lost three babes since that witch arrived in our village. That never happened before.'

I frowned. 'But why would you think Mistress Foley put a curse on you? Did something happen between her and your family?'

He pulled down his sleeve and shook his head. 'Nothing happened, that's what she's like. She just takes agin you and you're cursed. That's the way these witches are, that's what my mam says. There's no rhyme or reason to it.'

I sighed, realising the limits of his understanding as to the causes of happenings in the world.

'And she rotted the wheat and made the cows go bad. Will

she hang?' he asked, his eyes lighting up. 'Can we come and see her hang? I'd like that, I would.'

I ignored his question and pulled up the hood of my cloak. 'Take me to your mother, Tom. Can you do that? I'd like to talk to her.'

Tom nodded. 'Who are you anyway?' he asked as we made our way down the cottage path.

'I'm Hester Albright the wife of the Lichfield magistrate,' I said, with weight on the word magistrate.

We came to his mother's house, a freshly whitewashed dwelling in the middle of a row of mismatched buildings and he walked straight in, bellowing that a woman from town was here to talk about Gwen Foley.

'I need to get home to Mary,' he said. 'I'll leave you to it.' With that he grabbed a freshly baked currant bun from the pile on his mother's scrubbed wooden table and backed out the door.

'What do you want to know?' came a throaty voice. I turned to see a large-boned woman dressed in black and wearing a white bonnet that ill-suited her long face knitting in the seat by the window. 'I see it all from here,' she said, her needles clacking. 'Nothing happens in this village without me knowing about it.'

'I would like to know what you can tell me about Gwen Foley, please, Mistress Hardwick,' I said to her with what I hoped was the same tone of courteous authority that I heard my Matthew use in such situations.

The woman tutted. 'Gwen Foley is evil. She is in cahoots with the devil. She rides that ragged beast of hers to visit him at night and she suckles from him and comes back here to do his ghastly deeds.'

'Please, madam,' I said in frustration. 'Can we keep to the

specifics of the matter? What do you truly know about Mistress Foley?'

'What I told you,' the woman said, putting down her knitting. 'Isn't that right, Hilda? Gwen Foley's a witch, isn't she?'

I started as I realised a diminutive figure was sitting in a low chair at Mrs Hardwick's elbow, her ancient face almost completely concealed by the shadows in the corner.

'The White, we call her,' the old woman whispered. 'There is nowt more fearsome than a white witch who has been called to the darkness. She is full of vengeance and wrath.'

I cleared my throat. 'Have either of you ever seen Gwen Foley do any crime or misdemeanour with your own eyes?' I asked, wanting only the facts of the matter.

They looked at each other and burst out laughing.

'You don't see witches doing their mischief, lady,' said Mrs Hardwick slowly as if I were dim-witted. 'You just feel the suffering they cause. My knees have never been right since she turned up and Hilda's tremors get worse with every passing day.' I glanced at Hilda and she held out a wizened arm and shook it a little for my benefit.

'But what reason would she have to seek vengeance on the people of Little Aston?' I asked, trying to align my questioning to their slanted way of thinking.

Mrs Hardwick shook her head. 'That I can't tell you,' she said, picking up her knitting again. 'That would be for her to tell you, but I daresay you'll have to torture her first like they did in the old days.'

'Lay Bibles on her until she breaks,' croaked the older woman, 'or flay her with red hot pokers. That'll loosen her lips. The old ways are the only true way to deal with such a creature.'

I realised with a weary sigh that I was going to get no sense out of these women who seemed to take delight in having someone to blame for their every ill fortune and sickness, and thanked them for their time.

I left the house and walked across the village square towards the pond on the far side. I sat down on an upturned log to eat my bread and cheese and contemplated the afternoon's findings. It was clear that the villagers were convinced that Gwen was a force of evil, but this seemed to be based on nothing of any substance, other than Gwen's unusual appearance and her lack of family in the locality. Bad events in the village like the cattle dying and the crops failing were being attributed to her, but it was plain to me that they could have happened for other reasons if only I could find out what they were. The items belonging to Lady Aston that I had found at the cottage worried me greatly though. I wanted to discuss them with Amber before telling Matthew as I feared he might take them as clear evidence of Gwen's guilt. Such evidence would allow him to avoid any unpleasant crossing of swords with Lord Aston.

I had an hour or so to wait until George returned with the carriage so I took the opportunity to see if I could have a word with the Reverend Mr Brown who ministered from the village church.

The square church tower made a striking silhouette against the darkening afternoon sky and as I made my way through the graveyard and up to the heavy wooden doors, I was struck by how similar in style the building was to my father's church in Walberswick. Indeed, the high-ceilinged interior was so familiar to me that I almost expected Father to come raging out of the vestry demanding to know why I had not been back to visit this last twenty-seven years. Although it was cold inside, there were candles lighted on the altar which suggested the vicar was present somewhere on the premises.

I wondered whether I should call out, but decided against it as I imagined what my father's reaction would have been if a parishioner had shouted for him like a dog within the walls of his own church. Instead, I crept around the periphery of the nave peering into various recesses and small rooms until I came across the door to the vestry which was ajar, with small scraping noises coming from beyond. I hesitated before I knocked, listening carefully to the sounds within and trying to identify the familiar but unplaceable smell which was drifting from the room.

'Vicar,' I said tentatively as I pushed the door open a fraction wider. An unshaven, rough face looked up at me from a stool by the brassier where the Reverend Mr Brown was holding a blackening chestnut on a toasting fork in front of the flames.

'Oh dear,' I said, somewhat confused by the scene and sensing that my presence was unlikely to be a welcome one.

He blinked at me once or twice in the gloom and then his face unexpectedly broke into a wide smile. 'Mrs Albright,' he said, placing the toasting fork on the floor and standing up to greet me. 'How nice to see you. You must excuse me, my housekeeper has gone to Leicester to tend her sick mother so I am left to my own, rather inadequate, means in terms of meals at present. It is only when such women leave your service that one realises how much they do,' he mused as we both looked at the pile of crumbling chestnuts lying on a bed of cinders by his feet.

I laughed. 'It is balm to my ears to hear a man acknowledge that,' I told him. 'There's plenty who think that meals appear by magic and the house is kept by fairies.'

He blushed then and I saw that he had several nicks on his chin, of the sort Matthew was apt to give himself when he tried to shave in a rush using cold water and an unsharpened blade.

'See here,' I said, opening my bag and taking out the last of the bread and cheese. 'Would you like to eat this instead? It's leftover and will only go to waste.'

The vicar began to politely refuse and then, as I offered the bag towards him again relinquished his defence and took the food from me with bashful thanks.

'Come, let us sit somewhere more pleasant to talk,' he said. I followed him through a narrow door into a pleasant wood panelled room with padded chairs either side of a warm hearth. There was an ornate grandfather clock at the far end which gave a comforting tick, a bookcase along the back wall and two large latticed windows letting in the last of the light.

'This is my sanctuary,' he said, sinking into one of the chairs. 'Now, please do tell me the purpose of your visit. I assume it is in connection with the death at Little Aston Hall?'

He chewed thoughtfully on the bread and cheese as I explained to him the perplexing nature of the events that had occurred since the discovery of Lady Aston's body. I told him that the guilt had been laid by Lord Aston most forcefully at the feet of Gwen Foley with no evidence to place her in the Hall on the night of the crime, nor any clear motivation that she should commit such an act of violence.

'They say she is a witch,' I added, narrowing my eyes to catch his reaction.

He nodded calmly as he placed the last morsel of bread into his mouth.

'You show no surprise at that, vicar,' I said. 'Does it not shock you, as a man of the cloth, that such ungodly beliefs are rampant in your village?'

His hand went to the white collar around his neck and his eyes to the large crucifix hanging above the fireplace. I tried to decipher the emotion that clouded his face – somewhere between regret and amusement – but found myself unable to understand it.

'Do you know what a charlatan is, Mrs Albright?' he said suddenly, his hand falling into his lap.

'Yes. It's a pretender or an imposter of some sort,' I replied. 'Why do you ask me that?'

'That is I,' he said with a sad smile. 'I am a charlatan. I wear the clothes of a holy man, I speak the words of a holy man and I minister to my congregation as a holy man, but there is nothing holy in my heart.'

I waited for him to continue, listening to the clock tick heavily behind him.

'Now it is my turn to be surprised at your lack of shock at my words,' he said finally.

I shrugged. 'It doesn't shock me or surprise me, vicar,' I said. 'What we see on the outside of a person is often not commensurate with what lies beneath. Life has taught me that on many an occasion. Perhaps we are all merely actors in one way or another, playing the parts that have been ascribed to us?'

He put his chin in his hand, his elbow resting on the arm of the chair and looked at me with interest. 'Do you read?' he asked. 'You speak like a person who reads the thoughts of others, the great storytellers, the philosophers, the playwrights. Tis unusual in a woman.'

I nodded. 'My dear friend Sarah keeps the bookshop in Lichfield with her husband and I have the pleasure, the privilege and the opportunity of reading widely.'

'Yes, I know the shop,' Brown replied. 'You are a lucky woman to have such a friend, Mistress Albright. I fear I have no true friends, and no family of my own.'

'I am sorry to hear that,' I said, sensing his sadness. 'Please do call me Hester.'

'And me Nicholas. I am a lonely person, Hester,' he said. 'And I am alone in spirit as I garner no comfort from my faith.'

'Why did you join the ministry?' I asked him, 'if you had no calling?'

He shook his head. 'I was a fool,' he said bitterly. 'I fell in love with a girl, Tabitha, whose father was the local vicar. She was beautiful and gentle and kind. I wanted to be her husband. I couldn't sleep thinking of her, I was quite obsessed with marrying her, having her. I had no faith but she insisted she would only be wed to a holy man like her father so I joined the ministry and did my learning in cloisters and returned joyfully to our village ready to take her as my wife.'

'What happened?' I asked, seeing his face briefly lift and then fall at the memory.

'When I got back she had married another,' he said quietly. 'An engraver from town, a fellow named Ernest who had no more faith than I, but a good deal more money.'

'I'm sorry, Nicholas,' I said, 'that was a wicked betrayal.'

'I had already accepted this position in Little Aston and I had no other choice but to take it. I had planned to bring Tabitha with me and begin our married life together, but in the end I arrived here on my own and have remained so ever since.'

'My father was a vicar,' I said presently as we watched the latticed light on the hearth rug fade almost completely away. 'I grew up in a rectory in Suffolk by the sea with my parents and my sister Nell.'

'That sounds very pleasant, an idyllic sort of childhood,' Nicholas said wistfully.

'No,' I said, shaking my head. 'My father was a monster.' The words hung between us, chilling the room. 'We suffered terribly, my dear sister most of all, because of Father's unyielding religious beliefs, because of the shame taught to him by his God. If you are an unholy man, Nicholas, then you are in the presence of an unholy woman.'

Nicholas stood and walked across to the window. He opened a cabinet hidden under the sill and pulled out a bottle of brandy and two glasses. He poured us both a small drink and handed one to me. I took it gratefully.

'A toast then,' he said, raising his glass, 'to the secret unbelievers.'

I raised my glass in return before taking a sip of the fiery liquid.

'I married them here, you know,' Nicholas said, swirling the brandy round his glass and then swallowing it in one gulp.

'Tabitha and Ernest? Surely not?' I gasped.

He laughed. 'That really would have been cruel, wouldn't it? No, I married Lord and Lady Aston here the week after I arrived, twenty-one years ago. She was already with child, her belly was huge but no one mentioned it. They were very much in love.'

'Were they?' I asked in surprise, remembering her bitter, defiant words and manner in the Johnsons' bookshop. 'I was under the impression that she was unhappily tied to a man she didn't much like.'

'Perhaps she came to feel like that about her husband, but when they wed their eyes shone with love for one another. I remember it well because it was a painful reminder of what I had hoped for Tabitha and myself.'

'I'm glad she had some happy years at least,' I said, the image of Lady Aston's bloodied head coming unbidden to my mind.

'Indeed,' Nicholas replied. 'Unlike poor Joanna Baker. She must have rued the day she ever agreed to wed that merciless husband of hers.'

'I saw it was you that ministered to her at the end,' I said. 'But she wasn't from Little Aston, was she?'

'She was not. Joanna was born in the city of Lichfield, lived there all her life and went to the same church, St James, every Sunday. The vicar there, a devout old trout, had known her since she was an infant, baptised her, wed her to William and christened all her children. But he refused to accompany her to the gallows and read her the last rites. He said Joanna had forsaken her place as one of God's children by committing a mortal sin.'

I shook my head at the cruelty of such a denial to one in such great need.

'Joanna's sister Agnes came to ask me if I would take the role instead. She had heard that I am – how shall I put it? – somewhat less pious than others of the cloth.'

'It was a great kindness you did her, Nicholas,' I said. 'It's the mark of a man, how he treats those who have nothing to give in return.'

'I hope I gave her some comfort through my words. The notion of God has its uses in desperate situations, there's little doubt about that.'

'Will you speak to Lord Aston on Gwen Foley's behalf?' I asked him, emboldened by our shared confidences. 'She will hang too if we cannot dissuade Lord Aston from his accusation of murder or dismantle the charges of witchcraft against her and we have precious little time left. Gwen is an innocent woman, Nicholas, I am certain of it,' I said, pushing the nagging doubts that the findings of Lady Aston's effects in Gwen's cottage had planted to the back of my mind.

The vicar shook his head sadly. 'I cannot,' he said.

Seeing my frown he continued in an agitated manner. 'Who do you think pays for all this?' he asked, waving his hand above his head. 'The church, the graveyard, the vicarage. It is all part of Lord Aston's estate. I am paid by him. Little Aston church is a private enclave that the ecumenical council does not oversee.'

'Then it seems you work not for God, but for Lord Aston,' I said slowly, beginning to understand the scope of the man's power.

'I fear it is much the same,' Nicolas replied, staring into the fire.

6

SEAWATER

My dearest,

I write in this letter all that you should know about your beginnings. It is a sorrowful tale but one which I hope will give you comfort as full knowledge often does, and a better understanding of the source of your strength of character.

I am fond enough of Lichfield, but I'd not be truthful if I said I didn't miss the freshness of the salty water and the sound of the waves breaking on the shore in the place where I grew up – a small village called Walberswick in the county of Suffolk. We had to leave, Papa and I, because of you being born, else my father would have taken you away and you would have been lost to strangers, and to yourself.

It was my responsibility to look after my little sister Nell, that's what father said, and I always tried my best to keep her safe. We liked to sit on the pebbles, looking out over the sea while we told each other stories about singing mermaids and horned warriors from far-off isles. When Nell tired of that, we would set off along the beach searching for pieces of amber which we truly believed came from the land of fairy tales. We bit down on the stones that we found to see if they softened between our teeth, and if they did we would know they were amber and run home to give our finds to Mother. She would tell us we were good girls and sit polishing the nuggets for hours with her little bristled brushes until the golden honey colour was revealed. Sometimes there would be a tiny creature caught inside and we'd turn the glowing stone in our hands and marvel at how something that had lived such a long time ago could still be here with us and be part of something so pretty.

Nell once found a piece of amber that had a whole butterfly inside, wings and all. That was her special treasure and she didn't let anyone else hold it, apart from me, of course, because we shared everything. Nell was the beauty and I was the shrewd one, that's what Mother told us and it seemed that way in the eyes of others too.

The boys in the village had been nudging each other when Nell walked past since she was eleven or twelve. She was so fair of face that you couldn't help but be drawn to looking at her whenever she was near. Her hair was smooth, the colour of driftwood and she was slender as an oar. My face, with its freckles and wide forehead was pleasant enough, but not one to glance twice at. I looked much as I do now, although my skin was fresh and bright back then and my hair was a deep coppery red like my father's. I felt no envy towards Nell though. We were like the same person, me and my sister, two sides of one coin, and between us we had everything a person could want. We loved each other, and were miserable and full of unease any time we had to be apart.

Our mother had taught us both to read and write as early as we were able. Nell liked stories as much as I did, although she preferred to listen to Mother or me reading aloud than to take her own pleasure with books. Mother had been a governess before she married and had a shelf of books that we were allowed to choose from. My greatest joy was in going back to my favourites time and again, comforted by knowing what was going to happen and that there would always be a happy ending.

Father, who was the parson of the village church, had a small library of his own in the rectory where we lived. I wasn't allowed to go in there or touch any of the holy books that he drew on to write his sermons so I never did, even though I was curious about the powerful stories they must have held to spur Father to preach with such bursting passion when he gave his proclamations on a Sunday morning.

Nell was Father's favourite so she was allowed to go into his study, although she didn't have any interest in the books. She would sit sewing or drawing as he worked and it made him happy just to have her nearby, as it did us all. She had a special beauty about her Nell did, the kind that goes all the way through a person and makes them shine. She brought out a gentleness in Father that nothing or no one else ever had the power to do. But a pure love like that can hold danger in it too and make a person want to possess another all for themselves. I think it was that which made Father turn on Nell the way he did. That and his religion.

It was a fine June day when Nell had just turned fourteen and I sixteen that a sun-tanned lad with a broad smile and sparkling eyes came and sat next to us on the pebbles and began showing us how to skim flat stones and make them bounce over the sea. Eric, he was called. We didn't know anything else about him then or who his people were but Nell liked him right from the start and he would join us in our games and stories in the afternoons when we had all finished our chores. One afternoon Father bade me to clean the silverware in the church and Nell went to meet Eric on her own. I hesitated and told Father I would prefer to go with Nell, but he thundered his request at me again and I had no choice but to obey him or else feel the back of his hand. He was easily angered, my father, when anyone defied him, so we did as he said in our house and never thought about whether a man could be of a different type.

That evening as I was brushing Nell's hair ready for bed, Nell told me that she and Eric had walked together along the shore, looking for amber. I asked her if he had behaved nicely towards her and she told me that he had tried to hold her hand but she had said 'no' and I believed her because I didn't know much about men back then, and Nell had never lied to me.

I noticed the swell of her belly when the weather began to chill and the sea turned from blue to grey. Eric had already gone some weeks back, we didn't know exactly where to, but we knew by then that he was part of a gypsy caravan that had up and moved on to Norfolk for the harvest season.

Nell had no inkling that what had happened between her and that boy that afternoon in the sand dunes could make a baby.

I knew what could happen because Mother had told me the year before when I had turned sixteen. She was worried that I might get myself into trouble as I was a friendly and adventurous sort of a girl, even if I wasn't particularly fair. It hadn't crossed her mind, or mine, that our sweet Nell, who looked and behaved like an angel and was still so young, might have needed the warning too.

When Father found out it was as if a gateway to hell had opened up in our very house.

'Cornelia! Did you give in to temptation, girl?' he bellowed as Nell stood, trembling at the foot of the stairs on her way up to the bed we shared. Her shift had caught on the base of the candle stick she was holding as she turned and her shape was clear for all to see.

My mother ran up the hallway and put herself between Nell and Father as he lifted his hand, or else he would surely have struck her. We were all afraid of him with his mighty voice and raging temper, and we kept out of his sight as much as we could for fear of aggravating him and waking that demon of anger who lived inside.

'I am a man of the cloth and I will not have shame brought upon me,' Father said, his eyes rolling wild in his head so as we could only see the whites. 'Get her out of my house.' He banged the wall with his fist six times, once for every word, causing the sampler hanging above the door to crash to the floor.

'Please, Seth,' Mother had pleaded, 'where would you have our *daughter go? For pity's sake, let her remain here until her confinement has ended. She can stay in her room, we will tell people that she is afflicted with a sickness and must be kept apart. Hester and I will look after her.' She put her arm around me and we stood together in defiance of him even though our legs were shaking.*

'We will,' I said in a whisper.

'And when this bastard is born?' Father pointed at Nell's swollen belly. 'When the wages of sin makes its devilish way into the world? What will happen then? I will not have such a creature under my blessed roof.' Father put his hands together then and looked to the ceiling, his lips moving in a silent prayer.

Mother tightened her grip of my shoulder and bit her lip.

'I will marry and I will take the child far from here,' I heard myself saying, jutting my chin out in obstinate defiance, my love for my sister overtaking all reason.

Father began to laugh then in a mirthless manner. 'You will marry? And who will you marry, pray tell, Hester? What manner of a man would be willing to take you for a wife along with a bastard child to pass off as his own?'

'A kind one,' I said, nodding with surety that I could follow through with my designs and that it was right.

Nell let out a sob and Father narrowed his eyes. He ranged his pointed finger across all three of us and spoke in a low, threatening tone. 'I want it away from here, as soon as it is born. If you do not find a husband willing to take you both then I will arrange for the child to be collected by the papists at Campsey Priory and brought up in piety to understand the shame of its existence.'

I swallowed hard, realising the weight of my promise. The priory had a fearful reputation in our parts as being the most severe of institutions for destitute children who had nowhere else to go. It was a place where devout nuns believed in beating the sin out of children who had been born outside of wedlock as they prepared them for a life of servitude and submission. The thought of Nell's child falling into the hands of such people filled me with dread.

We agreed to Father's terms with solemn nods and I helped Nell up the stairs and into bed. We lay awake long after the house had fallen silent and I calmed her as she was sore upset. Nell put her hands on her belly and I put my hands on hers and we gazed at each other in wonderment in the moonlight as we felt the kicks and swirls of her little one dancing through the night, blessedly ignorant of the storm it had caused.

7

BLOOD

As soon as I arrived back in town from my visit to Little Aston I headed directly to see Amber at Dr Crouch's surgery to find out about Tamworth. To my dismay as I hastily turned the corner into Bird Street I collided with Agnes, her arms laden with muddy carrots which scattered across the cobbled street.

'I am sorry, please let me help,' I said, leaning over to pick up the vegetables.

'Leave them be, I don't need any help from you,' Agnes snapped, giving me a look that revealed her continued disgust at my failure to act on her sister's behalf at her time of greatest need. Shame coursed through me once again and I muttered another apology as I made my way past her and towards the low door of the surgery.

I was relieved to find Amber inside. She and the doctor had not long since returned from a house call and were readying to go out again to attend a squire who had broken both arms falling from his horse.

'Amber,' I said urgently as Dr Crouch went to pack the necessaries for their patient. 'Tell me about Gwen's dog.'

Amber smiled. 'I saved it. I stitched him up across his breast bone just like I would have done a man. I fed him marrowbone soup with a spoon and laid him down with a sedative of valerian for the pain and he woke this morning with a wet nose and bright eyes, all that he is still weak.'

I felt awash with relief as she spoke, and joyful at how happy Gwen would be at the news.

'You are a wonder,' I told her. 'Thank you. Will you come with me to tell Gwen? I'd like to speak to you on the way. I have been to Little Aston today and have made some pertinent discoveries.'

Amber asked me to wait while she spoke with Dr Crouch, and disappeared through a thick black curtain into the doctor's private quarters. I looked uneasily around me before sitting down in the consulting room – green painted it was, with a bookcase of medical books on one side next to a chest made up of hundreds of small drawers containing the herbs Dr Crouch and Amber prescribed and used in their treatments. On the other side of the room was a narrow wooden bed with shallow boxes of sawdust beneath to catch the blood from surgeries, and a collection of metal instruments on a high table beside. I gazed at the array of jars stacked atop the bookshelf and apothecary chest. They seemed to contain all manner of strange fleshy items. Most of them resembled dead fish to my unschooled eyes and I felt quite nauseous imagining how they had been acquired from human bodies.

The bell above the door tinkled as a skinny young man covered in weeping sores came creeping in, and lowered himself gingerly into the seat beside me. I noticed that his limbs were shaking and he tried to still them, one at time, sighing loudly and tutting in frustration as he did so as if his body were a disobedient animal that he was tasked to train. My heart lurched in pity for his afflictions. I wondered, not for the first time and with much pride, how Amber managed to remain so calm and measured in her dealings with people in such misery and felt thankful that there were those like her who had the stomach for such work.

Amber came back into the room and gave me a nod. 'He can manage without me this evening,' she confirmed. Then, turning to the poor soul beside me she said in a gentle voice, 'Peter, Dr Crouch will be with you shortly to apply your salve. Can I get you something to drink while you wait?'

Peter shook his head and gave her a pained smile revealing a set of teeth so strong and straight that I felt relieved the lad had at least one part of his body that didn't trouble him.

'Come, let us go to the gaol,' Amber said, and I followed her out of the surgery, happy to be away from the contents of the jars.

I told her as we walked about the villagers' hatred of Gwen and the unfounded nature of their accusations.

'It seems that these stories against her gather pace and become stronger with each telling,' I said as we rounded the corner of Bore Street. 'They have taken on a life of their own and Gwen has been powerless to defend herself. Every death, illness or misfortune is laid at her feet and with no other explanation they have fallen back on the old superstitions of witchery, egged on by some idle older women in the village who seem to be taking much gratification from it. It is a perilous situation and it worries me greatly.'

Amber furrowed her brow as she absorbed my words.

'There's something else,' I said, pulling her down an alleyway just before we reached the street door to the gaol. I opened my bag and showed her the glove, the spectacles and the lock of hair. 'I found these hidden in Gwen's cottage. They belonged to Lady Aston.'

Amber touched the items and looked at me in surprise.

'What are we to make of this?' she said. 'Does it point to Gwen being the culprit after all?'

I shook my head. 'Not necessarily. Someone could have placed these articles in Gwen's house to make her seem to be guilty. Don't you remember you and John used to play such tricks on each other when you were children? You once made John miss his dinner for stealing apples when it was you who'd eaten them and hidden the cores under his bed.'

Amber nodded slowly. 'I had forgotten that, Mama, but it now comes back to me. What a horrid sister I was,' she said, shaking her head. 'I hope John forgives me.'

'It was only tomfoolery,' I assured her, 'he did much the same to you, I'm sure. But my point is that these items may have nothing at all to do with Gwen.'

'We will ask her,' said Amber. 'Keep them from Papa for the time being.'

I nodded, pleased that we were of the same mind and we turned back on to Bore Street and knocked on the door of the gaol.

8

HECATOLITE

The next day, Amber and I went to see Sarah at the bookshop to see if she could recommend us any books that might provide alternative explanations of the stories being told about Gwen Foley in Little Aston.

We found Sarah clutching the bottom of a rickety ladder whilst Samuel placed some ancient volumes on the top shelf of a bookcase.

'Michael calls it stock rotation,' she said. 'He won't throw any books out so we have to keep them all somewhere, even if no one wants to buy them.'

'They all have value as tomes of knowledge, Mother,' Samuel explained pedantically from his position near the ceiling.

'It's a shop, not a library,' Sarah whispered to us. 'My husband and son seem to forget that.'

'I heard that,' said Samuel, carefully finding his footing down the last few rungs. 'Father and I are of the same opinion about books – that they are the most precious objects on earth.'

'Yes, dear,' said Sarah, raising her eyes at Amber and me. 'But you don't have to dust them all, do you?'

Samuel frowned and pulled a book from a lower shelf. 'If

you will excuse me, I have to return to my studies,' he said with a small bow.

I noticed with pleasure as he bent into the light that his skin was much improved, although the scars left by the scrofula made his face look older than his tender years.

'You need to stay up here, Samuel. You can work on the table in the corner,' said Sarah. 'Your father is in our rooms. He is in a tremendously black mood and doesn't want to be disturbed.'

Samuel, looking pained, carried his books over to the far side of the shop. I looked at Sarah in sympathy, knowing how much she and Sam dreaded Michael's frequent melancholic episodes.

'He refuses to come down,' Sarah told us. 'He hardly eats and he won't work. He sleeps constantly and when awake he stares at the wall, his face blank of all expression. I have had to send word to the city council that Michael is not fit to carry out his duties as sheriff at the current time. They will have to manage without him until he is well again.'

'How long do these bleak episodes usually last?' asked Amber.

Sarah sighed. 'It can be a few days, or a few weeks, several months even. Then when it is over he comes down the stairs, freshly shaved, eats a hearty meal and goes about his business as if nothing has been amiss. The boys and I know better than to comment upon it; we are just relieved to have him back.'

'Would you like me to see if I can help him?' asked Amber. 'Or Dr Crouch, if he would prefer?'

'Thank you, my dear, but Michael won't see a soul when he's like this. I find it's best to leave him be. Your prayers would be welcome though,' she said with a nod. 'Yours too, Hester.'

I pretended not to hear her request as I took off my cloak and made myself comfortable on one of the high stools beside the counter.

'So, Hester, tell me about Gwen Foley,' Sarah said, putting aside her husband's misery in favour of local gossip. 'Word is all over town that she has murdered Lady Loella of Little Aston Hall, God have mercy on her, and furthermore that she has been accused of witchcraft. That part can't be true, surely? These sorts of beliefs are far in the past, are they not, particularly in a civilised city such as our own?'

'The truth of the matter has yet to be uncovered in regards to the murder of poor Lady Aston,' I told her. 'But I am in agreement with you about the accusations of witchcraft. Such feverish thoughts are leading to dangerous actions in the village and at Little Aston Hall. It is muddying the water and making it unlikely that Gwen Foley will receive a fair hearing when the assizes court arrives next month.' I picked up the teacup that the Johnson's maid had placed in front of me and took a sip as Sarah pondered my words.

'They all but strung her up there and then the night Lady Aston was killed,' Amber added. 'Lord Aston is convinced that his wife was trying to protect herself against witchery when she was fatally wounded by a blow to the head from Gwen.'

'Does the post-mortem align with that?' asked Sarah, quite surprising me with her knowledge of lawful proceedings.

Amber nodded. 'Dr Crouch and I examined the body and we have concluded that she died from a head wound caused by a collision with a heavy object. Lady Aston was also found to be holding a witch's bottle in her hand when the body was discovered. Lord Aston took that as certain evidence that his wife was in mortal fear of Gwen and was holding the bottle to try and ward her off after she somehow managed to gain entry to their drawing room.'

'And how does he think Gwen got into the Hall and into the drawing room without being seen?' asked Sarah.

'Down the chimney,' said Amber, raising an eyebrow.

'Perhaps having changed her form to some spirit or animal in order to make access.'

'But Lord Aston is a man of learning, is he not?' Sarah turned to me in confusion. 'Why would he believe such nonsense?'

I shrugged my shoulders. 'We don't know. It seems these old beliefs haven't yet been buried; they lurk under the surface only half dead, ready to be pulled from the filthy ground when circumstances can't be explained by any other reason. Also, Gwen Foley is of a strange and unusual appearance that seems to make folk afraid. Her skin and hair are purest white and her eyes are a pinkish hue.'

Sarah looked surprised. 'She does sound unusual. Nonetheless, I doubt Lady Aston would have come to such a far-fetched conclusion about the woman. You remember, do you not, Hester dear, that that very lady was in this shop not long ago asking for books on science and philosophy?'

'I do,' I said. 'She presented herself as a woman with a keen mind and no time for superstitions.'

'Exactly. And a woman with a keen mind does not fear witches,' said Sarah. 'She told us herself that she would tolerate no talk of such things in her house.'

Amber rummaged in her leather bag and placed a small package wrapped in muslin on the table. She unwrapped it and we all three looked at the bottle lying before us. 'Then why was she holding that?' Amber said.

Sarah picked it up and ran her fingers across the clouded pale green glass. 'I can see a tooth, some hair, pins, a sprig of a plant, rosemary, is it?'

I nodded. 'Rosemary only grows in full sun, you see, so those who have a mind to think about plants in such a way see it as a defence against darkness.'

'What are the pins for?' Sarah asked, shaking the bottle gently and making them float around inside.

'They're meant to snag the witch's spirit and trap her inside so she can cause no more trouble,' I said as we watched the pins sink once again to the bottom.

Sarah raised her eyes at that. 'And what is the liquid?'

'We think it's urine,' said Amber.

Sarah wrinkled her nose. 'I have heard about these bottles, but I have never seen one before.'

'I have,' I said, taking the bottle from her. 'They were still quite common in Suffolk when I was growing up. Folk would build such things into the brickwork of their houses. "Just in case", they would say. The old beliefs die even harder in the countryside.'

A breath on the back of my neck made me jump. Samuel was peering over my shoulder, his interest piqued by our conversation and by the peculiar bottle. 'Prosecutions of witches may not be as far back in history as you think, Mistress Albright,' he said. 'Indeed, only eleven years ago a woman was found guilty of witchcraft at the Lent assizes in Hertford. She was charged under the Witchcraft Act and sentenced to hang but she was pardoned by Queen Anne at the last minute.'

I stared at him. 'How do you know of such a thing?' I asked.

He reddened and pulled a book from behind his back. 'It's all written down, recorded by men of letters, if you know where to look.'

'Samuel, we need to help Gwen,' Amber announced in her usual straightforward manner. She had spent the best part of an hour deep in conversation with the accused woman the evening before, after she had told her the good news about Tam, and was convinced of her innocence, as was I. When Amber had asked Gwen why Lady Aston's effects were in the chest in her cottage,

Gwen had begun to cry and told her that she had no knowledge of how they might have got there.

'She is in a desperate position and will be hanged, there is no doubt about that, unless we find a way to speak for her and speak for her well,' explained Amber. 'The villagers have pointed the finger of blame at her for all manner of ills; spoilt crops, aching bones, infant deaths, stumbling black-tongued cows. The murder trial itself will not be heard fairly unless we can dispel the other rumours and accusations about her, especially those of witchcraft. Will you both help us? Please.'

Sarah took a hesitant breath and looked to her son, who nodded at her with an eagerness and animation that I hadn't seen in him before. 'Yes we will, won't we, Mother?'

'I want to help, but I don't want Samuel involved in any danger,' said Sarah, 'and I don't think Michael would approve.'

'He won't know,' said Samuel, his voice rising in excitement. 'Especially in his current state. This will be between us and the books.' He indicated the shelves of volumes that surrounded us. '*Verba movent*,' he declared. 'Words move people: that is the truth of the matter and words shall be the weapon we use to defend Gwen Foley. Now what do we need to find out?'

I admired Samuel. This quiet studious boy who had suffered so with his weeping skin sores seemed to be growing into a man of stature and action before my very eyes. Sarah felt it too and she looked to burst with pride as she regarded her son. He fetched his quill and paper and we set to work.

'The Lunar Society,' Samuel said, interrupting Amber as she went over the charges set against Gwen.

'What do you mean?' Amber asked.

'That's what you group of women should call yourselves. "Lunar" for the moon which provides illumination in the darkness and for its feminine associations. "Society" meaning a community or group formed for a particular purpose. That is what you are. A group of women seeking the light of truth in the darkness of gossip, rumour and superstition.'

'The Lunar Society,' I repeated with a smile. 'I like that. What do you think Sarah? Amber?'

'It's perfect,' said Amber. 'But you are part of it too, Samuel, even though you are not a woman.'

Samuel's colour rose again and he lowered his head to his work. 'I would like that,' he said. 'Perhaps I could be an honorary member, keeping in the shadows, though.'

'Yes, that would be best,' said Sarah. 'Samuel must be hidden from view.'

'Hester, with your name you should be the leader of the society,' said Samuel, looking up at me under his thick fringe.

'Do you mean because my married name is Albright?' I said with a smile, emphasising the last syllable, pleased to have caught up with one of his wordplays for once.

He frowned. 'I hadn't thought of that,' he said. 'No, it's because the name "Hester" means "star". Didn't you know?'

Amber burst out laughing, and I saw the delight in Samuel's eyes that he had amused her. I'd suspected before that Sam was sweet on her, even given the age difference and Amber's disinterest in romantic alliances. But it is a fact nevertheless that where love is concerned the heart won't be ruled by good sense.

O ver the next few days we of the newly formed Lunar
Society met at all available opportunities to work on our
case of defence for Gwen Foley. With Samuel's extraordinary
knowledge of the location and contents of almost every book in
his parents' shop we began to compile a body of alternative
explanations for the villagers' misfortunes that exonerated poor
Gwen.

'Knowledge is of two kinds,' Samuel had announced with
confidence as we embarked on our task. 'We know a subject
ourselves, or we know where we can find information on it.'

'And there is none who knows better how to find
information in this place than Samuel,' Sarah had mused,
nodding at her son as he showed us a large corkboard hanging
on the back wall of the bookshop. Upon this he had pinned
various scraps of paper detailing page numbers and book titles
where he had found that which we needed to know.

The first book Samuel showed us was a large dictionary of
husbandry put together by a group of gentlemen farmers. It gave
details of many possible sources of crop pestilence and disease

and Sam had quickly identified the scourge of Little Aston's wheat failure.

'You see,' he announced in excitement, prodding the middle of a yellowing page, 'the red stripes on their harvest, it was due to a blight called leaf rust, it is not uncommon in years when a wet spring precedes an unusually cool summer. If you remember, that describes exactly the climate of this year past in Staffordshire. That is why their wheat was spoiled – the rainy weather – nothing to do with witchcraft.'

'The damp could also be the reason that many of the older villagers have suffered much with their aching bones of late,' Amber added and Samuel agreed.

'You are right, Amber,' he said with a shy smile, tripping a little over her name as if thrilled to have reason to say it aloud. 'Culpeper details herbs to relieve the ache of damp bones and restore the humours. According to his book, the old folk would have had more success in reducing their pain by chewing on willow bark than by pointing the finger at Gwen Foley.'

'What of the cows and their black tongues?' I asked, hoping for a similarly straightforward answer.

Sam shook his head. 'I haven't yet been able to locate the source of that problem, I'm afraid,' he said, 'but I will not be defeated!' He looked at Amber to ensure he hadn't lost her approval, but she was already on to the next item on our list.

'And Gwen's unusual colouring?' she asked. 'Have you managed to unearth any information regarding that?'

Samuel took a breath and reached for a clutch of volumes from the pile in front of him. 'My findings in this area were most interesting,' he said. 'But rather troubling.'

He pushed his hair out of his eyes and picked up a fragile book consisting of not more than a dozen tattered pages. 'The first mention of people similar to Gwen comes from an Italian,

Alberico Gentili who in 1614 wrote about white Aethiopians who were considered to be demons.' He held one of the pages open for us but had put it down again before we had a chance to read it.

'And see here,' he said excitedly, opening another volume, 'a fellow called Pellicer in 1649 came across the same phenomenon in the Congo where he was working as a missionary. He wrote: "some white children are born from black parents... These are deemed monsters. They have African features but are white and feeble-sighted and exceedingly rare."'

Sarah frowned in confusion and a look of deep concern settled across Amber's face.

'Here again,' said Samuel, pulling a candle closer so he could read the tiny text of the next book with more ease, 'in another place, this time Panama in 1702, a London surgeon called Lionel Wafer describes the skin of some of the children he came across on his travels as peculiar in being, *"milk white, much like that of a white horse."'*

'I don't understand,' I said. 'Does this mean Gwen is come here to England from some far-off place?'

Samuel shook his head impatiently. 'No, Hester. That is not the case at all. You are missing my point.'

'I'm sorry,' I said, a little embarrassed and taken aback by his abrupt manner.

'Please explain it to us, Sam,' said Amber calmly, quite unruffled by Samuel's intensity. 'We want to understand.'

'It's all here in this catalogue of human differences,' he said, holding up a slim blue volume. 'This is a recent publication and is more, shall we say, objective in its delineation of people's physical variations without the rather unhelpful moral speculation that we find in the missives from missionaries and the like.'

We waited for him to continue, hoping his meaning would become clear.

'In this taxonomy they label the look "albinism",' he said.

'The look?' I echoed.

'Gwen's appearance,' Sam explained. 'The milky white skin, the pinkish eyes. The learned physicians who penned this book name it "albinism" and identify it across all species of animals including human beings.'

Amber leant over Sam's shoulder to see the text he referred to.

'It is a human variation, that is all,' said Samuel, running his finger under the text for Amber to read. 'It is rare but essentially it is a meaningless diversity. A lack of colouration in the skin and hair. There is no reason to fear it any more than there is to fear a fellow with brown eyes or a maid with red locks. Gwen's misfortune, apart from the associated poor eyesight and extreme sensitivity to sunlight, is that no one in Little Aston, or indeed the Diocese of Lichfield, has ever encountered a person with albinism, an albino, before her. People are afraid of what they don't understand, but that doesn't mean that there is a reason to be afraid.' He sat up and blinked with the realisation that he had struck upon the key to our defence.

'This is what we will argue,' he said, 'that Gwen Foley has albinism as documented in this text written by esteemed physicians, and that no indication is given that this condition is associated with evil or wrongdoing. Surely the assizes judges as learned men will agree that physical difference is not associated with moral or spiritual degeneracy?'

Amber hooted with triumph and jumped up. She began gathering the sheets of paper that Samuel had pinned to the wall.

'Come, let us prepare some banners and leaflets explaining

these points so that we can hand them to passers-by outside the gaol. The more people we can get on Gwen's side the better her chances at trial,' she said. Amber was ignited with purpose and Samuel watched with ill-concealed delight at being the source of her jubilation.

'Samuel is not to join us in our protest,' said Sarah sternly. 'We agreed on that.'

'Of course,' I assured her. 'He has done more than enough already.'

'He certainly has,' agreed Amber. 'Well done, Sam!'

Samuel reddened and smiled broadly to himself as he reached again towards his pile of books, and I was happy that he felt a pride in his intellectual abilities, which truly were proving to be exceptional.

'By the way,' he said, not wanting his moment of glory, especially in Amber's eyes, to end. 'I also found out why they use urine as the liquid in witch's bottles. Listen to this: it's from Joseph Blagrave's *Astrological Practices of Physick* which he wrote in 1671 towards the end of the English witch trials. He uses the word "patient" here to describe a person who is supposedly under the curse of a witch. It is nonsense, of course, but interesting nonetheless: "Collect the urine of the patient, close up in a bottle and put into it three nails, pins or needles with a little white salt, keeping the urine always warm: if you let it remain too long in the bottle it will endanger the witches life: for I have found by experience that they will be grievously tormented making their water with great difficulty if any at all, and the more if the moon be in Scorpio when it is done."'

Amber and Sarah tutted and tittered at the folly of it, but I fretted silently as Samuel read, remembering the unused stone pot under Gwen's bed in her cell, indicating that she had not passed water during her first night in gaol. I decided against sharing my thoughts with the others, though, not wanting to cast doubts on the great strides we of the Lunar Society had made that afternoon in our pursuit of truth and rational explanations to shore up our defence of Gwen, and I dismissed the unpleasant words as mere coincidence.

10

STONES

I noticed the bruises on Liberty's arm when I was helping her into her nightdress. I brought the candle closer and examined them, concerned.

She frowned and pinched her fingers to show me how it had happened.

'At school?' I asked her, pointing in the direction of Dame Oliver's and she nodded. She picked up her pinafore dress and rummaged in the front pocket, bringing out a crumpled letter addressed to myself and Matthew. It was written in her teacher's distinctive spidery hand and I took it from her with a sense of trepidation.

Amber, John and Esme had all attended Ann Oliver's Dame School when they were young, so we sent Liberty there too as soon as she turned seven as Matthew and I were both of the belief that girls should be taught to read and write just the same as boys. The first few weeks of Liberty's schooling had gone smoothly enough and we were hopeful that she would thrive there as our older children had, but from the Dame's letter it was clear that, as with most things where Liberty was concerned, it was not to be that simple.

Dame Oliver wrote that Liberty had thrown stones at one of the other children when they were in the garden. One had split the girl's lip and cracked her tooth and another had broken a window. I was to go and see her the next morning for a consultation about Liberty's future at the school, and she conveyed her disappointment and displeasure at her behaviour.

I mimed the stone throwing and the broken tooth and window to Liberty to try and ascertain whether the Dame's version of events was true, but she turned her face into her pillow and wouldn't look at me. I rubbed her little back until her rapid breath slowed down and she finally fell asleep.

I lay awake myself much of that night fretting about the happenings at school that Liberty was unable to tell me about and feeling helpless with frustration at the way others treated her.

'Try to keep your temper when you speak to Dame Oliver,' Matthew had advised me over breakfast, although he was as concerned as I about the letter and about the bruising on Liberty's arm. 'It will do no good to Liberty for you to make a scene.'

I nodded as I sipped my tea, recognising the prudence of his words, although I was unsure if I would be able to do as he asked.

'Liberty has no friends. The children find her very strange,' Dame Oliver said in an accusatory tone as we sat down in the small room at the back of the house that she used as her office. Her silver hair was piled in its usual tangled bun and I noticed her black widow's dress shone with grease from constant wear. I had known the formidable Dame for over twenty years, ever since John had started at her school, and I had never seen her wear any other garment.

'That's as maybe, Dame Oliver,' I said with forced pleasantness, 'but I will not have my Liberty being pinched by another child.' I thought of the blue and brown bruises in the shape of two finger tips that lingered across the top of Liberty's arm and waited for her reply.

'One of the boys was simply trying to find out if your daughter was able to utter a sound,' Dame Oliver said with a dismissive wave of her hand. I went to protest but she spoke over me.

'Liberty doesn't speak at all, Mistress Albright,' she announced, as if I were unaware of the fact. 'How on earth am I supposed to teach such a child?'

'Master Albright and I discussed this with you when you agreed to take Liberty into your school,' I said tightly. 'You assured us that you had yet to come across a child from a decent home whom you were not able to instruct and you were happy to take a year's tuition fees in advance so confident were you that Liberty would be able to learn under your tutelage.'

'Oh, I don't believe she is an imbecile,' Dame Oliver said, shaking her bony finger. 'Quite the contrary. It is my belief that she wilfully refuses to speak or learn. A sharp rap across the knuckles to provoke her into words would be the most fruitful course of action, although I am aware you and your husband hold with a more...' she paused, struggling for a suitable word, '...gentle method of child-rearing than that which I would personally recommend.'

Dame Oliver gave me a pained smile indicating her impatience with such indulgence. 'Nonetheless, Mistress Albright, Liberty needs to understand that she is to do as she is told or there will be consequences.'

'She is not being wilfully uncooperative,' I said, trying to keep my temper in accordance with Matthew's counsel. 'Liberty cannot hear.'

Dame Oliver shook her head. 'I don't believe that,' she said, pursing her thin lips together and creating more lines on her ancient face. 'She understands perfectly well when it is time for luncheon or play.'

'Yes, Liberty knows routines and she recognises common words from the shape of your mouth when you say them,' I explained carefully.

Dame Oliver wrinkled her nose in distaste. 'I am sorry, but there is no place for a girl like Liberty in my school,' she said, unlocking her money drawer. 'The other children don't take to her, and neither do I.' She pushed a pile of coins across her desk towards me. 'She threw those stones at Isabella for no reason at all. In fact, the girl was trying to make friends with her, encouraging Liberty to talk by showing her how silly she looks when she makes her humming sound.'

I glared at Dame Oliver, struggling to hold my tongue.

'I am reimbursing you the fees that you have paid. Please take Liberty home and do not bring her here again.'

I counted the money back into my purse, my hand trembling with anger.

'This is five shillings short,' I said.

'Yes, it is less a three-shilling payment I made to Isabella's parents in recompense of her broken tooth and the two shillings it cost me to have the window pane repaired.'

'How can you know it was Liberty who broke the window?' I exclaimed.

'And how can you know it wasn't her, Mistress Albright, as she cannot speak to you?' Dame Oliver said, leaning forward with a smirk, satisfied that she had made her point.

I collected Liberty from the garden where she was sitting alone under a tree as the other children played pat-a-cake by the wall. She was confused, but I pointed towards home and I smiled at her so as she wouldn't think anything was amiss.

The afternoon sun warmed our faces as we walked home and I longed to explain to Liberty that she had done nothing wrong, that she was right to defend herself and that it wasn't her fault Dame Oliver wouldn't teach her anymore. My heart ached that she had no playmates or even a dear sister of a similar age as I had been fortunate enough to have, to make her silent world any less lonely.

But without words all we had were the feelings between us and I squeezed her hand as we made our way through the bustling streets so as she would know I was always on her side. As we passed the Guildhall I thought of Gwen inside – fragile, frightened and alone – and my determination to help her grew ever greater.

11

THORNS

The Lunar Society had agreed to meet outside the gaol on the following Sunday morning, but before then I had the opportunity to visit Little Aston Hall again with Matthew. As Lord Aston had requested and paid for it, the law required Matthew, in his role as magistrate, to take statements from the Aston household about events pertaining to the death of Lady Aston so as they could be presented to the assizes judges when they arrived in town.

I hadn't at that point told Matthew about the Lunar Society or the activities of Amber, Sarah, Sam and myself as I didn't want to compromise his legal responsibilities. I also didn't want to worry him as he was becoming more fragile in body and spirit with every passing day with the weight of Lady Aston's murder on his shoulders, and my involvement in Gwen's defence would have given him even more cause to fret.

Knowing me well and in light of my voiced desire to help Gwen on the night of her arrest, Matthew suspected I was up to something, but he preferred to turn a blind eye and that suited us both.

'Let me do the talking when we get there,' Matthew said as

we sat close together in the carriage, a blanket over our knees, trying to keep the chill of the morning from seeping into our bones. 'You know Lord Aston's opinion about women who don't hold their tongues or overstep their position.'

'God bless the squire and his relations,' I said dryly, wondering if Matthew was familiar with the ditty.

'And keep us in our proper stations,' Matthew finished for me with a hollow laugh. 'In all earnestness though, Hester, I know you are the equal of men in character, heart and mind, better than most in fact, rich or poor, but we need to tread carefully with these people. We don't want to antagonise Lord Aston any more than is completely necessary. Who knows what he might do next if provoked?'

'What worse can he do?' I asked in a voice louder than I had intended. 'He already has an innocent woman lined up for the gallows based on his word alone as far as I can tell.'

'Well, that is for the assizes court to decide. Our job, rather my job, is to collect the declarations from the occupants of Little Aston Hall, the scene of the murder.'

'It's ridiculous,' I said. 'He will have told everyone what to say.'

'That's as maybe, but this is the process of the law. I can't change it to suit our purposes. Unless you want to see your own husband being tried at the assizes for interfering with the course of justice?'

'Hmmph,' I said, turning away from him and staring through the misted carriage window at the rainy fields beyond. I knew he was right, but could not hide my disapproval.

Lord Aston was waiting for us on the driveway his face set in a scowl, his black mourning clothes sodden with the rain.

'I expected you at nine,' he said as I helped Matthew down from the stoop.

'My apologies, Lord Aston, the inclement weather meant the

road out of town was churned up by the early carriages to London,' explained Matthew. 'It took us a good while to make our way through.'

Lord Aston had stopped listening after the apology and we followed him into the hallway as we had on the night of Lady Aston's murder.

'I have gathered my family in the saloon,' he said, throwing an ornate door open onto a formally furnished room, dominated by an enormous painting over the fireplace depicting hounds tearing apart a fox. Herbert and his two younger siblings, a dark-haired boy and girl in their early teens, sat rigidly in seats along the far wall.

'You may question them now but I don't know what you think they will be able to tell you.'

Matthew was in pain after sitting in the carriage and we were both cold from the journey so I found the verve to speak, even after Matthew's warning not to. 'Lord Aston, my husband and I would like to take the opportunity to remove our wet cloaks and sit a moment by the fire to warm ourselves before he begins his duties here.'

Lord Aston opened and closed his mouth and glared at me, but before he could speak Herbert leapt up and rang the servant bell.

'Of course, Mistress Albright. How remiss of my father to neglect the comfort of you and your good husband. Won't you sit down, please? I will have Lena bring you some tea.'

He guided us to two stuffed chairs by the hearth and Matthew sat with relief.

We waited in silence until Lena came in with the tray. She was trembling so that the cups and saucers were rattling off each other and Herbert watched her with an impatient tut.

'Thank you, Lena, that will be all,' he said as she bit her lip and scuttled out of the room.

'We are extremely sorry for your loss.' Matthew began in his official tone, having had a reviving sip of his tea. 'It is with regret that the most unfortunate of circumstances have necessitated our visit to you today. Please accept our condolences once again on the untimely death of Lady Aston, your dear wife and mother.'

Lord Aston and Herbert nodded and the two younger Astons stared at the floor, the girl flushed pink with emotion, the boy stone faced.

'Well, come on, let's have the questions,' snapped Lord Aston, striding the length of the room to the window and squinting through the watery pane at the formal gardens beyond.

'Of course,' said Matthew, indicating for me to get his notebook from the saddlebag at his feet. 'Perhaps we could begin with the younger family members.'

The girl looked up startled and began smoothing down the black silk of her dress in readiness for the attention.

'Could you tell me your names and ages, please?'

'I am Claudia Aston and this is my brother Gabriel. We are both thirteen,' the girl said, surprising us both with her courage to speak first.

'Twins then?' said Matthew pleasantly.

'Oh no,' said Claudia, carefully correcting Matthew's assumption. 'There are ten months between Gabriel and I.'

'I'm the oldest,' Gabriel said in a high-pitched tone that fell to a deeper pitch within that one short sentence, reminding me of how our John's voice had changed at that age.

'I understand you were both at home on the afternoon of the eleventh, the day your poor mother met her demise. Did you hear or see anything unusual? Anything that might be useful for us to know?'

Gabriel and Claudia looked at each other and then at their father.

Lord Aston sighed heavily. 'They were in the school room in the garden wing writing out their French declensions. They heard and saw nothing.'

'Is this correct?' asked Matthew, addressing his question to Gabriel.

He nodded. 'We didn't hear a sound nor see an intruder.'

'Gabriel and I heard the screams, though, when Lena found Mama,' Claudia said in a shaky voice. 'We ran through the house to the drawing room but Herbert was already there. He said Mother was dead and he didn't want to let us in, but we pushed past so we could see it with our own eyes.' She paused at the memory and screwed her face up, forcing back tears until her composure had returned. 'Then Father came rushing in with Mr Brown behind him. When he saw Mama he howled at the top of his voice, like an animal caught in a trap.'

Lord Aston poured himself a whisky from the decanter by the window and drank it down in one large gulp.

'That must have been very frightening for you both,' said Matthew kindly.

'Not for me,' said Gabriel, standing so we could see the height of him. 'Claudia was scared but I wasn't. I go hunting with Father and Herbert. I'm used to seeing carrion.'

'Sit down, Gabriel,' Lord Aston bellowed and the boy sat immediately, his face resuming its earlier hard appearance.

I stared at the boy, quite shocked at his callousness, before turning my attention back to his sister. 'What happened next, Claudia?' I asked, forgetting Matthew's request that I stay quiet.

'Herbert told us to go to our rooms and to stay there,' she said, 'and that's what we did, until we heard the commotion with Father and Herbert in the hall getting ready to go to the village and we came down again to see what was happening.'

'When you entered the drawing room where your mother lay, did you notice anything unusual, anything different about the room at all?' Matthew asked, frowning briefly at me.

Claudia pressed her lips together and narrowed her eyes as she tried to recall the scene. 'The horses were missing,' she said at last.

'What do you mean?' Matthew asked, leaning forward.

'There were two marble statues of horses, one on either end of the mantelpiece. They had been Mother's, a gift from her parents when she turned twenty-one. They weren't there when we saw Mama lying on the floor. I couldn't bear to look at all that blood around her so I looked up instead and I remember noticing that the horses weren't there, as they usually were.'

'Do you mean these ones?' Herbert asked with a quizzical frown, rising from the settle to point at the two magnificent white marble horse sculptures on either end of the mantelpiece. 'They have always been here, Claudia, not in the drawing room.'

Claudia followed his gaze and flushed red as a beetroot. 'I'm sorry,' she gasped. 'I must have got muddled up and forgotten which room I was in. It was all such a shock and poor Mother lying there...' she tailed off, distressed and embarrassed by her mistake.

'Typical feeble-minded girl,' muttered Lord Aston. 'I don't know why you bother asking women anything,' he levelled at Matthew, studiously ignoring my presence. 'Waste of bloody time.'

Claudia stared at her lap, deflated with shame and I had to bite my lip to stop myself leaping to her defence.

'No matter,' Matthew said. 'Claudia, it is quite understandable that you might have become confused over a small detail given the high emotions at the time. Please do not let it trouble you, it is no trouble to me.' She gave him a small, grateful nod and I admired his gentle handling of the error.

'I have one more question,' Matthew continued, ignoring Lord Aston's heavy sigh. 'Have either of you heard of a woman in the village named Gwen Foley?'

Claudia shook her head, but Gabriel jumped up with animation. 'I've heard of her, the peasants say she's a witch, don't they?' he said excitedly. 'They say she looks like a spectre and flies around at night on her hound, smothering babies and ruining crops.'

Lord Aston poured another drink and brought it to his lips with a hand so full of shakes that a fair portion of it spilt onto the floor.

'Tell me, Claudia,' I asked quickly, sensing Lord Aston was about to send the children back to their rooms. He clearly hadn't shared with them his notion that Gwen was responsible for Lady Aston's death, or his and Herbert's brutal persecution of the woman on the night of the murder. 'Did your mother like books?'

Lord Aston froze, glass in hand and glowered at me. 'What nonsense is this? Did she like books? Do you think a volume from my study flew around the house and hit my Loella on the head?'

I ignored him and raised my eyes at Claudia, hoping to prompt a response from her.

'Oh yes,' she said. 'Mama loved books. She wanted to read Father's books on science but he wouldn't let her.'

'Certain areas of knowledge are not suitable for women,' said Lord Aston. 'Science is one of them. Law is another.' He glared at Matthew who shuffled through his papers so as to avoid his eye and his meaning.

'That has been most helpful, Claudia and Gabriel. Thank you for your time,' Matthew said. 'And please accept my condolences once again.'

Gabriel shrugged, but Claudia's bottom lip began to tremble.

My heart went out to such a sensitive child as she being brought up in a houseful of brutes as oafish as her father and brothers. I would have liked to throw my arms around her in place of her mother, she looked sore in need of it, but she made herself stand upright and blinked back her tears as all girls of breeding are taught to do in company.

'This is a waste of everyone's time and you two are becoming thorns in my side with your incessant questions,' said Lord Aston when the children had gone. 'That ghostly witch killed my wife and everyone knows it. She violated my house with impunity. She came down the chimney and smashed Loella's brains out on the hearthstones. And before you cast aspersions on that I can assure you that there is no other way to gain entrance to this building. I ensure doors are locked day and night and there are mantraps all around the grounds to catch poachers. Loella was trying to protect herself against that evil creature with a witch's bottle. You saw it in her hand with your own eyes, you know I speak the truth!' His colour was high and he was shaking again, but whether with anger or grief I couldn't tell.

Matthew waited a moment for Lord Aston to compose himself.

'It is most helpful to hear your opinion on the events leading to your wife's death, but I am still not clear,' he said. 'Are you accusing Gwen Foley of murder or of witchcraft?'

Lord Aston looked at Matthew as if he were a fool. 'Both,' he shouted. 'She murdered my wife. She came down the chimney by malevolent means. There is no other explanation. Loella must have been petrified of that woman, that's why she had the bottle. She was probably trying to hide it behind a brick in the hearth to protect herself, but Gwen Foley killed her before she could get it in place.'

'Forgive me, Lord Aston,' said Matthew, treading carefully,

'but I was under the impression that you are a learned man, a man of science and rational thought? It is 1723 not 1623, after all. Surely these antiquated beliefs about witches hold no sway in your mind? Nowadays such notions are held only by simple-minded peasants or... women, are they not?' He glanced at me apologetically, but I forgave him his slight, knowing he was trying to lead Lord Aston into rethinking his accusations against Gwen.

'I am drawing on rational thought, Master Albright,' Lord Aston hissed. 'My account is the only explanation possible given the facts of the matter and also given the recent history of devilish events in this village. There is evil afoot in Little Aston, make no mistake about that, and it emanates from the White. I will see her swing from a gibbet for witchcraft and murder. There will be no mercy for her as she had no mercy for my Loella.'

He stormed from the room and slammed the door behind him, making the decanters on the sideboard rattle on their silver tray.

A stunned silence filled the room until Herbert stepped forward from his position next to the mantel. I had all but forgotten he was there, not a word had he spoken since correcting Claudia on the position of the marble horses. 'I apologise for my father's passionate outburst,' he said, holding out his hands in a placating gesture, 'but I am certain you can understand his distress.'

In Herbert I saw a younger, thinner version of his father. The same steely blue eyes, the same bushy hair, albeit brown where his father's was grey, and the same confidence in his place in the world – right on top of the pile. I knew we wouldn't get any different information from him than we had from Lord Aston. For reasons that were as yet unfathomable to me and Matthew they were intent on blaming Gwen for the crime.

'Of course, it is a most disturbing time for the whole family,' Matthew said, reaching for my arm to help him to his feet. 'I will need to speak to the servants of the house and then we will leave you all in peace to mourn the Lady Aston.' He wrapped his fingers around the top of his stick and took a step towards the door.

Herbert's face fell and a little of his highborn poise left him. 'What? Why would you need to do that? I don't think Father would approve of you talking to the domestics. We are quite strict about servants knowing their place in this house. They are not given voice. They are given instruction.'

'Well then,' said Matthew pleasantly, 'please instruct them to answer my questions truthfully and then my wife and I will be on our way.'

Herbert huffed and puffed before finally showing us downstairs. He ordered the housekeeper, a shrew of a woman called Mrs Fox, to gather the staff around the kitchen table and we waited for everyone to appear. Matthew and I questioned them one by one in the little parlour by the scullery which was Mrs Fox's private quarters and we came up with nothing helpful from any one of them.

Nobody had heard or seen any stranger entering or leaving the Hall; nobody had heard any fighting or shouting; and nobody had any other ideas about who could have killed Lady Aston, or might have wanted to, other than the witch Gwen Foley. They were all in agreement about that, apart from the cook, a gentle soul named Matilda Syms – an unusually tall, well-padded woman she was, ten or more years older than myself, who pleasantly surprised us with her strongly-held, private opinions on the folly of accusing women of sorcery.

'I don't like that talk about witches and pointing the finger at them that's different,' she confided in me as she sat down and pulled her shawl round her shoulders. 'It's dangerous, to my mind. It's not how I was brought up, you see, to believe that sort of talk. I'm a Derbyshire Methodist through and through and we don't hold with tales of witchcraft or any of the dark arts. We believe we are all born God's children and none are in line with the devil. "Love thy neighbour and treat them as you would want to be treated yourself," that's what we are taught in our church. And that's what poor Gwen was to me, a neighbour. I quite liked her even though she looked a bit peculiar, but none of us is perfect, are we? She grew lovely cabbages and carrots in her grandmother's garden. I sent the kitchen boy, Robby, to buy from her a few times last summer. Thank goodness Lord Aston didn't know where his veg came from!' she said with a gasp that made the dewlap under her chin wobble. 'Imagine if he'd found out? I didn't know he had such a hatred for Gwen or I wouldn't have done it. I'd have thought talk of witchcraft and the like were below a man of his intellect, though, truth be told. His wife wouldn't hear a word of it, God bless her soul. You won't tell him where his veg came from will you?' Her eyes widened with alarm and her long fingers worried at the hem of her apron at the thought of Lord Aston's wrath for her accidental error.

I reached out to reassure her with a pat on her chubby arm. 'We won't tell him, Matilda, and may I say I admire you holding your own view on Gwen Foley. It can't be easy as it's different to most folks' opinions round here.'

She smiled at me. 'To be honest, ma'am, most of the time I find it best to keep everyone fed and keep my thoughts to myself,' she said and I found myself warming to her even more as I recognised the feeling.

'Thank you, Matilda,' said Matthew, noting down her

responses in his ledger. 'Is Robby the kitchen boy here? Can we speak with him?'

Matilda shook her head. 'No, sir, he left Lord Aston's service a few weeks back. He's over in town now I believe, doing odd jobs for folk. He has to fend for himself more or less.' She lowered her voice out of respect and said, 'His mother was Joanna Baker. That poor woman they hanged for doing away with her husband.'

I tutted and shook my head in sympathy and Matilda clearly shared my sentiments as she wiped a tear from her eye as she spoke of it.

'In that case will you send Lena Harris in, please?' Matthew said. 'She is the last, I think?'

'I will, sir,' said Matilda. She hesitated at the door. 'Be gentle with her, won't you? She's a frail one, is Lena, and frightened of her own shadow.'

'We will,' I said, appreciating her advice. Matilda hesitated again and went to speak, before changing her mind and closing the door gently behind her.

Lena came in almost immediately and sat down in front of us, her eyes darting nervously around the room. She was a pretty girl, I thought, with her coal black hair and big blue eyes, but there didn't seem to be much in the way of wits about her.

'Lena, we would like you to tell us about the afternoon of the eleventh of November,' Matthew began. 'You were the first person to find Lady Aston's body, is that right?'

'Yes, I was, sir. She rang the bell for tea and I got it all ready by meself and carried it up to the drawing room for her as usual and I thought it was strange because she hadn't opened the door for me. She usually does because she knows I find it hard to hold the tray and open the door and I've had a couple of accidents dropping cups and things like that.'

She paused and I nodded encouragingly.

'Anyway, she hadn't opened the door for me so I put the tray on the cabinet in the hallway and opened it meself and that's when I sees my lady's feet sticking out from behind the settle next to the hearth. I ran over to her because I thought she must have fallen or taken faint but when I got to her I saw she was dead.'

'How did you know she was dead?' Matthew asked.

Lena put her hand to her mouth and closed her eyes. 'Oh, sir, it were dreadful! There was blood all round her head like on the carpet and in her hair and her eyes was wide open but there was not a flicker of life in them. That's when I screamed and Herbert came running in and then he sent me out and that was the last I saw of her until you and Mistress Albright arrived and that coroner lady who looks like a gent.'

Matthew suppressed a small smile at her description of Amber before asking his most important question. 'Who do you think killed her, Lena?'

Lena took a deep breath. 'I think it was that witch they call the White from the village.'

'Do you?' I said, trying to catch her eye to see if she was lying. 'Why do you think that? Did you see Gwen Foley in the drawing room or anywhere in the Hall?'

Lena shook her head.

'Then why do you think it was she?' asked Matthew.

'Because Lord Aston says so,' Lena answered in a small voice. 'And Herbert says we must always agree with Lord Aston and not upset him.'

'When did Herbert say that to you?' I asked.

'When we were... on our own together one day,' she said shyly. Lena blushed and it seemed likely from her words and her reaction that her relationship with Herbert was more than was considered proper between a master and a servant in his house.

Matthew had clearly had the same thought. 'Has Herbert

been taking advantage of you?' he asked, rather too directly for the delicacy of the situation in my opinion.

I was right as Lena burst into tears and refused to say anymore. I glared at Matthew as she rushed from the room.

'You should have let me talk to her about it,' I admonished him. 'You jumping in with your big feet. You scared her off.'

'Yes, you're right, dear,' said Matthew tutting. 'That was my mistake. She may have more to tell, but we will not know it now.' He thumped the arm of his chair with his fist in frustration and I softened in my pique towards him.

'Don't be harsh on yourself, my love, it's been a long day,' I said. 'And a trying one at that.'

Matthew nodded. 'It has. And the worst of it is that we are no nearer the truth now than we were when we arrived.'

'Perhaps not,' I said, looking out the parlour window as Herbert and Gabriel strolled across the lawn holding their guns and a brace of dead pheasants. 'But the hunt has most certainly begun.'

12

FINGERNAILS

There was an early frost on the day of Loella Aston's funeral but by the time we had gathered around the freshly dug grave in the family plot of Little Aston church the white sparkles had melted away in the winter sun. The service, led by the Reverend Mr Brown, had been rightly solemn but there was an air of disquiet among the mourners which lent the event such an uneasy affect that I almost expected the lid to lift on Lady Aston's coffin and for her to rise up and point a bony finger at the scoundrel responsible for her death.

I admired Nicholas's ability to come across as quite sincere as he delivered an homage reflecting on the qualities of a good Christian woman, all of which he implied were embodied by the late Loella Aston, and his assurance of her spirit finding sanctuary in the arms of the Lord.

I had positioned myself at the end of a pew near the centre of the nave so that I could surreptitiously observe the congregated Aston family in front of me, and their domestic staff who were seated across the aisle. Lord Aston held his face stony throughout, although I noticed his eye twitching as a tearful Claudia read out a poem by John Dryden which had been a favourite of her mother's. Her voice almost gave out as she reached the final line. '*What has been, has been, and I have had my hour,*' she whispered, poor lamb, before having to be helped back to her place by Herbert.

As Herbert had turned to assist his sister I saw that there were three livid red marks down the left side of his face. They looked like scratch marks, so straight were they and my mind initially went to the altercation with Tamworth on the night of Gwen's arrest. But I could remember no attack to his face by the dog and, more saliently, I had noticed no such wounds on his face when we interviewed the household. No, these marks were recent, still oozing blood. He was clearly uncomfortably conscious of them too as I had noticed him dabbing a handkerchief at his cheek several times throughout the service.

Gabriel was seated next to Herbert and sniffed constantly throughout the service, though whether that was from crying or due to the symptoms of a cold it was difficult to tell.

The household staff in the pews to my left sat in silent respect as one would expect, although several of the older ones had fallen asleep, their chins nodding on their chests, whilst most of the younger ones gazed unseeing towards the front, lost in their own daydreams and concerns. Lena the housemaid was the exception. She was bent forward as if every word were of the utmost importance to her, her eyes burning with a rage that I found perplexing. It was only after I had seen Herbert's face that I realised her attention was directed towards him, rather than towards the coffin wherein lay her dead mistress.

A scattering of folk from the village had seated themselves behind the household staff. Those present included Tom Hardwick and a skinny, pockmarked woman with a restless toddler on her knee whom I took to be his wife Mary. The elder Mistress Hardwick and her companion Hilda sat with them, arms folded under their bosoms, watching the service as one might enjoy the cheap entertainments of a penny opera.

Matthew and I had been asked back to Little Aston Hall for the wake, and although Matthew was of a mind to decline the invitation I had urged him to reconsider as conversation at such a gathering might offer up a morsel or two of precious information that could help Gwen's predicament.

'I will stay only for a half hour,' Matthew whispered to me as we made our way slowly up the path from the churchyard and across the lawns to the grand Hall, his right arm leaning on his stick and his left held fast around my waist to give him balance.

'By the time we finally get there, my dearest, it will be all but over anyway,' I said under my breath as we paused once again for Matthew to rest his leg.

The small number of black-clad mourners were dwarfed by the size of the enormous reception room where drinks and small bites had been hastily laid out by the returning servants. After finding Matthew a chair I went straight over to Claudia. She was standing alone by one of the floor-to-ceiling windows which lined the right side of the room, staring forlornly out across the lawns of her grand family home.

'May I join you?' I asked and she started as if I had woken her from a deep sleep.

She nodded and we looked out onto the grounds together.

'It must have been delightful to grow up in such a place,' I ventured. When she didn't answer I tried a different tack. 'I enjoyed your reading of Dryden in the church. "Happy the Man" is one of my favourite poems too, it reminds us to live in the present day, doesn't it, and not worry too much about what's coming next? *Tomorrow do thy worst, for I have lived today.*'

'It is a comfort at least that Mama didn't know what was coming next,' Claudia agreed sadly. 'For tomorrow did do its worst, for her.'

I nodded in sympathy. 'You must miss her terribly,' I said.

Claudia's eyes misted. 'My mother was the only one who knew me. She knew I wanted to go away from here. My dream is to attend the University of Padua in Italy. It is where Copernicus studied, and Galileo. They have women teaching there as well as men. Can you even imagine such a wonderful thing? Mama was determined to help me learn about important things, not just the endless French and music and needlework that Father wants me to fill my head with to make me more marriageable. Mama understood that I wanted to find my own way. She bought science books and we were reading them together, and she was teaching me Italian. She spoke it because she lived in Milan when she was a child. She was going to ask Father if I could go and stay awhile with her sister who resides there still so I could practise the language. But all that's gone, I suppose, now she's dead.' She gazed at the grey clouds gathering above the copse at the far end of the lawn and sighed.

'Perhaps you could speak to your father about your ambitions?' I said uncertainly. 'I'm sure your happiness is of great concern to him.'

Claudia made a noise as if she had touched something unpleasant in the dark and then she gave a small laugh. 'My father cares nothing for the happiness of any woman,' she said. 'He cares only that they know their place in the world.'

'Claudia, your life is your own,' I told her. 'Would your mother not have wanted you to be the mistress of your fate? You are not a prisoner here.'

'Thank you, Mistress Albright, I shall think on that,' she said politely but without much hope, touching the tips of her fingers to the window glass.

I wanted to ask her again about Gwen Foley but before I could steer the conversation around, Herbert appeared at my shoulder and positioned himself between us. 'I see you have been consoling my sister. How kind you are,' he said as Claudia retreated behind her misty eyes once again. 'Please don't let us keep you from your husband.'

'What happened to your face?' I asked him with a boldness that surprised us both.

His hand went to his damaged cheek. 'A shaving cut,' he snapped. 'My hand was not as steady as usual on the morning of my mother's funeral. I'm sure you can understand that, Mistress Albright? Or perhaps my distress is difficult for you to imagine as you are of the good fortune not to have had a family member butchered to death by the local sorceress.'

Claudia went to speak, but Herbert silenced her with a look of such vitriol that she took an involuntary step backwards to enlarge the distance between them.

I raised my eyes at him and he held my gaze for several seconds, silently challenging me to contradict him. I was sorely tempted, but also keenly aware that I was a guest in his house and that, whatever his feelings towards her, his mother had been buried that very morning.

'Well,' I said at last, breaking the stalemate, 'I had better see to my husband.'

'Yes, you do that,' Herbert agreed with a sneer. 'Make yourself useful as a wife.' He spat the last word, so I would fathom his contempt for my position as a woman legally belonging to a man, and I refrained from retorting with my views on his position of unearned privilege and wealth.

Matthew was making stilted conversation with one of Lord Aston's elderly uncles. As I approached, Lena was reaching for his empty glass and I saw that the three middle fingernails on her right hand were ragged and caked in blood. I put my hand on hers and gave her a questioning look and she glanced up at me with a flash of panic. She pulled her fingers into a fist and shook her head. Over by the window Herbert was still talking to

Claudia, the livid marks on his cheek clear on his pale skin, even from across the room.

~

George came to collect us from Little Aston Hall at noon as arranged and we hoisted Matthew up into the carriage, me pushing, George pulling in a most inelegant, but effective, manner. Matthew let out a long sigh of relief as we set off down the driveway, the horses' hooves making a lively rhythm along the gravel.

'I shall be glad to get home,' he said. 'What an ordeal it is, making small talk with lords and squires. I don't know the first thing about riding or hunting and yet that is all they want to discuss. That and my war wound. They seem to think it is a badge of honour rather than a curse.' He tapped the wooden shaft below his hip. The injury necessitating it still pained him greatly and recalled in him such distressing memories that he often woke in the night shaking with terror.

'I know, my dear,' I said. 'You will rest as soon as we are home again and I will bring you a hot toddy to take the edge off that ache.'

He smiled at me in gratitude.

'But first I do need to have a quick word with Mistress Hardwick, the younger, in the village,' I said apologetically, and the smile fell from his face. 'George, stop here, will you?' I called to the front, leaning out the window and banging on the outside of the carriage door, before Matthew had a chance to object.

'I won't be long, I promise,' I said, jumping down onto the muddy lane by the pond in the middle of Little Aston.

I asked the first people I saw, an old couple minding a flock of geese, where Tom and Mary lived and made my way to the small cottage behind the farm where I had been directed.

The Hardwick's cottage was of the old style, squat and dark with a roof of straw and a doorway so low anyone larger than a child of Liberty's age would have to stoop to enter. The yard in front of the dwelling was messy, strewn with rusty farm tools and rotting vegetables picked over by an assortment of free ranging pigs and chickens. A small child sat on a patch of rough grass next to the cottage door digging in the dirt with a spoon. His dress and ruddy face were smeared with mud and snot streamed from his nose. He howled as he saw me approaching and the door was quickly flung open by his mother who greeted me with a suspicious frown as she lifted him onto her hip.

'Mary Hardwick?' I asked, in my friendliest tone.

She gave one curt nod and pulled her child into a closer embrace as if I had arrived to take him away from her.

'I am Hester Albright, wife of the Lichfield magistrate Matthew Albright.'

She eyed me suspiciously as I took a step closer towards her. 'I am very much interested in the death of Lady Aston and the role, if any, that Gwen Foley might have played in her demise.'

Mary shrank back at the mention of Gwen's name and made an exaggerated sign of the cross that encompassed both her and the child.

'I wonder if I could come in and talk to you for a few moments?' I asked, with little expectation that she would agree.

To my surprise she nodded and disappeared into the gloomy interior of the cottage. I bent and followed her in, nearly tripping over the pair of ragged chickens who preceded me and took a startled breath at the stench as I crossed the threshold. The one room that constituted the family's living quarters was damp and filthy, a pig and the poultry scavenging for food on the bare earthen floor. A small fire burned in a stone hearth at one end of the room with a blackened cooking pot hanging above it. Three low stools surrounded a roughly made wooden table in front of the fire and the family's straw beds and dirty bedding lurked in the gloom at the other end of the cottage.

'We don't have much,' Mary said defensively as I took in the meagre surroundings, trying not to betray my aversion to the filth in the room.

'Is Tom here?' I asked, peering around.

'He's gone back to the fields,' Mary replied. 'He's already missed half a day due to the funeral. Lord Aston wanted all the farm hands back at work straight after.'

'Lord Aston owns the farm as well, does he?' I asked, although it was clear enough from her words that he did.

'Yes,' she replied. 'But it's overseen by Master Duncan and Lord Herbert comes to look over the place once in a while too.'

I nodded. 'May I take a seat?' I asked, indicating one of the stools.

'Yes,' she said again, lowering herself onto one of the stools and placing her child on the floor beside her. He began chasing one of the chickens around the small space, narrowly missing knocking into the boiling pot over the fire, so she gave him a crust of bread and sent him to play outside.

I looked at her properly then and saw how drawn she was and how very young. Her face was covered with healing wounds and scars from what must have been an unpleasant malady and the marks took away any youthful glow she might otherwise still have had. An ill-fitting woollen dress hung from her thin frame and her hair was covered with a cotton bonnet that had once been white but was now threadbare and grey. I wondered what she had hoped for when she had married Tom Hardwick – surely not this? I felt a pang of empathy for the dreams she must have had of being a pretty wife with a pleasant home, dreams which did not, and now never would, come true for her.

'It's not an easy life you have here, Mary, but you do your best, I can see that,' I said in a gentle voice.

Her eyes softened a little. 'All the girls wanted to marry Tom,' she said quietly. 'He were broad shouldered and proper handsome. He used to dip his cap to the ladies and make them giggle, even the old ones.' She smiled faintly at the memory. 'And he always had a tale to tell, made me laugh he did.' She picked a splinter of wood from the tabletop and turned it between her fingers, deep in thought. 'We haven't had much to laugh about for a long time now, Mistress Albright,' she said, flicking the piece of wood onto the floor and watching as a chicken pecked at it before abandoning it in favour of a cluster of breadcrumbs.

'We had Jack the year we were married but I have lost three babes since then. Tom says it's the White's fault, that she put a curse on me because she is jealous that I'm married to him. He says she's a witch.'

'And what do you think, Mary?' I asked mildly.

'All I know is that I had my Jack with no difficulties – a good strong boy he is, too – and then as soon as she, Gwen Foley, arrived in the village, I can't keep a baby. There must be an association, mustn't there? One babe was lost on Christmas Eve.' She closed her eyes for a moment, before she could continue. 'She was perfect she was, and big enough to live, but she went blue and died not an hour after she was born. God wouldn't let that happen on Christmas Eve would he, Mistress Albright? That's what my Tom said. That's the work of dark forces. That's the work of evil, of a witch. Then Tom hurt his arm and couldn't work for months and we had no money left. That was her as well, wanting to finish us off, that's what Tom said.'

I let her talk and heard the desperation in her voice as she tried to make some sense out of the cruel misfortunes that had befallen her and Tom, and I understood why she wanted there to be someone to blame, a cause that could be stopped so good things could start to happen again. Gwen Foley was the simplest explanation to Mary's unschooled mind – an unusual-looking stranger, her arrival corresponding with a run of bad luck for the Hardwicks, the suspicions about Gwen that Tom and his mother had passed on to Mary. It was becoming plain to me how these stories about Gwen had begun in Little Aston, like a spark from a fire that caught alight the roof thatch of one cottage and was soon burning down all the houses in the village.

'I am very sorry about your lost babes,' I told her, placing my hand over hers. 'I know of that pain. It is a bleak place to find yourself in, there's no denying that.'

Mary sniffed and stared at the floor, so uncertain was she of how to respond to sympathy that I wondered if she had ever been offered any before.

'But, my dear,' I continued, 'there is no such thing as witchcraft and I think you know that really. The reasons women lose babes is due to hidden happenings inside our own bodies, or in the infants themselves, and from the humours all around us.'

She glanced up at me and I indicated the impoverished, unclean surroundings of her home. 'When you had Jack were you living here?' I asked her.

'I've lived in Little Aston all my life,' she replied with pride.

'No, I mean were you and Tom living here, in this farm cottage when you were pregnant with Jack and when he was born?'

Mary shook her head. 'No, the cottage was occupied then by Master Duncan's father. It was only when he died that we were able to move in. Jack was nearly one by then. Before that we stayed at Tom's mother's house, with her and Hilda.'

I thought of the clean, well-kept home of the older Mrs Hardwick and the bountiful food on her kitchen table and wondered whether the contrast to her current domestic circumstances was as evident to Mary as it was to me.

'Mary, has anyone ever spoken to you about household management, about keeping sanitary conditions? About making sure animals stay outside?' I asked her gently.

She shook her head and her eyes ranged around the room as if it were the first time she had seen it.

'Did you know that you can get a type of pox from chickens?' I asked her.

Her hand went to the pockmarks on her face and she shook her head again.

'And that having the pox when you are with child can lead to illness or death in the baby?'

She stood up quickly from the table, her voice rising in panic. 'No, I didn't know any of that,' she said. 'Tom always said that it's best to have the livestock indoors or someone could steal them and then we'd be left with nothing at all.' She put her hand over her mouth as a piglet ran across her feet. 'Is it my fault then, that my babes were lost?' she whispered, her eyes full of angst.

'It is not your fault, Mary, but nor is it Gwen's. There could be many reasons for your losses or no reason at all. I've lost babes of my own so I know the truth of that. But I am sure that, why ever it happens, it is not because of sorcery. And there are actions you can take to increase your chances of having another bonny child like Jack.'

'We must keep the animals outside,' she said.

'That would be prudent,' I agreed. 'And a good place to start.'

Mary shooed the chickens out of the open door and returned to the table, holding Jack's hand in hers.

I smiled at them, pleased that she had taken on board my advice. 'Do you think you might be able to talk to your husband about these matters?' I asked carefully as she sat down and pulled Jack onto her lap.

'About the animals?' she said.

'Yes that, and about Gwen Foley,' I ventured.

'I don't think my Tom would like me to say different about her,' Mary replied, biting her thumb nail.

'Say different about who?' a man's voice boomed behind us as Tom strode into the cottage, his face pinched with anger. 'What is she doing in here?' he shouted, pointing at me. 'She caused enough upset at my ma's house with her questions, casting doubt on the evil of that White woman.'

I stood up and tried to placate him but I feared he would strike me so enraged was he to find me talking to Mary.

'She wouldn't go, Tom,' Mary said, a strange look of power taking over her face. 'She said terrible things about our home and our lost babies. She said it was my fault, and your fault instead of that witch Gwen Foley.'

'I won't have anyone talk to my wife like that,' Tom said, pushing up his sleeves.

Mary started to giggle with glee and I realised she was excited at his manly defence of her.

I was beginning to panic that I would be unable to get past Tom without coming into contact with his fists when to my enormous relief George appeared in the doorway, an imposing figure in his great coat, holding his horsewhip in one hand and a purse of coin in the other.

'I am here to take my mother-in-law Mistress Albright home,' he said firmly, pulling himself to his full height having crouched to get under the lintel.

Tom took in the implications of George's two offerings and the men stared coldly at each other as I made my way around George and out into the yard. Tom grunted and nodded at the money and George placed it on the table and then backed out the door to join me. We hastened back to the carriage where Matthew was waiting for us and I was grateful for his comforting arms around me as we rode back into town.

It had been a discouraging end to my visit with Mary and I held little hope that she would convey to Tom the important aspects of our discussion about Gwen. But I was heartened by the thought that the Hardwick family would have the means to eat well, for a few days at least.

13

HAIR

I had arranged to meet Amber and Sarah outside the gaol on Sunday morning so we could pass pamphlets out to folk on their way to and from church and make them aware of the dire circumstances Gwen Foley found herself in. Matthew was unhappy about us not accompanying him and Liberty to St Mary's for the morning service as is our custom, but I assured him that what we planned to do was of more help in promoting goodness of thought and deed than Amber and me sitting on a hard pew listening to one of the Reverend Mr Connelly's interminable sermons. He agreed in the end but he turned his face away from me when I went to give him a kiss before I left just so as I would know I had irked him.

'Be careful, Hettie,' he couldn't help himself saying as I picked up my basket of food for Gwen. He never could stay cross at me for long.

Amber was already there when I arrived at Bore Street. She was holding Tam by her side on a short leash and having a heated exchange with Gregory at the door.

'How many times do I have to tell you?' Gregory was saying, pointing at the dog. 'You are not bringing that hound in 'ere.'

Tam lurched towards him and Gregory stumbled back and began pushing the heavy entrance shut.

Amber placed her boot in the door and held out a coin. 'Come now, Gregory, surely we can come to an arrangement. Is it not cruel to keep a dog from its mistress and a mistress from her pet? Let me take him in for a few minutes. To give comfort to the accused woman.'

'I have been given strict instructions that Gwen Foley's animal is not to be let anywhere near her,' Gregory shouted through the remaining crack in the door. 'Or she will ride it away straight out the window and be off to see the devil to cook up more wickedness.'

Amber saw me then and raised her eyes in exasperation at Gregory's stubbornness. I moved her aside and put my face up close to the gap. 'Gregory, it's Mistress Albright. Open the door, please,' I said in a voice I would use for persuading small children to eat their pottage.

He grunted and opened the door a fraction wider.

'Who has told you not to allow this dog into the gaol, my dear fellow?'

'Well, no one person exactly,' Gregory said slowly. 'But folks in the Star Inn been saying that the dog is Gwen Foley's creature that she rides on at night. To do her curses and spells and what not.'

Amber shook her head in disbelief.

'Gregory,' I said. 'I do hope you haven't been loose-lipped around town about a prisoner in your care. I fear that the assizes judges will not be pleased if that is the case. Perhaps they will recommend a new gaoler be instated here if the responsibilities of this job are too much for you. I can ask my husband to arrange that, if you like.'

Gregory was silent, no doubt dwelling on the consequences of no longer having his occupation as gaoler in the often empty, two-cell prison with a warm hearth of his own to sit beside and plenty of coinage coming his way. 'That won't be necessary, ma'am,' he said as he drew the door fully open. 'You can have ten minutes with her. But keep that thing on a leash.'

~

Gwen was beyond delighted to see Tamworth and he surely felt the same, the way he jumped up beside her and licked her face until she cried with happiness.

'My Tam, my Tam,' she said over and over in her peculiar little voice and Amber flushed with pride at having saved him for her.

He lay across her lap as we spoke and the pair of them looked like they were made to be together, like two broken pieces of a jug made whole again.

'Gwen,' I said, drawing her attention from the dog as I had sombre information to relay to her. 'I visited Little Aston Hall several days ago with my husband and we talked to the family of Lady Aston and the servants. I'm sorry to tell you that they almost all seem to be of one mind when it comes to pointing the finger of guilt at you for the murder of Lady Aston. That, along with the villagers' accounts of witchcraft, and the grim fact that Lord Aston and his household seem to believe it too, means that the outlook for your trial is not favourable.'

Gwen pressed her lips together and closed her eyes.

'Can you think why they are saying these things?' Amber asked her.

She sniffed and wiped her nose on the sleeve of her filthy dress. 'Perhaps no one dares to disagree with Lord Aston?' she said. 'If he says it was I, then they will all say it.'

'That could well be the case,' I said, thinking back to Lord Aston's furious, unpredictable temper. 'Matilda, the cook at the

Hall, told us that a boy, Robby, used to visit you to buy vegetables for the house. Is that right?' I asked her.

Gwen smiled. 'Yes, dear Robby. He liked sitting with me and Tam and helping me in the garden. He told me no one was kind to him at the house except for Matilda and Lena the maid. He told me that–' She pressed her lips together again as if she was keeping in words she wanted to say.

'Go on,' I urged her.

'He told me that Master Herbert, Lord Aston's son, was being improper with Lena and taking her into the chambers upstairs to lie down for him. Robby said that for all Lord Aston is a brute he will not countenance any fraternising or the like between family and servants under his roof as it disrupts what he calls "the natural order of things", and that he would most likely cut off Herbert's inheritance if he ever found out and it would all go to his younger son, Gabriel, instead.'

'Did Lena tell him this?' Amber asked.

Gwen nodded. 'She is scared to death of Lord Aston finding out. She didn't want to lose her modesty but Robby told me that Herbert bullied and charmed her into it. You know how men can be...' she said knowingly, surprising me with her worldliness.

'I do,' I said, a knot of anger rising up in my throat.

'Is Herbert aware that you know about him and Lena?' Amber asked carefully, her eyes narrowing.

'I don't see how he could be,' said Gwen, stroking Tam's ears. 'Only Matilda knew that Robby visited me and she kept that a secret as she is familiar with how folk think about me in that village.'

'Time's up,' said Gregory, banging on the door and making Tam sit up and growl.

'Gwen,' I said, taking hold of her hand. 'You may hear us outside the gaol today. We are going to be handing out pamphlets that we have had printed about the unfairness of the charges of witchcraft against you.'

Amber pulled one of the leaflets out of her bag and handed it to Gwen. She peered at it in the gloom of the cell, but it was obvious she couldn't make out the words.

'It tells how the misfortunes in the village have been blamed on you but that they are not your fault,' I told her quickly, aware that our time had run out.

'We have had help from a most learned friend in finding written accounts from men of science and philosophy that challenge nearly all the charges of black magic that have been made against you.' I felt a wave of gratitude as I thought of the excellent work that Samuel had done for the Lunar Society on Gwen's behalf.

'We want to prompt Lord Aston to withdraw the accusations of witchcraft against you. Without those, the charge of murder is much weakened as he claims you entered the Hall by unnatural means. Our hope is that if we can get enough people to understand that there are other, more reasonable, explanations for the misfortunes in Little Aston that Lord Aston will be ashamed ever to have held such archaic beliefs about sorcery and the like.'

'We need him to withdraw his charges before the assizes court arrives in Lichfield, Gwen, otherwise it may be too late,' Amber said, cutting straight to the heart of the matter as she picked up the end of Tam's leash. 'That is why we are taking action today.'

'Thank you,' Gwen whispered as she held out her hands for one more touch of Tam's wiry coat before Amber led him out the door.

We stood on the cobbles outside the gaol, handing out our missives to passers-by for the rest of the morning, determined in our intent to destroy the integrity of the accusations of witchcraft against Gwen. Sarah joined us after the first hour, bringing with her a small trestle table from the shop to place our leaflets on. Samuel helped carry the table but she sent him home straight after, much to his chagrin, fearful of what Michael would say if he found out we had involved his son in our actions. Besides which, Sam had to go back and look after Michael who was still laid up in his bed with the melancholia, so Sarah told us.

Much to my and Amber's admiration, Sarah had also brought with her a large piece of sacking tied across two sticks held on a pole on which she and Sam had painted the words: 'Gwen Foley is no witch'. I held it up and walked up and down in front of the table and it drew folk over from both sides of the street. Some were quite easy to persuade into our way of thinking, whereas others muttered or spat and carried on walking. Robby Baker, half-starved and wearing nowt but rags, poor lamb, walked straight up to Amber and told her he wanted to help and she set him to handing out leaflets just as soon as she'd bought him some hot gingerbread to eat from a street vendor.

I stiffened as Agnes approached me through the crowd. She was holding a small child on her hip, her long dark hair hanging over one shoulder. She stared up at my sign and shook her head. 'This woman you are helping,' she said. 'Let me guess, she is your kin or of your religion?'

'No, Agnes,' I said, 'I thought about what happened to Joanna and how it shouldn't happen again and I found the courage to act to try and save this woman, together with Amber and my friends. We call ourselves the Lunar Society.'

She snorted and turned the child towards me, his face

crumpled into tears at her bitter tone as she spoke. 'This is Joanna's youngest. He will never know his mother and will grow up in the shadow of her conviction. You can play at being good, Mistress Albright, and having worthy intentions, but I know you for what you are. A coward.'

Her words stung me as deeply as they had before. I passed the banner to Sarah as Agnes walked away, and leant against the wall of the Guildhall with my head in my hands while shame burned through me.

'Come, Hester, there is work to be done on behalf of Gwen,' Sarah said kindly. 'Don't lose heart. We are making good progress.'

As if to prove her wrong a spry old fellow chose that moment to point at the sign with a loud squeal. 'Gwen Foley is a bloody witch and she should burn not hang,' he shouted.

'Surely, sir, we are a civilised city and are moved onwards from such brutalities?' Sarah answered, hoping to appeal to his reason.

He smiled a toothless smile. 'I'd like to see a burning,' he said, his eyes shining. 'Whee, the sparks that would fly!' He laughed as he hobbled off down the street and I had to stop myself from taking the placard back off Sarah and thumping it down over his head.

'Lobcock,' I shouted after him.

'You can't get through to some folk,' I said, turning to Amber to share my frustration. She wasn't listening though. Her attention was taken by a large figure in purple finery pushing his way through the crowd.

'Mercy God, Mama,' she said. 'It's Uncle Philip.'

'What the hell is going on here?' Philip demanded as he reached our area of protest. His plumed hat was crooked on his head, pulled over an elaborate wig of grey curls and he righted it before accounting for who was present.

'Hester? Amber? And dear God, is that the woman from Johnson's bookshop?' He indicated towards Sarah who was deep in conversation with a richly dressed couple on their way back from morning song at the cathedral. 'Get off the street immediately, you recalcitrant women. Hester, I am ashamed of you. Does my brother know how his wife behaves in public?'

'Who's this puff-guts?' said Robby, kicking Philip smartly in the shins. Philip pulled back his hand to strike the boy and Tam leapt at him, knocking him from his feet. The crowd began to laugh as Philip struggled to heave his considerable bulk up from the cobbles, his face a shade of scarlet. They laughed even harder as the yellow plume of his hat drooped down over his eyes and nose and his wig fell clear off the back of his head and landed in a tangled heap on the ground behind him.

'His hair has escaped!' Robby shrieked with glee and he picked it up and pretended to struggle to keep it in his hands. The crowd cheered with mirth as I finally managed to swipe the wig away from Robby and handed it reverently back to Philip.

Amber had helped him up and was trying to brush him down, but Philip swatted her hand away and turned to me in fury. 'This ends now,' he shouted. 'The assizes judges will decide if this prisoner is guilty of witchcraft, not a scatter of feeble-minded women.'

'I don't believe in witchcraft, Philip,' I said to him, jutting my chin out in defiance. 'Do you?'

'My personal beliefs are of no relevance in the matter. God will guide the court members in their deliberations.'

'I don't believe in God either,' I said, wanting to provoke him further, so irate had he made me. A woman in the crowd gasped and began reciting the Lord's Prayer to save my soul.

Philip came up very close to me and spoke into my ear. 'Be very careful what you say in public, sister-in-law. The last blunderbuss to proclaim publicly in Lichfield that he didn't believe in God found himself being burned to death for heresy in the market square. Now get home before I have you and your group of vagabonds arrested. Tell Matthew that he is relieved of his duties and that the proper magistrate of this city is returned. And just in time it seems.'

Philip turned then to the people gathered with an ingratiating smile. 'There is nothing to see here, please go about your business,' he said.

A small fellow dressed in brown appeared at his side.

'Get rid of all this heretical claptrap, Bart,' Philip ordered him, picking up one of our pamphlets and ripping it in two. 'This is what comes of leaving a weak man in charge,' he muttered before turning and announcing to the street, 'I will see justice done for Lord Aston, by God I will.'

I braced myself for those present to cheer in support of Philip's words, but they didn't and I felt a spark of hope that perhaps our efforts to change people's hearts and minds hadn't been completely fruitless and that all was not yet lost for Gwen.

Matthew was as angry as I'd ever seen him when I told him what had happened in Bore Street. He was nervous as well, for he was scared of his brother's wrath and knew he would be coming soon to our home to take him to task for letting me follow my head in such a manner.

'I had heard Philip was making plans to return to Lichfield – he has set up some business importing fruit, I believe – but I didn't know it would be so soon,' he said, putting his hands on his cheeks. 'What have you done, Hester?'

'I won't see Gwen hanged. I had to defend her,' I said, urging him to understand.

'No. You have to allow the law to take its prescribed course.

That is the only way,' Matthew replied in an agitated tone. 'We may not always agree with the law in cases such as Gwen Foley's, but we have no choice but to align ourselves with it.'

'But what would it mean for Liberty if we let this happen?' I asked him. 'If we let Gwen hang for witchcraft because she is different and has been made a scapegoat, what if misfortune takes you, me, Amber, all of us away and Liberty is left alone in the world when she grows up? What is happening to Gwen could happen to her. Liberty is different too and she hasn't the voice to defend herself. We must at least try and change things before it is too late.'

'Our Amber is another woman who is different is she not?' Matthew countered. 'And no one threatens her, she is no scapegoat.'

'Amber is of an unusually strong character, Matthew, as well you know,' I replied, although I had my own private fears about her being different from most other women. 'She is clever and spirited and brave. She has a profession too and earns her own living. Liberty and Amber cannot be compared in such a way.'

Matthew came towards me, shuffling on his stick and put his arm around my shoulders. 'Don't upset yourself, Hettie. Our Liberty will always be protected. We are family enough ever to hold her safe.'

I took a step back and looked him sternly in the eye. 'You know as well as I, husband, the cruel nature of life and the turns it can take. Nothing is certain,' I said. 'Not a one of us is ever truly safe.'

He took my hand. 'Dear one, I do wish you would at least try to find solace in the teachings of Christ. I think it would give you succour in your times of doubt and fear.'

'I don't need God, Matthew,' I said, shaking him off. 'I need the law of our land to protect the vulnerable and not simply serve the whims of the wealthy. Do I ask for too much in that?'

Matthew went to speak but held his lip as Liberty came running in from the garden to show me a small beetle she had found. I held her to me and Matthew watched us embrace, his eyes heavy with the conflict between duty and love.

One firm rap on the door told us that Philip had arrived and I sent Liberty up to her room to work on her sampler before I opened the door to let the fury in.

'Hester, please go and join our daughter upstairs,' said Matthew as Philip marched into the room and stood glowering at him, the top of his hat almost touching the ceiling beams.

I thought it best I should do as he bid given the circumstances, and took my leave up the wooden staircase to help Liberty with her sewing. Liberty couldn't hear the shouting that ensued from below, but she noticed the bedstead trembling from the noise and frowned at me quizzically. I made the clapping sign we use for thunder and pointed to the sky and she smiled and went back to her needlework, her trust in me unwavering.

14

ASHES

The Lunar Society met at dusk in the bookshop the next day to take stock of Gwen's predicament and what the consequences of Philip's return might be for her ever-decreasing chances of being set free.

'We need a miracle,' said Sarah, turning towards her customary piety. 'Only God's hand can save her now.'

'We're not giving up,' Amber said. 'Uncle Philip is full of bluster and his own self-importance but he is a man of high society and of considerable learning, nonetheless. He has spent much time in London these last few years. I believe he would loathe such archaic accusations of witchcraft to be taken before the assizes judges when they arrive in Lichfield – it would make us seem like a city of simple-minded provincials. Philip is the type of man who wants to be perceived as sophisticated, as above the common rabble. Did you not see the fashionable set of clothes he was parading around in yesterday like a puffed-up peacock?'

'I did,' I replied with a smirk. 'If only they suited him better, he might have looked dashing. As it was he looked a buffoon.'

'I don't think we can make assumptions about Philip being

too intelligent to believe in otherworldly goings on,' Sarah said, frowning. 'Do you remember, Sam, how reading about the ghost in Hamlet gave you such a fright that you had to drop the book and run out into the street to compose yourself?' Sam went to speak but Sarah held up her hand so she could finish her point. 'And you won't find a soul with more book learning behind them than my Samuel,' she said with a definitive nod.

'Mother,' said Samuel, his ears pink with embarrassment. 'I was but eleven years old and I had never before read a story so vividly described as Master Shakespeare achieves in that play. The ghost of Hamlet's father seemed real to me for a fleeting moment, but a moment's more reflection assured me it was but fiction.'

'Hmm, perhaps,' Sarah said, still unconvinced. 'But we need to persevere with challenging these witchcraft accusations, nonetheless. Folks were coming over to our way of thinking yesterday weren't they, Hester? It seemed a fair few were open to a different explanation of the events in Little Aston.'

I nodded. 'I thought so, too, and so did Amber. If Philip hadn't arrived when he did, I think there is a good chance we could have had the crowd join us in our protests against Gwen's unfair imprisonment. Records of such support would have added weight to her pleas of innocence at the trial next week too.'

'Damn him to hell,' said Amber fiercely. 'Why did he have to turn up then, the corny-faced fool?'

Sarah, shocked, said a prayer under her breath to protect her shop from Amber's curses.

'Forgive her, Sarah,' I said, giving Amber a stern glare. 'She is upset, as are we all.'

'Action is the only route to change,' Samuel announced. 'And I for one am not ready to give up on saving Gwen Foley. I will spend the day constructing a clear written defence against all charges of unnatural behaviour which have been levelled against her so that it may be read out in court. Much of it is already stated in the leaflet, but there is more I want to add.'

'Who will read it out?' I asked. 'Gwen cannot afford a lawyer and neither Amber nor I can do it because of our kinship to both Matthew and Philip.'

Amber pursed her lips. 'This is true. Besides which, Dr Crouch has nominated me to take over as official coroner of Lichfield when he retires, so it would not be appropriate for me to present evidence which did not arise from the post-mortem, even if I wasn't related to the magistrate.'

'In which case I will do it,' said Samuel, sitting up straight on his stool.

'You will not,' said Sarah. 'I will.'

This surprised me, and my admiration for her grew: I knew the trouble that such action would cause between her and Michael, let alone the courage it would take for her to speak in public at such an official event.

'But your husband is the sheriff,' I reminded her, 'you have the same kinship limitations as Amber and myself.'

Sarah shook her head. 'Michael is considering stepping down from his position due to his continuing ill-health. If he does so then such a constraint will not apply.'

'Sarah, have you the verve to do this?' I asked her. 'Surely it would be wise to seek your husband's permission first?'

'Michael is not of this world at the present time, so deep in sadness is he,' Sarah said quietly. 'He cares not if the sun rises tomorrow, so it will be nothing to him for me to speak for Gwen at her trial.'

'Folk may not come to your shop if they disagree with your words,' Amber warned her.

But Sarah was resolute. 'It is God's will that I help this woman,' she said, her hand touching the silver cross that hung always on a chain around her neck. 'I am honoured to be part of the Lunar Society.'

Samuel came across the room and sat beside his mother. 'Kindness is the greatest of all powers,' he said, looking at her with a deep respect. 'I am humbled to be your son.'

Sarah welled up and pulled a kerchief from her sleeve to dab at her eyes. 'Just make sure what you write will convince them, Sam,' said Amber lightening the tone. 'It's tears of joy we want at Gwen's release, not of regret.'

'Rest assured I will persevere to craft a defence of the highest quality for Gwen Foley,' he said with a determined nod.

'I don't doubt that for a second, young Master Johnson, you have an uncommonly apt way with words,' Amber replied with a smile, and Samuel reddened to the roots of his hair.

I was in our garden a few days later scattering ashes from the fireplace around the roots of our old apple tree when Liberty ran out to join me with Tam at her heel. She loved the garden dearly, as did I, albeit of modest size and quite barren. Apart from the medicinal plants I grew in the raised beds by the back door, and the apple tree by the back wall nothing would grow in the flinty ground, however hard I had tried over the years to get flowers to take. Liberty liked to chase round outside with her stick and hoop and I was happier with her safe where I could see her, than out in the street where she might not hear a carriage or rider coming towards her and be deathly injured.

I showed her the valerian roots and camomile plants I was collecting to make a remedy for Michael Johnson that I hoped might help alleviate his gloom and she helped me gather them and put them in my basket. She pointed to the lavender, which was her favourite and I let her pull off a handful of spent blooms to put in a cotton twist under her pillow so she could have the scent of them with her all through the night. Liberty threw sticks for Tam and giggled with joy as he leapt to catch them and my heart warmed to see her happy.

So content were we pottering about together in the weak morning sunshine, I forgot for a while the troubles with Gwen. My shoulders eased and my breath grew calm for the first time in what seemed like a long while.

Our peace was soon interrupted, though, by the back door flying open and George standing there, his shirt hanging out over his britches and a look of wild excitement on his face. 'Come quickly, the baby's coming,' he said.

I dropped my secateurs and rushed after him into the house.

Liberty wanted to come too, but I left her with Matthew who was thrown into a state of panic by the news of our Esme beginning her labours.

He ran his hands through his hair and looked at me fearfully. 'It seems only yesterday Esme was the same age as this one is now,' he said, pulling Liberty onto his lap and holding her close. 'She is but a child, God help her.'

'Try not to fret,' I soothed him although I felt as anxious as he, the memory of Nell's terrible ordeal making me tremble with apprehension. 'All will be well. Esme is as strong as an ox. I will attend her along with the midwife and if needed we will call for Amber to assist. I will send word as soon as our grandchild is safely arrived.'

I kissed him and Liberty before packing my basket with herbs and clean cloths. I followed George out into the street and felt a prickle of trepidation as I noticed that grey clouds had gathered, covering the earlier blue of the sky. I climbed up onto the back of the horse he had brought and pulled my scarlet cloak over my head as heavy rain began to fall, wishing I had the comfort of a God to pray to for the safe deliverance of my daughter and her baby.

Despite my fierce hopes it soon became apparent that Esme was not going to have an easy time of it with the birthing of her child. Her hips were narrow like Nell's rather than wide like my own. My fear rose with thoughts of what difficulties the next few hours or days might hold for her. Esme clasped on to my hand so hard as soon as I arrived at her bedside that after I had spoken to reassure her, I had to prise her fingers off my own in order to prepare her a crampbark tincture to relieve her contractions.

'Where is midwife Anne?' I asked George as I held the cup to Esme's lips and pushed the hair out of her eyes.

'She is attending another birth across town,' George replied, staring at Esme. 'She will come when she can. What can I do to help?'

'George, leave us,' hissed Esme, reaching for my hand again. 'Go and see to your horses. Mama will call for you when it is done.'

George pulled on his cap and took his leave, relieved like all men, to be away from seeing his wife in childbed.

I attended Esme for the rest of the day, so brave was she and strong too. She recited the poems Amber had told her to learn over and over again and it helped to distract her a little from the pain that otherwise threatened to overcome her. George came up at three and told us that he had received word that the midwife wasn't coming, having unexpectedly gone into an early labour with her own child and I calmed Esme and told her that we could manage between us.

No girl could have tried harder to birth that baby than my

Esme, but I could see she was getting fatigued and at sundown I called for George to go and fetch Amber from the surgery.

'I was hoping it wouldn't come to this, but Esme needs a cut to get the baby's head out,' I told him quietly at the door. 'Amber is the only one I trust to do it. Go and fetch her and bring her back here as fast as you can.'

George ran down the stairs and saddled up a visiting squire's stallion that was stabled by the inn. I watched him gallop off down St John Street and felt washed with relief that in the shortest time Amber would be with us and Esme would be safe.

I heard the hooves thundering back into the yard thirty minutes later and looked out the gable window expecting to see Amber dismounting from behind George. I gasped when I saw he was alone, and ran to the door to meet him as he was taking the stairs three at a time up towards me.

'She isn't there,' he panted, trying to get his breath. 'Dr Crouch says she's been arrested. Philip Albright came to their door and had her taken away. Amber is in the Guildhall Gaol.'

I was aghast, but I knew I had to act quickly or else risk losing my Esme like I had lost Nell.

'Stay with her,' I ordered, grabbing my cloak from the chair. 'I'm taking that horse.'

George stepped aside and let me pass and I had to force myself not to look back or else I couldn't have left my daughter in such a pitiful state. But the consequences of not getting Amber to her were direr still, so I did what had to be done, as any mother would.

I was never a particularly steady rider and the stallion was big and unruly, but I somehow managed to direct him towards the middle of town and get to Bore Street without taking a fall. We clattered to a stop on the cobbles outside the gaol and I clambered off and banged on the door with one hand while holding the mighty horse's reins in my other.

The door was opened not by Gregory as I expected, but by Philip, dressed again in his purple finery, his face smug with satisfaction.

'Well, who do we have here?' he said. 'My favourite sister-in-law. What a pleasant surprise.'

'Where is she, Philip?' I demanded, trying to look past him. 'My Esme is in difficult childbed and we need Amber's help without delay.'

Philip shook his head. 'I'm afraid that won't be possible. Amber has been arrested on charges of impersonating a King's coroner at the home of Lord Aston and will be held in this gaol until next week when she will be tried at the assizes.' He let his words sink in and tilted his head in mock sympathy. 'Isn't that a shame,' he said, his eyes gleaming.

'But she's your own niece,' I said, trying to appeal to his decency.

'Amber is no niece of mine,' he said with a dismissive grunt. 'I know your and Matthew's sordid secret about your sister's bastard child that you passed off as your own. Do you think my brother didn't tell me that when you first arrived in this city? It was evident to me that you somehow tricked him into marrying you. Why else would he have lumbered himself with an infant that wasn't his – a girl at that – and a wife full of such wilful disobedience?'

I stumbled back against the door frame and dropped the reins. It came as a shock to me that Philip knew about Amber's true parentage. I was shaken by the realisation that he had the power of life and death over my family and plainly felt no kinship loyalty to any one of us.

'Amber has to come with me. Esme is in danger. Her child

too. Please,' I begged, 'do something to save your brother's grandchild.'

'Well,' said Philip, revelling in his moment of command. 'Perhaps we could come to an arrangement regarding the charges against Amber.'

'What do you want from me?' I asked urgently, my heart with Esme and her unborn babe.

'I will have Amber released if you and your group of...' he struggled to find a word to describe us, his nose wrinkling in distaste, '"associates", this so-called Lunar Society, agree to cease all efforts to defend Gwen Foley from the accusations of witchcraft that have been made against her by my esteemed friend Lord Aston.'

I stared at him in disgust. A cry came forth from one of the cells behind him. I knew it wouldn't be Amber, she would never show an emotion in such a way, so it had to be Gwen. I closed my eyes as I grappled with my conscience, but we both knew he had found my one weakness, my love for my family, and that I had no choice but to do as he wanted.

'I agree,' I whispered.

'What's that?' Philip said, cupping a hand to his ear. 'I didn't quite hear you.'

'I said I agree to your request. I... we of the Lunar Society, will no longer seek to discredit Lord Aston's accusations of witchcraft against Gwen Foley. Now please, release Amber.'

'Certainly,' Philip said with a smile, 'as soon as you have signed this document legally binding you to your promise. It is a shame that we can't even trust the word of our own kin these days is it not, Hester?' he said, handing me a paper and quill.

I signed it and he shut the heavy door in my face and pulled the cover over the hatch. I was about to begin banging on it again when it opened and Amber came out, her eyes flashing with anger.

'Let us make haste,' she said. I turned and saw Robby Baker standing on the cobbles, holding the stallion's reins which I had dropped to sign Philip's papers. I thanked him, weak with relief that the horse hadn't had a chance to run away, and Robby kept it steady for us while we mounted.

The cries of my newborn grandson an hour later and the gladness of Esme's smile when she saw him, despite her soreness, brought me such joy that I thought I should burst. Amber stitched Esme up, her brow creased in concentration, as I washed the tiny boy and kissed his hands and feet. George came in and stared agog at his son. I handed the babe to his father and George cried like a baby himself and told Esme she was his sweetheart, which made Amber and me smile at each other in delight.

It was only afterwards, when Amber and I were making our way back through town in the moonlight that we had a chance to deliberate over the earlier events at the gaol.

'Poor Gwen,' I said. 'She is truly on her own now and I pity her greatly. I am overcome with regret at having let her down.'

'Philip gave you no choice,' Amber reassured me. 'He is a wicked and self-serving man. It's hard to believe he comes from the same blood as dear Papa.' She kicked a stone along the road and shook her head.

'I'm sorry for the things Philip said about you,' I said tentatively, not sure whether or not she had heard him from inside the gaol. This had always been difficult for me to discuss with Amber. Other than acknowledging the bare facts surrounding her parentage – that she was my sister Nell's illegitimate child – Amber had always declined my offers to tell her more details about the circumstances of how she came into the world, despite me bringing up the subject on a number of previous occasions.

Amber carried on walking, her eyes fixed on the road ahead.

'You know Papa and me have always thought of you as one of our own, as our first child,' I continued, desperate for her not to have been hurt by Philip's words.

'I know that,' Amber said at last. 'I'm not ashamed of my beginnings and I don't care who knows. It's just been easier, I suppose, all these years to keep the secret between you, me and Papa and not talk about it further. I never really think about how I came into the world. It's understandable that Papa told Philip, though, when you first arrived in Lichfield. Pa always says they were close back then, like brothers should be.'

I nodded, remembering the warm rapport that Matthew and Philip had shared when they were younger.

'It's a pity Philip turned into such an avaricious brute,' I said, 'and a nasty one at that, bringing up your parentage in such a situation, blackmailing me, knowing I would agree to anything to keep Esme safe. That's how mothers feel about their children. It's how your mother felt about you.'

Amber didn't reply and I felt my usual sadness that she didn't want to know more about Nell and that when I was gone there would be no one left to remember my gentle sweet sister, as though she had never lived at all. I thought about the letter that I had written for Amber, my latest attempt to capture Nell's story for her, and I wondered whether she would ever want to read it. I didn't know how to approach giving it to her but I deeply wanted her to have it.

'Sometimes I do wonder what my parents looked like,' Amber said after a while, pleasantly surprising me and igniting a hope that she might be becoming more open to knowing about her mother.

We walked on together and I told her about Nell and how she had had the prettiest eyes and how her little nose screwed up when she laughed and how her hair shone in the sunlight. I couldn't tell Amber much about her father apart from he was a good-looking lad with a tanned face but she laughed anyway and said she had always imagined him so.

I told Amber that I'd written it all down for her, everything I could remember about her being born, and about Nell and my parents, and how Matthew and I had brought her with us to Lichfield to start our life together here as a family.

When I asked her if she would like to read it she got a faraway look in her eyes and turned her face up towards the starlit sky. 'Perhaps I will read it one day,' she said at last. 'But for now the past can stay in the past. We have more than enough to be thinking about in the present, do we not?'

'That we do, my dear,' I said, taking her hand, heartened by the steps forward we had taken at last on this delicate subject. 'Come, let's go together to tell Papa he has a precious new grandson.'

'And a namesake at that,' said Amber. 'Another dear Matthew to join us in the world. What a day it has been.'

15

SHELLS

The day after Father's furious condemnation of Nell's condition was a Sunday. Mother had sent word around the village that Nell was weak with an illness and was resting in bed; and no one had any reason to doubt her.

I watched Father preach his sermon on forgiveness as though he were a stranger. His familiar burly limbs and dark red beard became repulsive to me and the origins of pure hate towards him and all that he stood for began to take root. Whoever I married would have to be a man who bore no resemblance to my father, either in appearance or character.

I closed my eyes and said my own private petitions to a different kind of deity than the one that resided in Father's church and in his books. Instead, I thought of the power that works through the natural world to move the tides and change the seasons and bring people into life, and I moved towards it in my heart and mind, allowing Father's enraptured voice to become untethered from all that was dear to me.

When I opened my eyes I saw a trim young man who I realised to be the new tutor at the manor house come in the side door of the knave and begin looking for a space to sit down. He squeezed onto the end of the pew in front of mine with so many polite apologies and thanks that it made me smile. Even from the back and even though I had never before set eyes on him, he felt familiar to me from that very first moment. I stared at the shape of his shoulders in his formal Sunday frock coat and the way his fair hair curled under the ribbon that held it at the nape of his neck and some deep part of me recognised him with joy. I knew without any doubt that he had come for me and for Nell and for our unborn babe.

After the service I waited for him by the back gate of the cemetery as I anticipated he would take that little used path back to the manor house and that I would have a good chance of speaking to him in privacy there.

'Can I walk with you?' I asked as he strode past. 'I'm Hester Moore, the Reverend Mr Moore's daughter. What's your name?'

'Matthew Albright,' he said, looking at me in surprise and then back to the church where Father was shaking hands with the congregation as they left by the main door.

'Father asked me to welcome you to the parish and show you around the village,' I said quickly, sensing his concern that it would be impolite for him to walk with me unaccompanied.

'Thank you, that would be most pleasant, Miss Moore,' he said with a smile. He opened the gate and let me pass through it in front of him. 'I put myself in your hands. Lead me to what you think I should see of Walberswick.'

'There isn't much to admire,' I admitted. 'Apart from the church and the manor house, which of course you have already seen.' I bit my lip and tried to think of where else I could take him.

'Hmmm,' he said, rubbing his chin with mock concern. 'You've lived here all your life?'

I nodded.

'Therefore, you must have a favourite place here, do you not?'

I nodded again.

'Well then, that is where you will show me,' said Matthew with a laugh.

I took his hand – I know it was improper but I felt such affection for him straight away and was so happy at his timely arrival – and I led him down through the sand dunes to the place on the beach where Nell and I liked to sit and watch the boats on the horizon.

'I grew up far from the sea,' Matthew said as he lifted his face to the salty breeze. 'As far from the sea as you can get on our little island, in a place called Lichfield in Staffordshire.'

I found it almost impossible to imagine a childhood without the sea and felt a prick of pity for Matthew's lack of it. 'What is Little Field like?' I asked, never having heard of it.

Matthew laughed at my error. 'Lichfield,' he corrected. 'It is a busy city of considerable size where many carriages stop on their way between London and Chester. There is an impressive cathedral at its heart and markets every day of the week that bring farmers and village folk from across the county.'

'But no sea,' I mused, watching the waves rock back and forth against the shore.

'No, no sea. We have Stowe Pool, though, where men catch crayfish, and the River Tame is to the east.'

'Where is your favourite place in Lichfield?' I asked, pronouncing the unfamiliar place name carefully.

He sighed and looked up at the gulls circling overhead. 'I suppose I should say the cathedral or perhaps St John's church, but in truth, my favourite place is the King's Head tavern on Bird Street.' His serious face broke into a grin and I giggled at his irreverence.

'And may I ask why you left?' I said, picking up a small white shell from between the pebbles and turning it in my fingers.

Matthew took the shell from me and held it in his palm. 'My older brother Philip is set to inherit my father's house and business when he dies, which will not be too long, I'm afraid. There is nothing else for me in Lichfield. My mother is gone and I have no sweetheart.'

He glanced at me and I lowered my eyes so he couldn't see how much his last admission pleased me.

'An old friend from school wrote and told me that he was leaving his position at Walberswick Manor in order to move to London to train as a solicitor. I asked him to recommend me to his employers, and being a valued and trusted tutor they accepted his word and offered me the position forthwith. I teach Latin, French, history and arithmetic to their four sons, while their daughter listens in secret at the door. I have told her parents she is welcome to join the lessons but they will not agree to it. They don't want her chances of a good marriage ruined by an education.' He shook his head. 'Tis a pity, but that is the way of the world, I suppose, and we have to damn well accept it.'

He put his hand across his mouth. 'I do apologise for my language, Miss Moore. And you a vicar's daughter.'

'Call me Hester,' I told him. 'I don't care what words you use and I don't care about being a vicar's daughter.' I pushed my chin out to show him my character lest he thought I was a feeble type of girl.

He handed me back the shell. 'I can see we're going to be friends, Hester,' he said in amusement.

We met often over the following weeks, always on the beach, usually at dusk. I would leave a shell on the alms box by the church gate in the morning if I could meet him that evening and he would take it away at some point during the day if he was also able to meet me. If the shell was still there in the afternoon it meant he could not escape from his duties at the manor house or that some unforeseen responsibility or engagement had arisen. On such days I would sit instead with Nell and Mother making tiny bonnets and dresses to clothe the infant as we fretted wordlessly about what would become of the babe once it was born. Father spent all day and evening in his

study when he was not in church and at meal times he ate in silence, his eyes locked on the crucifix above the fireplace. Once, as we were clearing away the platters after supper and Father had returned again to his books, I asked my mother why she had married him.

'I was governess to his younger brothers at a grand house in Aldeburgh,' she said in a low voice after a moment's hesitation. 'Seth was away at university in Cambridge studying theology. When he came home to visit his parents he was forever trying to do me favours around the house or read to me from the Bible. I felt sorry for him as he seemed a well-meaning but lonely fellow. I breathed easier when he returned to his college and left me in peace, though.

'One day he came home unexpectedly and forced himself upon me in my room. I don't know what came upon him. He was like a man possessed. He sat and wept afterwards and even in my misery I tried to comfort him. Seth turned nasty to me then, I suppose he saw a way to put the blame on me and away from himself. He told me I had tempted him by walking and talking in a suggestive manner, like a harlot. He said I had made him a sinner and he must marry me to make amends or I would go to hell.' She placed the pewter dishes back on the dresser with trembling hands, although her voice was clear as she recounted the events.

I sat motionless at the table, waiting for her to continue.

'Your father said that if I wouldn't marry him he would tell his parents that I led him into temptation. They were very religious people, Hester, and they were filled with pride that Seth was going to be ordained. I was frightened to say no to him. My parents in Bury St Edmunds had died by that time and I had no other home or kin to go back to. So Seth and I were wed.'

I stared at her in the flickering candlelight and saw the lines of strain that the sorrow of being married to my father had etched on her once beautiful face. Mother opened the drawer of the dresser and pulled out a breadknife, its blade reflecting the orange light from the candle as she held it tightly in her hand.

'I would have him dead,' she said. 'I would kill him myself if it meant we could be free of his tyranny. I would like to stick him through with this and see him bleed out over the flagstones.' She looked at me as if surprised that I was still there and a cold chill travelled up my spine. She had gone to quite a different place in her mind.

'Please don't ever do such a thing,' I beseeched her, afraid that father's harshness towards Nell would prompt her to carry out her threat. 'Such an act would make our situation worse not better. You would be done away with. Nell and I and the child would be destitute. What triumph would that be?'

Mother slowly nodded her head as the sense of my words reached through her anger.

I took the knife carefully out of her hands and laid it down on the table. I held her hands in mine and made her look into my eyes. 'Mama, I will make this right, I promise,' I told her. I stepped forward and embraced her, hoping she might let herself cry at last and let out the bitterness that she had swallowed down for all those years, but she remained silent and rigid in my arms and wouldn't let out a single tear.

My meetings with Matthew were the beacon of my days as that mild winter turned into a gentle spring and Nell's time for childbed drew near. I knew I had to tell Matthew what I needed and also wanted – for him to agree to marry me and for us to take Nell and her baby far from there, far away from Father and the Campsey Priory nuns, even pass the child off as our own if need be – but I feared greatly that he would say no to such wild plans.

As I got to know Matthew and found myself falling in love with him, I feared even more greatly that I would lose him completely when the picture became clear and that he would think of me as *nothing but cunning, and himself a fool for falling in step with my scheme of deception. Finally, when Nell's belly was so round that she could no longer disguise it to leave the house I decided I could wait no longer to tell Matthew of our predicament.*

We were sitting close together in the dunes, in a sandy cove out of the wind as he read to me aloud from a book of verse. I remember his face was touched with emotion as he read the lines and that he laughed when my hair came loose from its plait and billowed around me. As he tried to help me catch it back he held the back of my head in his hands and looked at me as if I were the fairest girl in the world.

'Dear Hester,' he said his eyes softened with love. 'Being with you makes me so very happy.'

He leaned forward to kiss me and I was filled with joy of a magnitude I had not anticipated.

'Matthew,' I said, leaning my face into his neck. 'I have something I need to tell you and something I need to ask you.'

He took his arm from around me and reached into the pocket of his waistcoat. 'Firstly, my love, there is something that I need to ask you,' he said, arranging himself onto one knee.

I crept into the bed I shared with Nell that night and found her wakeful and full of angst as was her usual state of being since Father's proclamations on her being with child.

'All will be well,' I told her, finding her hand under the counterpane and stroking it gently. 'Matthew and I are to be married. I have told him of your situation and he has agreed that we will all travel together to Lichfield after you have the babe. We will set up home there and tell people your husband is dead. Matthew will support us with his teaching and money from his father until such time as you can find work, and a husband before too long, I am

sure. Matthew is happy to help us, dear kind soul that he is.' I spoke quickly tripping over my words, excited to share the wonderful news.

Nell clung to me in the dark and I felt the baby moving inside her through her shift. 'Thank you, Hester,' she whispered. 'I knew you would save us.'

'You can rest now, all will be well,' I told her, kissing her forehead, for I did not know the disaster that was to come.

16

COAL

I made my way to the bookshop with a heavy heart to tell Sarah and Samuel about my agreement with Philip.

I was greeted by Samuel, beaming with enthusiasm and keen to recount to me his visit to Little Aston village the previous day.

'I was becoming increasingly vexed at being unable to find a conclusive reason for the cows staggering and dying,' he said. His face lit up with the pleasure of finding a solution to a thorny problem and it pleased me to notice that his scrofula scars had become almost invisible, except in bright daylight. 'So I went to explore the pastures outside the village where they graze.'

'He came back fair covered in mud,' said Sarah, tutting indulgently at Samuel.

'I had found one rare, but possible cause of such an affliction in an ancient text written by a monk, Brother Cassius, who looked after his monastery's dairy herd near Winchester. Brother Cassius described a fever that had swept through his cows who grazed in a field outside the monastery walls and I was determined to find out if the cattle in Little Aston had suffered the same fate. You see, Cassius found that the affected cattle in his herd had been eating snails in wet grass along the river bank that adjoined their field and had contracted from them a grave disease just like the cows in Little Aston.'

'Go on,' I said, intrigued.

'I examined the meadows by the stream in the village and found these.' He held up a pail and I peered inside seeing five or six large snails. 'They concur with Brother Cassius's description in every detail. He named the disease anthrax – it's the Greek word for coal because the disease turns tongues black as coal. That's what killed the cows in Little Aston, anthrax, an unpleasant, but completely explicable, natural phenomenon, not some devilish curse by Gwen Foley.'

Sam put the pail down with a flourish and gave me a satisfied smile. 'This will surely be of the utmost expediency in our defence of Gwen, will it not?' he said, clearly unsure why my reaction to his discoveries was unexpectedly reserved.

'You are such a clever lad, Samuel,' I told him after an awkward pause. 'And you have undoubtedly found the cause of the cows' affliction. But I am afraid the Lunar Society cannot help Gwen any longer.'

'Whyever not?' exclaimed Sarah as Amber ducked in the doorway and threw off her hood.

We explained as best we could and I could see that Sarah, being a mother herself, understood the awful dilemma which Philip had put before me. But Samuel was of a different mind on the matter, beset with the idealism of youth in the face of such unfairness.

'Philip Albright is not playing by the rules,' he declared. 'Surely you aren't going to let that oaf control you in this fashion?'

'In these circumstances the rules are his to make, Sam,' I told him. 'It would be worse for us all, and Gwen, if we continued in our efforts.'

'Gwen is going to be sentenced to death. How could it be any worse for her?' Samuel exclaimed, his faded scars livid again on his reddening face.

'Only God can save her now,' muttered Sarah, touching her cross.

I shook my head. 'My faith is not in an invisible God, I'm afraid. Only in the actions of good people.'

'Is it not the same thing, Hester dear?' Sarah asked, placing her hands in the prayer position in front of her chest. 'The Lord does his noble work through us, that's what the Bible teaches.'

'Hmm,' I replied, not wanting to engage in such a discussion with Sarah, knowing the conflicting points of view we had on the subject.

'Well, either way, acting on our own or as instruments of God, I have an idea of how we can continue to help Gwen,' said Amber, shrewdly moving us past our differences. We turned to her expectantly as she stood up from her stool and Samuel gazed at her with barely disguised adoration.

'As I understand it,' she said, 'Philip has – through foul means, I hasten to add – left Mama with no choice but to sign his declaration stating that she, and the rest of us of the Lunar Society, will desist in our attempts to construct a defence for Gwen Foley in relation to the charges of witchcraft that Lord Aston has brought against her.'

I sighed with disappointment. 'Yes, that is the state of affairs,' I agreed. 'I thought you might be saying something else in addition to that.'

Amber lifted a finger. 'I haven't finished yet. The document you signed said nothing about desisting from defending Gwen against the murder charge, is that right?'

I nodded. 'That is correct, but as you know the two charges are entirely entwined.'

'I see where you are headed with this, Amber,' said Samuel,

his eyes lighting up. 'You mean that we, the Lunar Society, are still free to help Gwen in relation to the charge of the murder of Lady Aston.'

'Exactly,' said Amber. 'And if we find the genuine culprit, then the charge of murder against Gwen Foley will have to be rescinded by Lord Aston and, in all likelihood, the witchcraft charge as well, as all attention will be laid upon the individual who is truly responsible for killing Lady Aston and their ensuing trial.'

'Of course,' I whispered in relief and Sarah gave a small clap of appreciation.

'So that is what we must do,' said Samuel. 'Let us change the direction of our efforts to help Gwen towards finding the real murderer of Lady Aston. Are we all in agreement?'

Sarah and I agreed heartily, and we of the Society shared a cheerful feeling that a door had opened up where before there had been only a stone wall.

Sarah sent her maid to fetch tea while Samuel set out the notes he had made throughout all the previous meetings of the Lunar Society. He pursed his lips in thought as he re-read them to himself. 'We are missing something,' he said at last, setting down his teacup and wiping the corner of his mouth with his handkerchief. 'I believe there to be a vital piece of information that we have overlooked or not yet found which will point to the true perpetrator of this crime. My suggestion is that we part company now and cogitate on the circumstances of Lady Aston's murder. We shall meet again on Saturday afternoon to share our thoughts.'

'That will be the last chance we have to come up with an alternative felon for this crime,' I said solemnly. 'Gwen's trial is on Monday. She will be hanged the next day if found guilty.'

'Then let us use our reasoning and our knowledge and understanding of the world and of the ways of people to work out this most challenging of problems once and for all,' said Samuel with all the optimism and enthusiasm of youth.

'We can but try, I suppose,' said Sarah doubtfully. 'Godspeed you all and we will meet here again on Saturday.'

Amber left immediately to attend a patient, but I took a little longer getting into my cloak and talking to Sarah and Samuel about the Aston family and the villagers, and their vitriol against Gwen.

It was nearly dark by the time I left although it wasn't quite half past four, and I had to watch my footing on the stone stairs so that I didn't fall. I reached the street with a relief that was short-lived. Before I had taken two steps towards home, a strong hand grabbed my arm and nearly pulled me off balance.

Philip glared at me beneath his wig and hat. His breath was foul as rancid meat. 'What have you been doing inside there?' he demanded. 'Plotting against the King no doubt and the laws of this land. And that bastard daughter of yours is in on it too, isn't she? I saw her leave not ten minutes since.'

'Get your hand off me,' I shouted, refusing to be cowed by his rough manner and accusations. 'How dare you follow me? I am free to go wherever I please in my own city. I don't need your permission or that of any man.'

'That is your problem, Hester,' Philip spat back, twisting my arm up my back so that I was nearly on my knees on the filthy cobbles. 'You don't seek permission and you don't respect the God-given authority of men over women. You are of the weaker sex and you will bow down to me as a man of standing in this city.'

Our altercation had brought several faces to the windows of the shops and houses lining the street, but such was Philip's wrath that none came to my aid – apart from young Samuel, that is.

He bounded down the stairs of the bookshop, slipping

nearly off balance on the last one and stood face to face with Philip, his eyes flaring with outrage. 'What do you mean by this, sir?' he said. 'Unhand this woman at once.'

Philip didn't move to let me go, so Sam used force to pull his hand off my arm and helped me up to my feet.

'I heard the shouting from the shop, Hester. Are you all right?' he asked, glaring at Philip.

'This is none of your business, boy,' Philip roared. 'I have every right to show dominance over this woman, she being my brother's wife. I am also magistrate of this city.'

'A man may be so much of everything that he is nothing of anything,' Samuel told him, leaving Philip open-mouthed and speechless.

Finally, he lifted his finger and pointed at Sam. 'You listen to me, boy,' he brayed, 'if I find out that you are part of this unlawful defence of Gwen Foley then I will see to it that any ambitions you might have with your book learning and fancy ways with words come to nothing. You'll spend your days shovelling shit like the rest of the Lichfield peasants, raised in a bookshop or not.'

Samuel looked not the least bit afraid. He stood up to his full height, which I was pleased to notice was a good two inches taller than Philip, and silently held his gaze.

'Do you have no more to say, boy?' Philip mocked. 'Your beloved words fail you now do they?'

'Prejudice, not being founded on reason, cannot be removed by argument, so I will waste no more of my words on you, sir,' Sam said at last, looking at Philip as if he were a rotten turnip.

Philip pursed his lips and smoothed down his purple outer garments as he tried to think of something pertinent to say back to Sam, but he knew he'd been bested by a mere lad and we knew it too.

'Know this,' he said, straightening his hat. 'Gwen Foley will hang because Lord Aston wants her to hang. All the words and all the pleading in the world won't save her now. Her die was cast from the second Lord Aston made his charges against her. You play with fire, Hester, and you will get burnt.'

He swept away down the street, his portly frame swinging from side to side.

I leaned into Samuel who put a protective arm around my shoulder. 'Sam, if you wish to have nothing more to do with the Lunar Society or the plight of Gwen Foley, I would understand, my dear,' I told him as we watched Philip's figure melt away into the darkness. 'You have your future to think of, and what a bright future it will be with a mind like yours.'

Sam answered me in a loud voice, clearly hoping Philip might still be able to hear. 'Philip Albright is a scoundrel. I will not take instruction from such a man. I fully intend to continue my association with the Lunar Society and in the defence of Gwen Foley.'

'I do hope you don't come to regret that decision,' I said, Philip's dreadful threats still ringing in my ears. 'Your mother would never forgive me.'

Sam smiled. 'A fellow cannot stay entwined in his mother's apron strings forever,' he said with a shrug. 'And now I insist on walking you home,' he announced, inclining his head towards Dam Street, 'in case any other buffoon should try to interfere with your progress.'

Calmed by Sam's presence I walked with him in companionable silence for a minute or two while I recovered myself from Philip's rough handling.

'Will your father be joining us at the St Clement's Day dinner on Wednesday evening at the Guildhall?' I asked him presently as we made our way up Conduit Street.

'That is doubtful,' said Sam. 'In all probability I will attend in his place. Is it true that the grand dinner is being hosted by Philip?'

'Yes, he is taking the opportunity to introduce Lichfield society to the new sweet oranges he is importing from China by way of Portugal. Matthew is insisting that we go. Philip's new oranges will feature in every course of the banquet and will also be sold at the St Clem's street carnival.'

'And St Clement's is the perfect feast for Philip to present the city with his fare because of the rhyme associating oranges and lemons with the bells of St Clement's.'

'Indeed,' I said, knowing it wouldn't take Sam long to make the connection.

'Let's hope the fruit is not as bitter as the man,' said Sam and we laughed gently together as we approached my front door.

17

BITTER ORANGE

I laid my best frock out on the bed the following morning and
sighed at the scattering of moth holes all across the back.
Neither of us had much enthusiasm for attending the St
Clement's dinner or in supporting Philip in his latest business
venture, but Matthew had insisted we go else the rupture
between our family and his brother might grow even deeper and
end up causing more trouble for us as time went on.

Liberty stood with me as we examined the garment and
copied the way I pursed my lips in annoyance as I turned the
gown over in my hands.

'I suppose it is five years since John's wedding when I last
wore it,' I said, shaking my head. 'I'll have to take it to Madame
Cottrell to see if she can mend it before tomorrow eve.' I mimed
pulling a needle and thread so that Liberty would understand.

'Here, help me try it on to see the fit of it,' I told her, undoing
my day dress so my meaning would be clear. I stood in my
petticoat while Liberty helped me into the red and pink brocade
gown, its linen lining feeling cold and unfamiliar against my
skin. The bodice fitted well enough, although the lace at the end
of the sleeves was starting to yellow, and the heavy silk skirt fell

to the floor with a satisfying thud. But when Liberty tried to do up the hooks and eyes to attach the stomacher it soon became evident to us both that they weren't going to meet. Liberty tapped the rolls of fat that had gathered round my belly and we hooted with laughter as she pulled even tighter to try and get the garment to fit me.

'It's no use,' I said, wiping my eyes with mirth. 'I'll have to get Madame Cottrell to enlarge it as well as mend the moth holes. We'll take it to her now and ask her favour.' I pointed towards town and again mimed pulling a needle through the fabric so Liberty would know my intention.

I struggled out the dress and was relieved to slip into my more comfortable daytime attire as Liberty went downstairs to put on her shoes and coat.

The preparations for the annual St Clement's festival in the city, celebrating the trades of metalworkers and blacksmiths, had begun all over the marketplace. A raised wooden platform for the smithies to fire gunpowder out of their anvils was being erected next to St Mary's church and any number of booths selling food and sideshows of various entertainments were appearing around the square. Liberty skipped along next to me in excitement and her face shone with wonder at the transformation of the city, although she could hear neither the music from the fiddlers nor the songs from the troupe of players as they rehearsed their performances.

We slipped down an alley off Bakers Lane and rang the bell hanging over a barred black door about halfway down. Madame Cottrell's daughter Odette opened it almost at once and we followed her into her mother's workroom where Madame sat sewing, surrounded by dresses and undergarments and gentlemen's breeches hanging from strings crisscrossing from wall to wall. The French seamstress had lived in Lichfield for as long as I could remember but she had no English. She had no need for it, I suppose, as she had her daughter to assist her, and her work was with a needle and thread and not with words. I began explaining the problems with the dress to Odette, but Madame Cottrell shushed us and took the garment from me to examine under the light of the only window. She pointed to the moth holes and I nodded and Liberty managed to make her understand it needed taking out as well by pinching gently at my belly.

Madame Cottrell nodded curtly and spoke in French to Odette who told us the price. It was very expensive and when I explained I needed it by the next day it increased still more. I went to protest, but so shameful was the thought of bursting out of a moth-eaten dress as I sat down with the gentlemen and ladies of the city in all their finery that, truth be told, I would have agreed on any price.

St. Clement's Day dawned clear and crisp and it seemed that the whole town was abroad for the festivities. We could hear the shouts from the crowds as they gathered for the boxing tournament and cock fighting that would take up the daylight hours until the evening entertainments began with a re-enactment of the fate of St Clement.

Matthew had little interest in such cheap amusements so Liberty and I left him at home with the *Gazette* and his pipe while we took in the sights. We avoided the fighting and the betting and instead found much delight in the performance of a 'Learned Pig' who guessed my age and told the time by rapping his trotters, and all for a penny.

We were eating hot pies and enjoying the antics of a group of tumblers when Gregory and the constable, overseen by Philip, led a man and a woman from the gaol and placed them in the stocks set up next to the water pump where we were sitting. The woman was wearing a buckled metal contraption over her head with bands covering her mouth preventing her from speaking, and the man was covered in vomit and stank of gin. They truly were a sorry looking pair.

'Come and see how the city punishes wrong-doers,' Philip announced to the crowd that had almost immediately gathered. 'Jed Borman and his wife did become so drunk yesterday that he broke a window in the cathedral by throwing a bottle, and his wife Marion did steal a dress off Goodwife Ludgate's washing line and then speak such foul language to the Goodwife when she tried to regain her property that the air turned blue around her. Jed Borman will spend two days in the stocks as he has not the means to pay for a repair of the said window. Marion Borman will spend one day in the stocks as punishment for theft and tomorrow will be whipped and led around town in her disgrace. She wears the scold's bridle as her neighbours all do attest to her gossiping and cursing.'

I pulled Liberty away as people began jeering and throwing rotten potatoes at the wretched pair and we entered instead a covered walkway behind the church where human and animal curiosities were displayed. I paid a penny each for us to enter, relieved to be away from the Borman's sufferings and not giving much thought to what might be found within.

We were greeted by an overly friendly man with long red hair and a top hat. 'I am Gideon Fitchett,' he announced, spreading his arms wide, his showman's smile revealing a set of wooden teeth. 'Welcome to Fitch's great spectacle of curiosities. You will be amazed and bedazzled at what is within.'

He asked Liberty twice what her favourite animal was and shouted the question at her a third time despite my telling him she couldn't hear, and I took him to be a conceited fellow not much taken with listening to the words of others but rather more enjoying the sound of his own voice.

He held aside a curtain and we wandered into his display holding tightly on to each other's hand. I jumped with fright as a terrific growl emanated from behind me and turned to see a thin orange and black striped tiger standing miserably inside a small cage, with not room enough to take a step. I had only seen such a creature in picture books before and marvelled at the size of the beast and its fearsome teeth. Liberty put her hand through the bars to stroke the animal and I pulled her arm sharply back.

'No, Liberty,' I told her and snapped my own teeth at her so she would understand, 'it'll bite you.'

Liberty stared at the tiger for a long time and it stared back at her, its amber coloured eyes simmering with rage. She was becoming sad about it being locked up like it was, so we moved along to look at the rest of the display which was made up of men and women who had various unusual characteristics sitting on stools underneath signs that read of their fame.

The first lady stood up as we approached and her head nearly touched the ceiling of the tent so tall was she. 'The Nottinghamshire Giantess' her sign said and we smiled politely at her as she gazed down at us. The next human curiosity was a fellow the size of a five-year-old child, but with sturdy limbs and the face of a grown man. 'The Midget Man of Manchester' he was called. I had seen such small folk before: there had been a whole family of them in our village in Suffolk and they had gone about their business like anyone else, so I didn't consider him particularly odd but Liberty was fascinated and giggled with glee as he mimicked her surprised face.

We made our way along to the last stool where sat a woman of huge girth under a sign that said 'The Fattest Woman in all of England'. She glared at us as I peered at her, trying to make out her bumpy shape. I noticed that a cushion had fallen out from underneath her skirts onto the floor and I pointed it out to her so she could keep up her pretence. She gave me a small nod of thanks as she picked the cushion up and tucked it back inside her dress while Liberty gasped and put her hand over her mouth at the lie.

'Well, what did you think of Fitchett's Spectacle? Was it or was it not the most incredible, most amazing, most jaw-dropping display of animal and human curiosities you ever saw?' The man in the top hat was upon us as soon as we left the tent, drawing attention to his attraction by speaking loudly and encouraging us to do the same.

'What did you think, little girl? Were you afraid of the wild tiger? Were you startled by the enormous height of the giantess?'

Liberty shook her head in bewilderment and stepped behind me, away from the man. He would not desist though. He grabbed her by the arm and held her in front of a passing family.

'You see, this child has been struck dumb by my display,' he told them with exaggerated excitement. 'Come inside and see for yourself.'

Enraged I pulled Liberty away from him. 'I wouldn't bother paying to see this shambles of a show,' I told the father as he was counting out coins to pay for himself and his children to go inside. 'This man's a swindler and his attraction is worthless.'

The man tutted and walked away with his children much to Fitchett's chagrin. He opened his mouth to insult me but I spoke first.

'Touch my daughter again, sir,' I said, 'and I'll let that pitiful orange beast out of its cage to take its revenge on you for stealing its freedom.'

The showman turned his lip up into a snarl and turned his back on me, letting loose his false charms on a pair of lovers looking to be entertained.

'Come, Liberty, let's see if Madame Cottrell has finished her alterations of my dress,' I said, taking her hand and leading her away from the square, feeling downcast at the thought of poor Gwen still locked in her own cage in the Guildhall.

~

'You look quite lovely, my dear,' Matthew said, pulling himself up on the mantelshelf as I came down the stairs, dressed in my hastily, and expensively, repaired gown. I had pinned my long plait out of sight under a tall white wig I had rented from Madame Cottrell, and Odette had powdered and rouged my face using little pots that she said were from a fashionable salon in Paris, although they smelt suspiciously like chalk and jam syrup to me.

Matthew was wearing his best breeches and midnight-blue frock coat, and his waistcoat was embroidered with silver thread in an intricate teardrop pattern. He wore a light grey wig and one black leather shoe with a silver buckle which Sal had polished to a high shine with vinegar and carbonate.

I took his hand and we admired each other in our finery.

'My, what a handsome couple my parents do make,' said Amber as she came in the front door. 'You will do yourselves proud at Uncle Philip's dinner this evening. I have heard that the guest list is very esteemed.'

Matthew nodded. 'The senior bailiff, the deputy bailiff, the magistrate, all the almsmen of the city will be there, apart from poor Michael Johnson, of course, who remains indisposed.'

'And don't forget the gentry and the prosperous burgessmen and businessmen of Lichfield too,' I added, 'along with their wives.'

'Yes,' Matthew agreed with a sigh. 'Philip wants everyone

with any means to attend this supper so he can peddle them his oranges.'

Amber looked quizzically at Matthew and he continued. 'It has been Philip's business in London this past year he has been absent from Lichfield – organising the import of oranges by ship from Portugal. They sell well in London it seems, to the rich and the poor, and he is keen to open the market for them here. He has found a new supplier in the Algarve, a fellow named Almada. He has brought him here with him as well to persuade the locals of the quality of the fruit.'

'I always think of oranges as the type of fruit grown by lords and ladies in their orangeries and saved for their own table,' said Amber. 'I have only eaten them once, when a box of them were given as a gift to Dr Crouch and me by Lord Warrington when we cured his wife of dropsy. Dr Crouch poured away Lady Warrington's Madeira wine and told her to take a walk outside morn and eve. She was cured within a week!'

'I remember you brought a bagful home with you,' I said. 'Quite delicious they were, I have some preserved still in the larder. Every course of the meal tonight will be using Philip's oranges according to the handbill, so it's fortuitous I am fond of the taste.'

'You might not be after five courses of them, Mama.' Amber laughed.

'You are welcome to come with us,' I told her. 'You were listed on the invitation.'

Amber took in my dress and wig and shook her head. 'No, not for me,' she said. 'I would be uncomfortable in such formal company.'

'Walk with us at least,' said Matthew, picking up his stick, 'you have seen nothing of the fair yet.'

'You share your father's dislike of coarse entertainments,' I said. 'Papa has not been either so you can tut over it together.'

'Very well,' Amber agreed, 'I will walk with you to the Guildhall but then I am coming home to my bed. It has been a tiring day.'

'We are picking dear Samuel up on the way,' I said as I turned sideways to get the width of my dress out our narrow front door. 'He is coming in place of his father.'

We paused on our way across the square to watch the story of St Clement played out on the wooden platform and were much impressed by the actors' portrayal of the tragedy of the saint as he was tied to an anchor and thrown overboard to drown in the Black Sea. The blacksmiths finished the play in the usual way by firing their anvils, and a young lad from the foundry dressed as Old Clem led a procession of smiths holding hammers and tongs through the streets. We watched them begin their tradition of stopping at every tavern and taproom in the city, singing and demanding free ale, causing much mirth and good cheer as they went.

Samuel was waiting for us on the steps of the bookshop wearing white breeches and a rather old-fashioned frockcoat of Michael's which swamped his boyish frame. His face lit up when he saw Amber was with us.

'Happy St Clem's,' he greeted us, jumping down onto the cobbles, 'I hope you are looking forward to your supper of orange delights?'

Matthew smiled. 'Not particularly,' he said. 'But we are duty-bound to attend at Philip's bidding.'

'Did you hear, sir, that Gwen's trial will not be heard by the assizes court after all?' Sam told us in a low voice.

We stopped in our tracks. 'No,' I said, concerned. 'We hadn't heard that. Do please tell us what you know.'

'Apparently the assizes court are detained hearing a complicated trial in Leicester and won't arrive in Lichfield until the end of the month at the earliest. A meeting was held yesterday at the Guildhall. In attendance were Philip, Mayor Robinson and James Robinson the junior bailiff. They have decided that Gwen Foley's case is too important to wait and will be tried in the local Lichfield court on Monday. They, as justices of the peace, will hear her defence and decree her sentence.'

'But they need a sheriff, surely, to be quotient?' Matthew said. 'And your father is unable to carry out such duties at present.'

Samuel nodded. 'Yes, that is correct. Therefore they will invite another sheriff to take his place. James Robinson came and informed Mother of it yesterday while I was at school. Mother went upstairs and told Father, although she said that for all he reacted she may as well have told the news to the wall.'

'Dear God, I hope they don't ask Sheriff Drummond to come,' said Matthew. 'That man would send a pig to the gallows for rolling in mud.'

'We don't yet know who it will be,' said Samuel. 'Perhaps they will tell us tonight?'

'Perhaps,' said Matthew, adjusting his stick which had become caught between two cobblestones. We began walking down Breadmarket Street towards the Guildhall.

'Have you seen the wax tableaux of famous battle scenes, sir?' Samuel asked, falling into slow step with Matthew. 'They are one of the novel attractions for this year's fair.' He indicated down the side of the church and we followed him a short distance to where the models were displayed.

'Good grief,' said Matthew, leaning forward to inspect the first montage. 'It is quite startling in the authenticity of its portrayal.'

I gave the assistant a couple of pennies and Amber and I joined him and Samuel as they discussed the scenes.

'See here, this is Hastings, 1066,' said Sam, 'look at poor Harold being pierced by an arrow to the eye. But then here, justice is restored at Agincourt as the French are defeated by Henry V.'

Matthew nodded. 'And here is displayed the battle at Naseby. The New Model Army are depicted thrashing the Royalists. What a spectacle.'

'Where did you fight, sir?' Sam asked. 'I heard it was in Scotland that you sustained your... injury.'

Matthew stuttered and the colour drained from his face. Amber glanced at me in concern as she offered him her arm to lean against.

'My dear fellow, please accept my apologies for my indelicate querying,' Sam said, quite upset that he had caused Matthew distress.

'No,' Matthew said, righting himself. 'It is perfectly all right. I will tell you the tale, although it is not one I am proud of.' The familiar shame was in his eyes.

'You don't have to tell Sam,' Amber said, but there was something about Samuel's intelligent curiosity that made Matthew want to continue.

'It was the Jacobite uprising,' he began in a faltering voice, 'so that is the Scottish connection. But it wasn't on Scottish soil. I fought at the Battle of Preston as part of General Charles Willis's regiment. He had sent an envoy of recruiters to Lichfield and I signed up after hearing a rousing speech at the King's Head. Buoyed up with patriotism I was and with ale. Hester was furious when I got home.' Matthew gave a mirthless laugh. 'If I had known what hell awaited me, I would have done her bidding and hidden in the attic when the soldiers came to our door the next day, but I was committed then and I am a man of my word. I believed in the cause too.'

'Father always says that all men who do not fight regret not being a soldier,' said Samuel.

'Regret comes in many forms,' Matthew replied. 'I would still be whole had I not been foolish enough to be carried away with dreams of valour. A Scotsman took my leg clean off with his claymore as I scrambled over the city wall. It is a miracle I am alive at all.'

'How did you survive?' Sam asked. 'If you don't mind my asking?'

'A local washerwoman took me in, she pulled me off the street into her home and managed to stop the bleeding, I don't know how. She wrapped what was left of my leg in strips of cloth and I lay in a fever for days, concealed by her laundry hanging all around me. My company must have thought me dead, for they never came looking for me. The woman fed me like an infant with a spoon and cup, so gentle was she. I never even knew her name. I left in a covered cart after the fighting had stopped. She paid a man to take me out of Preston and as far south as he could. He left me in Manchester and found me some sturdy sticks so I could at least move forward, if only in a reduced manner. I managed to get back to Lichfield through the kindness of strangers who wanted to help an injured soldier and let me ride on the back of their drays. I fell into Hester's arms when I arrived home, so relieved was I to see my wife and children again. So you see, I am no hero, Sam, quite the opposite in fact.'

Sam shook his head. 'I disagree, sir, I am honoured to know you,' he said softly. 'It is not only our victories that define our character.'

'You came home,' I said to Matthew, as he gazed forlornly at a model of Henry V holding aloft his longbow in triumph. 'That's what mattered to us.'

∾

The Guildhall was alight with candles on sconces on the outside and along the corridors within. It felt peculiar turning left inside the huge oaken door to go up the stairs to the grand hall rather than down to the cells to visit a prisoner as was my usual reason to enter the building. As Sam and I supported Matthew up the stairs and into the high-ceilinged banquet room my mind turned again to poor Gwen, locked in her frigid cell not ten feet below where we stood, her fate in the hands of the very people who supped in good cheer in the hall above. 'Good evening, Master Albright, Mistress Albright.' We were welcomed by James Robinson the junior bailiff who indicated to a maid to take our cloaks. 'And this must be young Samuel, Michael Johnson's son.'

'Yes, it is,' Matthew replied. 'Do we have the honour of the Mayor's presence this evening?'

James sighed. 'I fear my father is enjoying the entertainments of the players and the smiths outside a little too much at the moment to join us. He will come inside presently to warm himself, I am sure, as it turns cold out does it not?'

'It does indeed, Master Robinson,' Matthew replied. 'The chill of a winter wind has undeniably arrived in the air.'

James nodded and stepped forward to greet the next group of guests.

Samuel bent down and spoke into my ear. 'Tell me, Hester, why is it that when two Englishmen meet, their first talk is of the weather? They are in haste to tell each other what each must already know, that it is hot or cold, bright or cloudy, windy or calm.'

I stifled a giggle at his droll words.

'What is it you find so amusing?' Matthew asked. 'We spoke only of the weather.'

I caught Sam's eye and we both stared at the floor. I gathered my composure before taking my place at the long table in the middle of the room.

I was seated between Matthew and Samuel in the middle of one side. Gilbert Walmesley, the registrar of the Ecclesiastical Court who lived in the Bishop's Palace by the cathedral was on Matthew's other side and Theophilius Levett the recorder and town clerk was seated next to Samuel, his buxom wife beside him.

Philip sat at the end of the table dressed in a silk coat the colour of marmalade and an immaculate periwig, beaming with conviviality at the esteemed guests who had gathered for his dinner party. His square-faced wife Helen was to his left, looking very much like she would prefer to be somewhere else and his son Jasper, who shared his mother's pained expression was to his right.

The rest of the guests were local businessmen who were bursting with pride to have been invited to such an event and a smattering of landed gentry who had not received a better invitation for the evening. I was perturbed to notice that Gideon Fitchett the showman from the curiosities attraction in the square was also at table, sitting near Philip, accompanied by his heavily rouged and powdered young wife.

'Welcome, ladies and gentlemen,' Philip announced, standing up to address the room. 'I am delighted that you have been able to join me tonight for this very special St Clement's Day feast.'

There was a screech of wood on wood as the door to the hall slowly opened and a dishevelled Mayor Robinson entered, holding up his hands in apology. 'Carry on, Philip,' he said in a slurred voice as he was shown to his place. 'Got delayed conferring with a constable on Bird Street.'

'Got delayed conferring with a molly-mop at the bawdy house more like it,' whispered Samuel.

The Mayor surreptitiously buttoned his breeches as he sat down.

Philip blinked several times and took a deep breath before continuing. 'What we have for your pleasure tonight is a fine dinner of several courses including soup, fish, meat and puddings all of which have been prepared using my newly imported sweet oranges as an ingredient. As you may know from eating such fruit previously, the oranges which are now and then on sale in Lichfield market are sour oranges from Seville and are most displeasing to the palate and the gut.'

There was a murmur of agreement along the table. 'Some of you may have had occasion to taste sweet oranges from your own orangeries,' he paused here to indicate Lord and Lady Warrington and the few other gentry who were dotted around the table, 'or as generous gifts from those in ownership of such rarefied growing houses. However, it is only now that such oranges will be plentiful in Lichfield as I have arranged for an importer from Portugal, Vicente Almada, who ships the fruit from China, to supply them to us in our fair city. Senhor Almada's countrymen currently supply a large amount of oranges to the great markets of London and they have become a common fruit in that town. It is time we joined the orange revolution and welcomed this nourishing and delicious fruit to our tables.' He nodded at Jasper who dutifully called, 'hear hear,' and we at the table joined in for fear of offending our host.

'So come, let us enjoy the fare which is being artfully prepared for us by the best cooks in Lichfield and celebrate the feast of St Clement's. We begin with a most exquisite orange and carrot soup.'

Philip sat down, quite flushed with his own self-importance, and took a long draft of wine which left a red stain along his upper lip.

The lids of the two large tureens on the table were lifted

simultaneously by maids wearing orange bonnets and we were served a ladleful each of hot yellow liquid.

Samuel, Matthew and I looked at each other in trepidation as did most of the other guests, until James Robinson took a large spoonful from his bowl and pronounced it, 'Quite delicious.'

I took a small amount onto my spoon and sipped. It tasted fresh and sweet, but was rather too thin to be rightly called a soup in my opinion. Matthew and Samuel enjoyed theirs well enough although both commented that had they been at home they would have preferred to lift the bowl to their lips and drink it as it would have made it easier to consume.

The fish course was next – trout baked with a parcel of sweet herbs and butter covered with orange slices – and was pleasant enough. I wondered what Gwen had eaten today as the meat course was brought in, and looking around the table I fretted that her fate now lay in the hands of the local justices of the peace who were present – the senior bailiff who was also the Mayor, his son James the junior bailiff, Philip who was the magistrate and whoever would stand in for Sheriff Johnson – and none were known for their leniency.

'Do you know yet which sheriff will replace my father at Gwen Foley's trial?' Samuel asked James.

'It will be Sheriff Drummond from Brummage,' replied James, gesturing for more wine. 'Isn't that right, Father? Oliver Drummond will be overseeing Gwen Foley's trial?'

Mayor Robinson tore his eyes away from the bosom of Theophilius's wife and nodded. 'Yes, Oliver said he would step in as Michael Johnson is in too bleak a mood to think coherently. Oliver is no weakling when it comes to ordering harsh punishments, and he is a friend of Lord Aston whom I believe brings the charges against the woman. There will be no mercy for that murderess and rightly so.'

He held up his glass and James did the same. I shared an anxious look with Samuel, and Matthew cleared his throat to speak, but Mayor Robinson hadn't finished.

'Tis a pity we cannot have her in the stocks for St Clem's,' he continued with a gleam in his eye. 'Folk used to like to see a witch rendered powerless. Could we do that, James? As a pre-trial punishment?'

James agreed with enthusiasm and repeated the request to Philip.

'With all due respect, sir, this is most irregular in respect to the law,' Matthew protested, putting down his fork and pushing himself up from his chair into a standing position. 'Gwen Foley cannot be sentenced until she has had a trial. Punishments cannot be meted out at random on the fancy of a Justice of the Peace.'

'Oh yes they can, brother,' cried Philip in amusement. 'Do you think the Bormans had a trial before they found themselves in the stocks this morning? It is up to my discretion to decide on punishments for lesser crimes.'

'And what is Gwen's lesser crime?' Matthew cried. 'She is being accused of witchcraft and murder, neither of those is punishable by time in the stocks.'

'Perhaps causing public affray?' suggested James thoughtfully. 'According to Lord Aston there was quite a disturbance in the village on the night of her arrest.'

Mayor Robinson smiled. 'And perhaps a whipping, too, for that?' he said, taking another draft of wine.

I thought Matthew might explode with anger. His face was furious as he lowered himself back down into his seat, unable to stand any longer. I put my hand on his lap to calm him, although I too was trembling.

'Gentlemen, I would not advise you to sanction such an act.'

It was Samuel who had spoken up and the table fell to a hush around him as he continued in his brave defence.

I hoped his voice would remain steady and not crack as he sounded like a grown man so confident was he.

'Your reputations are as men of moral standing and of great learning. Why would you risk opening yourselves to reproach from the Crown or from liberal reformers simply to carry out such a meaningless act? Gwen Foley will be hanged anyway for her crimes. There is no need to extend her punishment.'

It was a clever combination of flattery and common sense that played on the men's vanities and their cowardice. There was silence for a moment as the guests glanced uneasily at each other, then to our relief, Mayor Robinson cleared his throat and acquiesced.

'Yes, well young Johnson's probably right eh, Theophilius? We don't want irregularities chronicled in the city's records. We never know when the Crown will call an audit. Best to stick with the regular course of action and try the woman in court.'

Philip tutted in disappointment and gave Samuel a furious look. He turned to Gideon Fitchett who was seated next to his wife and spoke to him in low tones. Although I couldn't make out all that was said, I distinctly heard Gwen's name mentioned by both of them and it sent prickles up my back to imagine what they might be plotting. When Philip showed the man a key, I decided I could hold my tongue no more and stood up with the intention of making my way around the table to confront them. Fate meant to intervene, however, as no sooner had I got to my feet than the first mutterings of disgust began around the table as the guests began to eat their meat course – duck with an orange sauce in the French style.

Philip looked up from his conference with Fitchett with a frown, and Matthew pulled me back down into my chair as we sensed the atmosphere in the room was changing.

'What in God's name is this revolting dish?' exclaimed Mayor Robinson spitting his duck out into a napkin and throwing it onto the table.

Others around the table followed his lead and murmurs of 'horrible', 'bitter' and 'horsemuck' accompanied their rejection of the orangey meat.

'Please, ladies and gentlemen, duck *à l'orange* is an acquired taste. I assure you it is most favoured in the highest of French society.'

'The French can keep it as far as I'm concerned,' Lord Warrington announced as his wife feigned a swoon. 'What is this filth you have served us, Albright?'

Philip was aghast and placed a forkful of the duck in his mouth. 'It is perfectly pleasant,' he said, his cheeks stuffed with the foul fowl. He attempted to smile but as the rancid taste permeated his senses he began to choke and joined his guests in spitting out the offending mouthful.

'Hellfire and God's teeth, that is repugnant. Get the cook in here now,' he barked the last order to Jasper who leapt from his seat and ran downstairs to the kitchens. The hall waited with bated breath until Jasper returned with the bewildered cook, his apron covered in orange juice and his eyes wide in fear.

'What have you put in this?' demanded Philip, pointing at the platter of duck.

'What you said, sir, nothing more. The oranges you gave us are in the sauce.'

'Taste it,' Philip said, passing him a spoon.

The cook hesitantly did as he was bade and wrinkled his nose in disgust. 'These aren't sweet oranges, sir,' he said, shaking his head. 'These are the bitter ones from Seville and they've started to go off too.'

'What?' said Philip, a blush of anger starting at his neck and rising up to his wig. 'I paid Almada for the highest quality sweet oranges from China.'

The cook frowned. 'The ones at the top of the barrel were, sir. The soup and the fish were good, weren't they?' he said meekly. 'It's the oranges lower down that must have been the cheap ones. They don't taste nice. You can't eat them ones 'cept with large amounts of sugar in a marmalade.'

'I know that,' Philip hissed. 'That is why I paid through the nose for the very best sweet oranges from China which Senhor Almada receives in Portugal. Where is Almada? Get him here now!' he shouted as the guests began to tut and titter.

'He's gone, sir,' said the cook, his eyes wide with surprise that Philip didn't know. 'Said he had to board a boat back to Lisbon. He took the eight o'clock stage to London.'

The titters erupted into laugher around the grand hall as Philip stood in humiliation among the remnants of his orange feast.

'Dinner is over,' Jasper announced, flapping his napkin at the gathered guests as Philip followed the cook out of the room and down to the kitchen. 'It is time to leave.'

'Good grief,' said Matthew. 'Even by Philip's standards that was quite a drama.'

'Indeed,' said Samuel, his face shining. 'What entertainment. Better than any out on the street.'

'Hmm,' I said, looking at the showman as he waited for his wife to rise from the table. 'I will see you at home, Matthew. There is somebody I need to speak to first. Samuel, could you please assist my husband?'

Samuel nodded and offered Matthew his arm. I took a deep breath and approached Gideon Fitchett with a smile that didn't reach to my eyes. 'Good evening,' I said. 'I am Hester Albright. We met earlier at your curiosities attraction.'

'Gideon Fitchett,' he said with a low bow, his long red hair falling forwards to reveal a bald pate. 'Known to all as Fitch. You are another satisfied customer, I trust?' he said, turning on his easy charm and clearly not recognising me in my finery.

'Oh yes,' I agreed, 'I was most impressed by your human oddities.' I lowered my voice. 'You know the cells here hold a woman of even more curious appearance, do you not? I think my dear brother-in-law spoke to you of her earlier this evening. Her name is Gwen Foley.'

Fitch nodded and pulled me slightly aside, his interest piqued. 'I have heard, yes. Magistrate Albright has told me of this woman – she is a monster he says, with white skin and pink eyes. The White they call her. They say she is a witch.'

'Indeed she is,' I said. 'She has wreaked havoc in a village near here. But I consider it a pity that a person of her uniqueness should be put to death, Mr Fitchett. I wonder if there might be money to be made from such a curiosity – if you take my meaning?'

Fitch rubbed his pointed beard. 'Go on,' he said, shooing away his wife who grew tired of waiting to leave.

'I believe my brother-in-law has shared a similar notion with you, Mr Fitchett?' I asked, hoping I had read the situation accurately.

Fitch gave me a wary look. 'What do you know of my arrangement with Magistrate Albright?'

'I know, whatever Philip has told you, that Gwen Foley will not go willingly with you,' I told him. 'But I can help you with that.'

Fitch narrowed his eyes. 'Albright has assured me that the woman will jump at the chance to be part of my travelling show rather than face the hangman's noose.'

I shook my head and pretended to laugh although my stomach had turned sour with anger. 'Dear me no, Mr Fitchett, I fear you have been misinformed. I visit Gwen Foley regularly taking her food and such like and I can assure you that she is a woman of considerable pride as well as malevolent gifts. She will certainly not accompany you like a docile puppy should you unlock her cell door – of that you can be sure.'

Fitch frowned and pulled again on his beard. 'I have paid Albright five guineas for the key to her cell,' he said. He held out his right palm and the key slid onto it from up his sleeve. 'Are you telling me that I have been tricked out of my money?'

I raised my eyes. 'It would seem so,' I said.

Fitch looked around in fury. 'Where is he? I will thrash him for the swindler he is and expose his doings to the Mayor.'

'Please be calm, Mr Fitchett. There is a way in which this matter can be resolved without recourse to violence or wrath. I told you, I can help you with obtaining Gwen Foley. For a price.'

Fitch went to speak but was interrupted again by his wife. 'Gideon, I want to go home now. I'm cold and I'm tired and I'm sick to my stomach of the stench of these putrid oranges.' She pouted prettily.

Fitch's face softened. 'Yes, dear, I will be with you in just a minute. Please take my cloak to warm yourself and wait for me at the top of the stairs, away from the smell.' He touched her cheek lightly and she gave him a small smile as he wrapped his mantle around her shoulders.

When she had gone, he turned to me in frustration. 'Tell me what needs to be done and how much you want. I don't much fancy having to drag the woman kicking and screaming from her cell.'

'Give me the key to Gwen Foley's cell and I will go down there directly and explain to her that you are a good man and that going with you and doing as you bid will give her the chance of a life and a livelihood. She trusts me and she will come with me, I am sure of it. I will take her to an agreed place and you will meet us there later. You will leave with her then, taking your show and curiosities with you. No one will notice her missing until the morning and by then you will be long gone. All I ask is two guineas for my trouble. You don't pay me until you collect Gwen.'

'Here,' he said, passing me the key. 'I have already paid Albright his money so I want no mistakes made with this. Where shall I meet you to collect the woman?'

'I will meet you at the north door of the cathedral at midnight,' I said, 'and I promise you, I will have Gwen Foley with me and that I will have persuaded her to willingly accompany you and be part of your travelling attraction. You can pay what you owe me then.'

'You had better not be tricking me,' Fitch said fiercely. 'If you and the woman are not there, I will tell Magistrate Albright of your meddling.'

'You have my word, Mr Fitchett,' I told him, feeling no qualms for my lie as I had not the slightest intention of procuring Gwen for him to own and use as a human curiosity. Rather my intention was to free her and send her on her way out of the city and the certain threat of death that it held for her. I had no fear of either Fitch or Philip's anger when they found out I had deceived them, as both would have much to lose from making public their sordid and illegal plans for Gwen.

Fitch bounded across the hall to meet his wife and I waited a little while longer to make sure they had gone. The maids were busy clearing the table of the remnants of dinner and I watched as they dared each other to try a mouthful of Philip's duck and made each other laugh pulling faces at the sour taste.

Finally, after the hall was cleared and all was quiet, I made my way down to Gwen's cell, being careful to tiptoe silently past the slumbering Gregory. I rapped quietly on the door.

'Gwen,' I called. 'I am here to let you out.'

I placed Philip's key in the lock and turned it but it jarred and would not move round. I put it in at a different angle and then another but still it wouldn't unlock the door.

'Hester, is that you?' Gwen's voice sounded weak and confused.

'Yes, dear, it is I. I am trying to undo the lock so I can help you get away from here.'

I tried again to open it but it soon became clear that Philip had given Fitch a false key and simply pocketed the five guineas. I leant my head against the rough wood and groaned with frustration. 'I'm sorry, Gwen,' I said, feeling wretched with regret that I had failed her once again just as I had failed my Nell in her hour of greatest need. Gwen was silent but I heard her fingers tapping on the door and I tapped back.

'Don't give up, please don't give up,' I pleaded with her. 'There is still hope.'

I crept past Gregory who was beginning to stir and let myself back out onto Bore Street, hoping I wouldn't come across Fitch or Philip. I consoled myself with the fact that Philip knew nothing of my involvement in his deal with the showman, and that Fitch would be leaving tomorrow with or without Gwen. Should Fitch seek me out for revenge, then his anger would surely be directed at Philip's trickery rather than mine when I told him about the fake key.

In the market square Philip's bitter oranges were strewn half eaten everywhere on the ground, and the stall that had been set up to sell them had been overturned and broken in half. The sideshows and booths that had made up the St Clem's Day festivities were being packed up and taken away on carts, whilst the wretched Bormans were still in their stocks being pelted with rancid oranges by a crowd of drunken blacksmiths.

It was nearly ten by the time I pushed open the door of our house and Matthew was sitting at the table waiting for me. 'Where have you been all this time?' he asked. 'I was worried, I feared Philip had accosted you in the street again. Sam has been out looking for you. I sent him home not five minutes ago.'

'I'm sorry, Matthew. I thought I had found a way to set Gwen free,' I said, sinking into the chair by the hearth and unpinning my wig. 'But it was not to be.' I put my hands to my face and Matthew's ire towards me lessened.

'You can't save everyone, my dear,' he said gently. 'Not every story has a happy ending.'

'You don't understand,' I told him, suddenly overcome with fatigue at the events of the evening.

Matthew smiled sadly. 'I think I do. Whatever you do to try and protect others, Hester, you can't go back and save your sister. Gwen isn't Nell.'

'They are all Nell to me,' I said, looking up at him sadly. 'All of them.'

18

KEYS

Father wouldn't allow us to call the village midwife or the doctor for Nell however much Mother and I implored him. He said that if someone came to assist her with the birth then all of Walberswick would know by morning and he would be crucified with shame. That's the word he used, 'crucified', and it echoed around my head as I stood by the door watching in horror as Nell writhed on our bed, her arms flung out to the sides and her belly heaving as the baby struggled to move down inside her narrow hips.

'Come, Hester, let us try and move her into a different position.' Mother beckoned me, her face creased with concern. 'I once helped a midwife tend to a woman in a similar state when I was a governess. It is coming back to me what she did.'

I rushed towards her, my heart lifting at the possibility of alleviating Nell's suffering, but as I reached the bedside Father burst into the room his eyes full of madness and fury.

'I will not hear it any longer,' he shouted, dragging Mother out by her hair as I tried to pull him away from her. 'You will not bear witness to this scene of retribution. Only prayer will save Cornelia's soul,' he bellowed as he sent Mother and me flying into the

*passageway. He pulled a key out of his pocket and locked the door,
leaving Nell screaming behind it.*

'Open it,' I begged him, 'let us go to her.'

Father refused. 'This is your fault,' he said, pointing at me with a
trembling finger. 'You were told to look after her, yet you let this sin
happen. The guilt is on your shoulders, Hester, and can only be
relieved through penance and supplication.'

He stood in front of the door reading aloud from his Bible as Nell
sobbed and shrieked in the room within. Mother sank to the floor and
wept, while I ran at Father and tried to push him aside, but I could
not move him an inch so solid was he. He swatted me away as if I
were no more than a fly, and continued with his preaching. I ran
downstairs and out into the garden, thinking to climb up the back
wall of the house and get in through our attic room window, but
there were not sufficient footholds for me and I fell and cut my knee
trying to scale the flat bricks. By the time I got back upstairs Nell had
fallen silent and Mother was rocking herself backwards and
forwards in the corner of the hallway by Father's booted feet.

'Please, Father, have mercy on her. Give me the key,' I repeated
until my voice went hoarse, but he looked straight through me and
read his verses with fervour.

Finally, when the sun began to sink and his shadow grew long
along the floorboards, Father had no choice but to stop his preaching
so as he could go and use the privy. He gave me a warning look as he
placed his Bible on the floor outside Nell's room and told me if I tried
to gain entry then God himself would strike me down.

As soon as he had gone I rushed at the door and pulled and
kicked at it to try and get it open. I urged Mother to help me, but she
could do no more than stare ahead as she sat on the floor, her eyes
vacant of expression. I ran downstairs and threw open the dresser
drawer which contained all the keys for the house. I tried each in the
lock in case any were the same as the one Father had in his pocket,
but none would turn it and I stamped the floor in frustration.

'Nell, I'm here,' I shouted, but she didn't, couldn't, reply.

Father gave a mirthless laugh when he returned and saw the keys strewn about the floor. I truly think he had crossed over into madness by then, perhaps we all had. He pushed me aside to resume his Bible reading and it was then that I realised Mother had gone and that if I was going to save Nell I was going to have to do it on my own.

I stood firm in front of my father as he ranted and told him that if he didn't let me in to help my sister then I would run into the village and shout aloud what was happening inside our house, and that I would go to the manor house and fetch Matthew to fight against him. That made him stop. The humiliation of his congregation seeing his family in such disarray snapped Father back to what was left of his senses. He closed his Bible and stepped aside, throwing the key from his pocket onto the floor behind him as he went into his bed chamber and shut the door. I bent down to pick it up and saw Mother coming back up the stairs holding the breadknife in front of her, her face as pale and blank as a sheet of parchment.

I held up the key for her to see and she nodded and turned silently on her heel, taking the knife back down to the kitchen. I fear the horror that would have ensued had Father not already given up the key, for Mother had that distant look that folk get when they don't care about the consequences of their actions anymore. Sometimes, when I think about that moment I wonder if Father heard her tread on the stair and got a feel of the violence that was coming for him and that's what compelled him to withdraw and hide himself away in his room, rather than because of any pity for his daughter.

My hands were shaking as I unlocked the door and burst into the room. Nell was lying motionless on the bed and I feared she was dead but she revived a little when I went to her and I held her face in my hands, covering her with kisses. She had bled all over the sheets and Mother shook her head in anguish when she saw it. 'Help me,

Hester.' She pressed a linen cloth against Nell to try and stem the blood, but it was too late by then even if we had managed to fetch the midwife.

'We're here now,' I said, as I assisted Mother.

'All will be well,' I told Nell in the calmest tone I could muster, but I could see in her eyes that she knew she was going to die and that the hours she had spent labouring in agony alone had robbed her of her strength and her spirit.

Mother and I took turns mopping Nell's brow and holding her hand, trying our best to give her comfort so she would know at least that she was loved. When she finally died it was a terrible sort of relief as we could take no more of seeing her in such pain. Our sweet Nell.

Mother told me afterwards that there were ways we could have tried to help Nell birth the baby sooner, but we never got the chance to do that for her. I had the dreadful knowledge then that she might have lived if I had been able to get Father to open that door and I felt wretched with guilt that my begging and pleading had not been enough. Father had held the power over Nell's life and had wielded it in the cruellest way. He had decided on her fate based on his immovable faith and I had been helpless to save her.

Nell somehow found the determination inside herself to push one final time before she died and you were born into the world with her last few breaths. Our mother lay next to her on the bed, exhausted and held Nell's lifeless hand while I cut the cord and wrapped you in a linen cloth. You let out a hearty cry and I held your little body to mine and I told you that I would look after you and love you always. I sank to the floor with you in my arms and watched through the window as the sun rose above Father's church and the gulls flew past on their way out to the fishing boats, as if it were a day like any other.

When I found the strength to stand, I passed you to Mother and ran to fetch Matthew to tell him what had happened. He kept true to his promise and Father married us later that morning in the empty church, the words of the marriage ceremony devoid of all joy and muffled by his hoarse voice.

Afterwards I returned to the rectory to pack our belongings and waited at the gate for Matthew to return for us with his bags. I pleaded with Mother to come, to leave Father, but she would not be persuaded. 'This is where I belong,' she told me, staring at the grey clouds gathering on the horizon. 'It is my duty.'

The last time I saw Father was as he walked past us down the lane back to his church. I willed a lightning bolt to strike him from the sky or a tree to fall upon him but he strode purposefully forward as if nothing uncommon had occurred and all in the world was well and as God intended. It was when he reached the oak at the end of the lane where the swing still hung that he had put up for Nell when she was a child that he faltered as if he had tripped on a stone. I thought he would right himself and continue on his way but he fell to his knees and crumpled onto the ground at the sight of it and I was glad that he suffered so, and that he would feel her loss as well as I.

We left soon after in a pony and cart that some kind soul had gifted to the parish to help the needy. We were certainly needy, my dear husband and I, as we clattered across the country east to west not knowing a thing about how to care for the infant I had strapped to my bosom. By some miracle of nature, milk began to come from my breasts that first night and I was able to feed you. I can only think the sustenance was from Nell and it came through me, flowing like the love we had had for each other all our lives. Matthew held me in the moonlight as we sat by the roadside and I suckled you, your tiny hands grasping at my shawl. Matthew and I didn't need to speak in that moment to communicate our sentiments towards each other and towards you. We were family by then.

The only possession we had for you from your mother was Nell's *butterfly necklace that I had taken from around her neck after she had died. That and your name which she had chosen before you were born. Boy or girl, she wanted you called after the special stones that she had treasured all her life. She wanted you called Amber.*

19

KNOTTED THREADS

I stayed awake most of that night, stabbing at my embroidery until the threads were all of a tangle. I worried constantly about Gwen and her imminent sentencing, and fretted on the way I had falsely raised her hopes in my failed attempt to set her free. My misery was compounded by the decision I had been forced to make prohibiting the use of Samuel's defence against the charges of witchcraft in Gwen's trial, and by my lack of a clear insight as to who murdered Loella Aston. As far as I could see, no one had any reason to want her dead. Lord Aston and Claudia loved her, her sons seemed indifferent to her and none of her servants appeared to profit in any way from her demise.

'Could it have been an accident?' I asked Amber the next morning as we went through the statements from the Aston household that Matthew had collected on Lord Aston's behalf. I had told her about the events of the previous evening and about Philip's trickery, and it had made her even more determined to discover the truth about Lady Aston's death.

'No, it wasn't an accident,' she insisted. 'Dr Crouch was adamant that Lady Aston received a blow to the head with a heavy object. The injury to the back of her head was most probably obtained as she fell back onto the hearth, but the first and fatal blow was directly on top of her crown and couldn't have been inflicted with such force accidentally. Somebody killed her.'

'But how did they get in?' I pondered. 'The Hall is like a fortress.'

'It must have been somebody in the household,' said Amber. 'You and Pa spoke to all the servants. Did any one of them seem suspicious?'

I shook my head. 'Only Lena seemed to have something to hide and that has now been revealed as being her dalliance with Herbert. She would have no reason to kill Lady Aston. Her emotions when she recounted finding her mistress were wholly convincing to me and your father. Lena would have had to be a great actress to keep up such a charade, not a frightened mouse of a housemaid.'

'What of that chimney then? Could someone have climbed down it and then back out?'

'Matthew peered up it when we were following Lord Aston and Herbert to the village. He said it was too narrow for any adult to get through and what child would have cause or means to do such a thing?'

'A child whose own mother was hanged perhaps?' Amber suggested, holding my eye to gauge my reaction. 'A child who had worked at the Hall.'

I shook my head. 'If you're meaning Robby Baker you are on the wrong path,' I said. 'What reason would that poor boy have to kill Lady Aston? He knows well enough what happens to them that murder others, child and adult alike.'

'I think we should speak to him,' Amber said. 'Perhaps he wanted to protect Gwen in some way. You told me that cook said they got on well. We can't leave a stone unturned.'

'And if he did do it?' I whispered. 'I'll not stand by having him arrested and meeting the same fate as Joanna.'

Amber pursed her lips. 'No, me neither.'

'Gwen wouldn't want that, I know she wouldn't,' I said, standing up and pacing the floor.

'We should speak to Robby, nonetheless,' Amber said. 'He may be able to shed light on what happened even if he didn't do it himself.'

'And if he did do it?' I asked again.

'Then we give him a bag of coins, tell him to leave the city and never speak of it to a soul,' Amber said resolutely. 'Come, I think I know where to find him.'

We hastened to the coaching inn and found George dripping with sweat in the midst of rubbing down a half dozen fine black horses recently arrived from London. He smiled when he saw us and put his rag back in its bucket. 'What brings you here? If you've come to see Esme and Matt you're out of luck I'm afraid, she's taken him to visit my sister.' He pushed his wet hair out of his eyes and reached for the ladle in the water barrel.

I was pleased Esme felt strong enough to go for a walk with the baby and told George so.

'She fairs well, Hester, as does the babe. He has a hearty pair of lungs on him, wakes us at all hours with his hollering till Esme nurses him,' he said. 'I am ever grateful to you both for how you looked after her in her labours. I was scared out of my wits, I don't mind telling you, and felt as useless as a fifth wheel on a cart.'

'You did her proud, George,' I told him. 'She is a lucky lass to have a husband as devoted to her happiness, and that of your child, as you are.'

He looked to the ground shyly but I could see my words pleased him.

'We aren't here to see Esme,' Amber said, bringing us back to the matter in hand. 'We are looking for Robby Baker. I thought he might be here as I know he helps you out sometimes.'

'Aye he does,' said George, nodding, 'and good with the horses he is, too. But he's not here today, I've not seen him.'

'Do you know where he might be?' Amber asked.

George shook his head. 'I've no inkling. Robby comes and goes as he pleases.'

'Has he ever told you of anywhere else he goes?' Amber persisted.

George looked up to the stable rafters, searching his mind for memories. 'He did go off with the intention to visit Gwen Foley the other day,' he said slowly. 'But that old guard wouldn't let him in. Maybe he's gone to the Guildhall to try again?'

'Thank you, George, that's very helpful,' I said. I turned to speak to Amber but she was already heading towards the archway that led back into town.

We found Gwen ailing when we finally persuaded Gregory to unlock the door to her cell. Her pure white face was a pallid grey and her eyes were weepy and sore. Her hair stood out from her head in a tangle and she trembled with cold. I placed my cloak around Gwen's narrow shoulders and Amber rubbed her feet until they were warm.

'Tam?' she asked in a weak voice.

'He is fine,' I assured her. 'He is asleep on my hearth as we speak and fills his belly from our table morn and night. My Liberty has found a friend in him and they play together often with sticks and a ball.'

She smiled. 'I dream he is here with me,' she whispered, 'and then I awake and he is not and I don't think I can bear being apart from him any longer.'

I stroked her hair and tried to soothe her the best I could but she wanted to speak again. 'If I don't ever leave this place except to be taken to the gallows...' she said, pulling away from me and looking towards my eyes. 'If that happens, Mistress Albright, will you keep Tam for me and look after him?' she said. 'The thought of him being lost and alone again...' She put her hand to her mouth.

'Tam can always have a home with us,' I assured her, 'but there is still hope for you, Gwen. Don't give up yet.'

She pulled my red cloak more closely around herself and nodded bravely, although I could see her faith in the possibility of a good outcome was all but gone.

'Has Robby Baker been here to see you?' Amber asked. 'We are trying to find him.'

Gwen shook her head. 'Why are you looking for Robby?' she said with a frown.

'We are trying to find out who killed Lady Aston, to help your defence.'

She was aghast. 'And you think it was Robby?'

'We don't know. We need to talk to him; he may be able to help us. Help you,' Amber said.

'It wasn't Robby,' Gwen said, her hands flailing up and down. 'You can't think it was Robby. I beg you to leave him be. He is the only friend I have apart from Tamworth.'

'Gwen,' said Amber in a solemn tone. 'You have my word that nothing will happen to the boy whatever he tells us or whatever he has done. That is not our intention, but we need to know the truth of what happened to Lady Aston so that a conceivable alternative can be put forward in your defence at the trial. I promise you that Robby Baker will be safe.'

Gwen wrung her hands together and stared at the filthy floor. 'Robby was full of anger about his mother's death and that nobody tried to help her or save her from hanging,' she said at last.

I could see Amber shared my regret that we hadn't tried to find a way to save Joanna. I thought with deep gratitude then of Samuel and the Lunar Society and how the activities of our little group were giving a chance, at least, to try and save Gwen.

'Robby told me that his Aunt Agnes, Joanna's sister, used to work up at Little Aston Hall as a scullery maid some years back,' Gwen continued.

'He said that Agnes screwed up all her courage and went to ask Lady Aston for her help in saving their mother. Agnes wanted her to ask Lord Aston to try and get a pardon from the King for Joanna so she wouldn't be hung. But Lady Aston refused. She said it was none of her husband's business, that he wouldn't want to get involved in such a scandal and that he didn't have any direct communication with the royal household anyway. She scolded Agnes for asking, told her she should know her place and respect the laws of the land.'

'What happened then?' Amber asked, although we both knew.

'Then the assizes court arrived, Joanna was tried and sentenced to hang for her husband's murder. Robby had been working at Little Aston Hall himself for a year or so by then, helping out in the kitchen and the garden sheds and around the grounds. I doubt Lady Aston had any idea who he was, or any reason to care.'

'What did Robby say about Lady Aston?' Amber asked. 'Did he have violent intentions towards her?'

'Not that he ever told me,' said Gwen, shaking her head.

My heart sank at the prospect of Robby having carried out the terrible crime against Loella Aston; but from Gwen's words about Agnes' failed petition it seemed possible that he could be culpable, impelled by anger at Lady Aston's refusal to try and help his mother.

'Matilda, the cook at Little Aston Hall, may know more,' Gwen added. 'She was fond of Robby and he talked to her often – she'd let him sit at the kitchen table and eat titbits from her pots and pans, kind-hearted lady that she is. Is it Thursday today?' she asked suddenly.

'Yes, it is,' replied Amber.

'Then Matilda is most likely at the fish market on Wade Street. Robby told me she doesn't trust any other soul to choose Lord Aston's hake and crab so she is always to be found there when the fish is delivered fresh on a Thursday.'

We came across Matilda haggling hard over the price of a piece of turbot at the far end of the market. She was surprised when she first saw us, and then greeted us with a warm smile.

'You ladies appreciate good seafood too, I see,' she said, tucking the wrapped fish into her basket. 'This is the only place in town I buy fish and only ever on a Thursday when it comes in just a day after it's caught. One of the many shortcomings of living so far from the coast that is, the scarcity of fresh fish to eat.'

I thought it an odd comment from one born and bred in the Midlands – most of those dwelling in Lichfield never gave a thought to the sea as they had never seen it – but I didn't ask her to expand on it, eager as I was to speak to her about Joanna Baker's son.

'Mistress Matilda, we wanted to ask you about your former kitchen boy, Robby Baker,' I said, leading her gently by her arm to the side of the stall where the smell was less pungent. 'Do you know where he is?'

'Why are you looking for Robby?' Matilda asked, narrowing her eyes. 'He's a good boy he is and he's had enough bad luck to last him a lifetime, poor lamb.'

'We want to protect him,' Amber said, without expanding her point. 'If there's anything you can tell us about what Robby did at the Hall or where he might be it would be most helpful,' she added, putting her hand to the coin purse hanging from her belt.

Matilda shifted her basket from the crook of one arm to the other, and blew a puff of air from between her plump lips. 'Well,' she said. 'I don't know if it's useful but if it helps protect him, I'll tell you this. He still sometimes hangs around at the Hall even though he left after his poor ma died. He climbs like a squirrel, does Robby. I see him sitting in the oak trees or his favourite place up on the roof. The family and the other domestics don't see him because they're not looking for him, but I do and when I see him I put food out for him, like he's a stray animal. It's always gone after a while but I don't see him take it. I know he must be hungry, I saw him kill a pigeon once with his bare hands and shove it in his bag so as he'd have something for the pot, I suppose. I just wanted to help him, felt it was my Christian duty.' She tucked her chin down towards her ample bosom and nodded at the rightness of her actions in the eyes of God.

'Did Robby ever say anything to you about Lady Aston?' Amber asked.

'He didn't like her,' Matilda said in a confiding tone. 'But he never told me why.'

Amber gave her two coins and Matilda slipped them into her apron pocket. 'Thank you, miss,' she said. 'I'll buy some marchpane with that, and me and my sister Lizzy can have a little treat – we both of us have a sweet tooth.' She headed with enthusiasm towards the confectionary shop on the other side of the street.

Amber sighed heavily. 'It's looking ever more likely that it was Robby who killed Lady Aston,' she said and began counting the reasons off on her fingers. 'He had a good reason to hate her after she refused to help Joanna; he is good at climbing up on roofs without being noticed – which means he could have got down the chimney at Little Aston Hall; and he is small enough to have got down it, too. Furthermore, we know that he has a stomach for bloody acts and that he was full of anger at his mother's death.'

'But surely Robby wouldn't be letting Gwen take the blame for a crime he committed? She is his friend,' I said.

'He is a frightened little boy. Who knows what he would do?' said Amber, looking up at the top of the black and white buildings overhanging Wade Street. 'We must find him.'

'Where is he, though?' I asked, following her gaze.

'I think he's watching us from the rooftops,' she said, pointing at a flash of movement by the chimney stack above the sweet shop.

'Come quickly, before he disappears again.'

I followed Amber as she ran off down a narrow alley to get to the back of the row of buildings on the far side of the market and caught up with her as she began scaling the rear wall of the shop. The bricks were uneven and had been added to with no regard to order over the years so there were plenty of footholds for her to use as she made her way up towards the red tiles on the roof. I watched from the yard as she reached out for the chimney stack and heaved herself onto the peak.

'Is he there?' I shouted, shading my eyes from the noon-day sun which shone bright through a gap in the clouds.

'I can't see him,' Amber shouted back, standing upright in a way that made me flinch with fear as she looked out over the row of rooftops.

'Come down! You'll fall,' I insisted, wondering if we had gone quite mad the two of us, in our quest for the truth.

'No, I see him now,' she said and leapt across the gap over the alley onto the roof of the house next door. She was lost from my view for a few moments and then reappeared clambering across the tiles sideways like a crab. I gasped as her left foot found a loose tile and she slipped down the side of the roof, mercifully managing to grab on to a scantling and saving herself from a nasty fall.

'Hold on, I'm coming up,' I announced, looking around for something to stand on to give me a good start. I pushed a barrel against the wall and picked up my skirts so I could get on top of it. Once there I found I could reach the bottom of the roof and imitated Amber's way of finding footholds to take myself higher. My petticoat got caught on a nail about halfway up and I ripped it off so I could continue, cursing the clumsy clothes I wore and envying Amber's leather trousers and boots which were much more suitable for such exertions. I got to a position where I could see over the top of the roof by clinging to the chimney breast but I knew that I had not the ability nor the strength to go further, not in my heeled shoes and frock. I hung on and peered over.

Amber had found Robby and they were sitting together not three feet away on the other side of the roof overlooking the street.

I was prevented from hearing their conversation at first by a fishmonger down below in the market ringing a bell and proclaiming his catch of the day. When he finally fell silent, I was grateful that the voices I had been straining to hear came to me clearly in the still air.

'Did you like Lady Aston, Robby?' Amber was asking him.

Robby shrugged. 'She was just a lady. I didn't know 'er. Why would I know 'er?'

'Your Aunt Agnes knew her. She went to talk to her about your ma.'

Robby stared ahead at the mention of his mother and the breeze ruffled the thick brown hair that poked out under his cap. 'No one 'elped us,' he said at last. 'No one would. Those Astons have cold 'earts, that's what Agnes said.'

Amber turned her face towards him and she winced with guilt at the knowledge that she – we – had not taken action to help Joanna or her family either.

'Why do you sit up here on the rooftops?' Amber asked him gently.

'I like it up high,' he said. 'I like looking at the clouds and the birds. The sky it changes all the time but it's usually grey like it is now, with little bits of blue coming through. My ma used to say if there's enough blue to make a sailor a pair of trousers then it can be called a fair day. I dunno what she meant by that, really, but I can hear her saying it in me 'ead like, when I look at the sky. I can't remember her saying nothing else. Or what she looked like 'cept her face when she saw that rope hanging there for 'er. I won't never forget the look on her face when she seen that.' He picked up a piece of broken tile and threw it hard across the narrow street so that it landed with a click on the rooftop opposite.

Amber rested her chin against her fist and shook her head. 'It wasn't right, Robby, what happened to your ma. I'm sorry nobody helped your family and I'm sorry you are alone now.'

He sniffed and threw another piece of clay, hitting the

chimney breast of the facing roof this time and startling a pair of pigeons who fluttered off to find a quieter place to perch.

'It's my fault ma is dead,' he said bluntly, watching as the birds settled on the top of a market stall awning.

'What do you mean?' Amber asked, her brow creased in concern.

'I got 'er the poison, didn't I? The poison she used to kill da. I got it for 'er; she used it and he died. Then she got hanged for it. It's all my fault.' His voice faded as he repeated the words, and Amber shook her head.

'No, Robby, you're wrong,' she said. 'Even if you did get the poison for her, it was your mother's choice to use it in the way she did. And she did that because your father was cruel to her and to you all. So if it is anyone's fault that she is dead, it is his and it is also the fault of the judge that he showed her no pity. The fault does not lie with you. You don't have to carry that burden. Your ma wouldn't want that.'

Robby's shoulders relaxed a little and he gazed up as another shaft of blue opened up in the sky.

'Where did you get the poison from?' Amber asked after she had let her words sink in.

'Can't say. I promised I wouldn't say. Don't make me,' said Robby, pressing his lips together.

'I won't,' said Amber. 'I don't suppose it matters anymore anyway.'

They sat together watching the clouds part and rejoin and I thought of Joanna and the dreadful decision she had been forced to make – poisoning William or enduring years more suffering at his hands. I wasn't sure if I would have done anything different if I had been in her position and felt a wave of gratitude that dear Matthew had never lifted a hand to me or to any of our children. I thought of my own poor mother too, and how close she had come to committing a murderous act towards Father on the day we lost Nell.

'Are they going to hang Gwen Foley like they did Ma?' Robby asked.

'A group of us are trying very hard to stop that from happening,' Amber told him. 'Will you help us?'

Robby turned to look at her. 'Course,' he said. 'I like Gwen, she's a nice lady.'

Amber took a deep breath. 'I'm going to ask you a question and I want you to tell me the truth. It doesn't matter what the answer is, nothing bad will happen to you, I promise you that, but you must tell me the truth. Do you think you can do that?'

Robby nodded and sat up straight waiting for his question.

'Did you climb down the chimney in the drawing room at Aston Hall and hit Lady Aston on the head? Perhaps because you were cross that she didn't listen to your Aunt Agnes or help your ma?'

Robby burst out laughing. 'You what? That chimney ain't wide enough for a four-year-old to get down it, let alone me. They 'ave to clean it with sticks it's that bunged up with soot. And me clobber Lady Aston on the nut? Why would I do a thing like that? I don't want to swing from a rope, Miss Albright,' he said, rubbing his throat and frowning. 'I want to live my life, for what it's worth anyway.'

'Of course you do,' Amber said. I sensed her relief at the boy's words and I shared it too. 'That's what your ma would want for you, for you to live your life,' she continued. 'She'd be proud of you, being so brave, carrying on without her.'

'I ain't got no choice 'ave I?' Robby said, staring back at the clouds. 'I'm all alone now.'

'Could you not go and live with your Aunt Agnes?' Amber suggested. 'Like your other siblings? Aunts can be just as good as mothers, you know.'

I smiled to myself, knowing she knew I was listening, but Robby wasn't to be persuaded.

He shook his head. 'Naw. I can't be looked after no more. Not by no one. That's passed for me, that has. I want to work. Look after myself.'

'I understand that,' said Amber, reaching into her pocket. 'Here, I want you to have these coins as a thank you for helping me today and for telling me the truth – which I have no doubt you have done.'

Robby's eyes lit up as he took the purse. 'Thank you very much, Miss Albright,' he said.

'Amber, it's time for us to go,' I called from my position beside the chimney. 'I don't think I can hold on here much longer.'

Robby spun round and laughed in surprise when he saw me peering over the roof ledge, my bonnet halfway down my forehead.

'You go on home. There is something further I want to discuss with young Robby,' Amber called back, leaving me to navigate my descent back into the yard of the sweetshop, grateful that there was no one below to see my garters as I made my ungainly way down the brickwork.

I was awash with relief at Robby's innocence, even though we were no further in our hunt for Lady Aston's murderer. After my adventures on the roof and having walked back through the busy market square on a day when the world and his wife seemed to be out bartering and bargaining, I felt the need to be quietly at home with Liberty and Matthew.

I decided to make Suffolk harvest cakes using my mother's special recipe as a treat for Matthew as it was his favourite.

Liberty helped me measure out the currants and cinnamon and mix them with treacle and eggs in my largest bowl. The activity of the baking soothed my troubled mind greatly, even though I was a little disappointed that a new revelation in relation to Lady Aston's murder did not occur to me as I stirred in the flour.

Liberty grinned from ear to ear as she ate her first slice of the cake warm from the stove, and she fed her second slice to Tam who was perched salivating at her knee. She ran to show Matthew what we had made when he limped wearily though the door at five after a long day's tutoring.

'What's this? Harvest cake?' he asked, taking a piece from her and taking a bite. 'My very favourite. Have you been helping your mother with her baking?'

Liberty understood him as he mimed stirring in a bowl and she nodded happily.

'I know you like my mother's cake, Matthew, and I haven't made it for an age,' I said to him as I helped him off with his coat and settled him in his chair by the fire.

'Funnily enough I had it at Little Aston Hall,' he said as I buttered him another slice. 'The cook, Matilda, had made the very same cake. She brought me a piece to have with my tea as I waited for you and Amber to return from the village on the eve of Lady Aston's murder.'

'How curious,' I said, passing the plate to him. 'I didn't think that recipe had travelled out of our corner of Suffolk. I've never heard of anyone in these parts making it.'

I paused as I went to cut another slice, as a thought struck me just as hard as if a beam had fallen from the ceiling and thumped me on the head. 'Matthew,' I said with such urgency that he almost dropped his plate. 'What if Matilda is not a Methodist from Derby? What if she lied and in truth, like me, she hails from Suffolk?'

'Why on earth would she lie about such a thing?' Matthew asked, baffled by my outburst.

'Perhaps kind-hearted Matilda is not as generous in her spirits as she would have us believe?' I said slowly, the idea still forming in my mind. 'Perhaps she has the same old ideas about witches that took such a hold in my part of the country in years gone by. Perhaps Matilda didn't want us to have any reason to suspect that?'

Matthew blew air from between his lips and shook his head. 'She doesn't have the Suffolk burr in her voice. The woman sounds like she comes from where she says, Derby through and through.'

'Listen to me, would you know I was from Suffolk if you didn't already know? Matilda might well have lived in the Midlands for years, lost her accent along the way.'

'In truth, Hettie, yes I would know you were from Suffolk because you sound precisely the same as you did the day I met you.' Matthew raised his eyebrows at me as if that settled the matter, but I wasn't to be put off my chain of thought.

'Well that's me, isn't it? I don't change easy, you know that. Folk are different though. Some are more various in the ways they present themselves. Take your brother Philip: he used to be a modestly dressed, studious man, albeit he was always of an unpleasant nature, and look at him now! A year in London and he thinks he's cock of the hoot.'

Matthew had to agree with me about Philip and it brought him to weigh up what I was saying about Matilda.

'If Matilda was afraid of witchcraft then perhaps it was her who led Lord Aston to blame poor Gwen in the first place?' I said. 'A woman who was alone and different from the rest, Gwen was an easy target for such tattle-tales.'

'I can't imagine that Lord Aston would care much about Matilda Syms' opinion on any subject, or that of any domestic servant,' Matthew said doubtfully. 'I suspect his reasons for accusing Gwen lay elsewhere, although I have to admit they remain unfathomable to me.'

He sat watching Liberty play with her wooden doll in the corner, locked in her own silent little world, as he thought through what I had suggested to him. 'I suppose it would do no harm for us to take a trip to Little Aston tomorrow morning and speak to Matilda again,' he said at last.

'Philip will never allow that.' I tutted in frustration. 'He has reclaimed all magistrate duties from you so you would have no authority to pose further questions to Lord Aston's household.'

'Ah, but the folk downstairs at Little Aston Hall don't know that yet, do they, my dear?' he said, tapping the side of his nose. 'And if we get let in through the servant's entrance at the back none of the family need know we are there.'

'Matthew Albright, you are a wily fox, my love,' I said, planting a kiss on his forehead and he reddened with pleasure at my approval of his plan.

20

BRIMSTONE

The following morning, I went up to see Esme while George was preparing a modest carriage to take Matthew and me to Little Aston Hall. She was sitting in a low chair nursing the baby and my heart melted at the peacefulness of the scene.

'How are you, my pet?' I asked, touching my grandson's downy head as I sat down next to her.

'We are well, Mama,' she said, 'although Matty seems never to stop feeding.'

'I've brought you some ointment to help with the healing and some cabbage leaves to soothe your breasts,' I told her, pulling the items out of my basket and setting them on the table. 'And a harvest cake,' I said with a smile.

She smiled back and passed me the baby to hold while she poured us some tea.

'So what takes you back to Little Aston Hall today?' she asked, settling back into her chair and taking a slice of the cake.

'There are secrets in that house, I am sure of it. If we can uncover them, we might yet be able to save Gwen Foley from the gallows,' I told her.

'I hope you do,' she said, her mouth full of crumbs. 'I've never liked that family.'

Esme surprised me with that as I didn't know she had had occasion to meet the Astons.

'Lord Aston comes to the inn on occasion to wait for carriages from London bringing acquaintances or kin. His son Herbert too,' she told me. 'They both drink too much and Herbert is forever reaching up the serving girls' skirts or pressing his face to their bosoms when his father isn't looking. He is truly a vile young man.'

'We suspected as much about the younger Lord Aston,' I said. 'But now you have told me that I have even more reason to believe he was dallying with the maid, Lena, at Little Aston Hall.'

'His youngest son – Gabriel, is it? He has also been with them the last couple of times. He's as bad as his brother, hands all over the serving lasses. It's a sport to those Aston boys, I think, pouncing on the girls as soon as their father's back is turned in conversation or he's gone to the jacks.'

'Young Gabriel behaves in the same way as Herbert, does he? Thank you, Esme, that is all very helpful to know.'

Esme beamed, happy to be of use. I kissed her as I passed the baby back and made my way down the stairs to join Matthew in the carriage. We set off clattering along St John's and I put my thoughts to weighing up how the titbits I was collecting might fit together in a way that would shift the blame for Lady Aston's murder away from Gwen Foley.

We picked up Amber and Sarah on our way through town. As fortune would have it, Sarah had a delivery to take to Little Aston Hall – school books for the children ordered weeks ago before all the trouble started. The Johnsons didn't deliver in person as a general rule, but it was useful to have an innocent reason to be visiting the Hall in case our carriage drew attention. While Sarah made the delivery, Matthew and I intended to slip into the kitchen to question Matilda again.

That was the plan we had in mind although as with so many of our schemes of late, it didn't go quite as expected.

'Matilda's not here,' Arthur the hallboy told me, as he leaned against the range eating a handful of dried apricots from a bowl on the table. 'She's gone to visit her sister in the village, won't be back till tonight.'

'And Lena?' I asked. I waited for the answer while Arthur tossed a piece of apricot into the air and caught it in his mouth.

'She's in her bed with a headache,' he said with a smirk. 'Probably just fancies a day under the blankets if you ask me.'

'No one did ask you,' said Matthew. 'Do you happen to know where in the village Matilda's sister lives?' he asked, watching with distaste as the boy picked pieces of apricot out of his back teeth.

The young man patted his pocket and raised his brows. Matthew sighed and placed a penny down on the table.

'It's the cottage next to the church,' Arthur said. 'With the sagging roof. You can't miss it, looks like Lord Aston himself has sat on it with his big arse.' We left the lad chuckling to himself as we made our way back out to the carriage.

'I'll have to wait here,' said Matthew, wincing as I helped him up into the chaise. 'My good leg is seizing up in this cold weather. I need to rest it for a while. It is probably easier for you to walk to the village from here than take the carriage down that narrow lane anyway.'

'I'll stay too,' said Sarah. 'I will take the books to Gabriel and Claudia and see if I can find anything out about their mother that we didn't already know.'

Amber and I agreed and walked to the village on our own. We found the house we wanted easily using Arthur's uncouth, but undeniably accurate, description.

I recognised Matilda's sister with her distinctive round face and wispy grey hair as soon as she opened the door, but I couldn't recall where I had seen her before. We introduced ourselves and told her we were here to talk to Matilda on official town business. She told us her name was Lizzy and shuffled ahead of us into a stuffy parlour dotted all about with cats of various sizes and furs.

'Am I wanted to give evidence at Gwen Foley's murder trial?' Matilda asked nervously when she saw it was us.

'No, I'm sure that won't be necessary,' I assured her, relieved that she still saw me as a person connected to legal authority.

'We wanted to ask you again about Gwen Foley,' Amber said as a large tabby jumped from the windowsill and began rubbing itself around her legs.

Matilda shifted uncomfortably in her overstuffed chair, the dewlaps under her chin wobbling as she drew her head back and forced herself to smile. 'I can't think what else I can tell you about her,' she said, glancing at her sister.

'You told us the other day when we spoke that in your opinion Gwen Foley was a nice woman and that you held none of the old ideas about witches and the like which many in this village seem to share. Is that truly your opinion?'

Matilda's eyes hardened. 'Yes,' she snapped, her pleasantness falling away. The black and white cat on her lap looked up, startled at her tone.

'Why do you want to know my sister's thoughts on the White?' asked Lizzy with a frown.

I realised with a start why she was familiar to me. She had been the plump woman walking beside me chanting 'witch' on the night that Lord Aston and Herbert had hauled poor Gwen from her home.

'Tell me, Lizzy,' I said. 'Where did you and your sister grow up?'

It was Lizzy's turn to glance at Matilda and they shared a look of alarm. 'Derbyshire,' she said slowly.

'Whereabouts in Derbyshire?' asked Amber, ignoring the tabby as it curled round her heel and began to tap the flap of her leather boot.

Lizzy opened and then closed her mouth and Matilda jumped in. 'You won't know it; it's but a tiny village; not even on the map is it, Liz?'

Lizzy shook her head, then nodded.

'Nonetheless, it must have a name,' Amber persisted, standing strong and firm in the centre of the room where she could see them both clearly.

'Erm,' Matilda bit her lip. 'I can't rightly remember.' She gave a shrill little laugh. 'I must be getting old, things slip my mind.'

'And you, Lizzy, do things slip your mind too?' asked Amber. 'Or can you tell us the name of the village in Derbyshire where you grew up?'

'I can't,' she said quietly, staring at her feet.

'Where did you grow up, then?' I repeated. 'If it wasn't in Derbyshire?'

The cat on Matilda's lap purred loudly, oblivious to the rising tension in the room as we waited for one of the sisters to answer.

At last Matilda said, 'We were born in Lowestoft. Then when we were a bit older Father got a position in Bury St Edmunds so we went to live there.' Her voice was suddenly different, the Suffolk burr clearly evident in the 'R's.

'Lots of witch-hunting in that neck of the woods,' I said, looking from one sister to the other to see their reaction. 'Lots of bad history, and not so very long ago. In your living memory I'd say.'

'We saw it when we was girls,' said Lizzy, her face hardening. 'We saw the last few hang and we were happy about it and Bury was better for it. Father helped lead those trials and he knew what he was doing. Cleansed we were and life went on better than before once those filthy beasts were gotten rid of. We know many folks nowadays don't agree with what happened at the trials back then, so we sometimes hide our origins and pretend to be Methodists from Derby if we are talking to modern types, like you people. We do it so they don't suspect what we really believe about the scourge of witches who still befoul this blessed country.'

'You stupid fussock,' snarled Matilda. 'You didn't have to tell them that.'

'Why not?' shouted Lizzy, frightening away the small cat who was perched on the arm of her chair. 'What does it matter now? Gwen Foley's a witch. She's caused nowt but misery in this village and she's going to hang like all witches should hang. I'm just thankful that Lord Aston sees it that way, too, and is a man of standing who can get his will done.'

'Did Gwen kill Lady Aston?' I asked Matilda.

She sniffed. 'I don't know who killed that stuck-up toad, and I don't rightly care,' she said. 'Always going on with her fancy ideas about the world and thinking she was better than everyone else 'cos of her book reading. But I'll tell you this, that Gwen Foley is a witch and we are all safer in our beds now that she is locked away and we'll be safer yet when she is dead and can do no more of her mischief.'

'Why did you send Robby to buy vegetables from Gwen if you were afraid of her?' asked Amber.

'I wanted to know what she was up to. I wanted Robby to report back to me. But he wouldn't say a word against her, the little urchin. Took to her he did. I told him not to go and see the White anymore but he went anyway.' Matilda tutted at the memory.

'And Lena?'

'What about her?' snapped Matilda.

'Did she know Gwen?'

'No, no. She's nothing to do with anything,' Matilda said quickly, looking across at Lizzy. 'There's nowt to be gained from pressing that one, she's an empty-headed blowsabella. Best leave her be.'

The four of us were silent for a moment, taking in all that had been said. The sisters were flushed and had clearly been rattled by our questions. We would have liked to press them further but given the unofficial nature of our visit, Amber and I could do no more than thank them cordially for their time and take our leave.

We waited until we were back on the track leading up to Little Aston Hall before we started to speak.

'What a nasty pair,' said Amber. 'I don't trust anything either of them says. We need to talk to Lena as soon as we get back.'

'I agree,' I said heartily. 'Those sisters are hiding more than they've told us. Let's hope Lena can give us the missing piece of the puzzle we need to put a stop to Gwen's trial.'

We found Matthew and Sarah sitting in the carriage when we returned, their fingers tinged blue with cold, blankets around their shoulders and across their knees.

'Did you uncover the truth?' asked Sarah expectantly.

'Not quite yet, but we have found out much that is helpful,' I said. 'Did you discover any more from Gabriel and Claudia?'

Sarah shook her head.

'No matter. Amber and me are going inside now to talk to Lena the housemaid, and then we will tell you all we know. If we get Arthur to let us in the back way and go straight up to the servants' quarters no one from the family will see us.'

'Be careful,' said Matthew. 'I don't want you finding yourself at the sharp end of Lord Aston's wrath. Or his cutlass.'

I nodded as I closed the carriage door and Amber and I made our way to the back entrance where the hallboy let us in without question. We could hear echoes of voices in the rooms around us, but we saw no one as we climbed the back staircase to the eaves at the top of the house where the maids slept.

Only one of the four doors was closed and I rapped gently, not wanting to frighten Lena. There was no response.

'Knock louder,' Amber whispered.

I did so and still Lena didn't reply. I peered through a knot hole in the wood about halfway up and could make out a figure lying in the narrow bed, but could see no details of the form.

'She must be fast asleep,' I said to Amber.

Amber frowned and shook her head. 'No one sleeps that soundly, unless they've taken a draft,' she said as she pulled on one of her leather gloves and took a firm grip of the handle. She twisted it so hard that the latch broke and she was able to push the flimsy door open.

We rushed to Lena's bedside and as Amber turned her over I saw with dismay that her lips and tongue were a mottled grey and she was struggling to breath. Amber sat her up and pushed her fingers straight down the girl's throat making her gag and then vomit, as I quickly grabbed the pot from under the bed to catch the mess. Lena opened her eyes then, much to our relief, and Amber gave her some water to drink while she came to her senses.

'What's happened to me? Why are you here?' Lena said in a plaintive voice, confused as a little child waking from a bad dream.

'It's all right, my pet,' I said, taking her cold hand in mine and wiping her face with a cloth.

'Someone poisoned you, Lena,' Amber said, running her finger along the top of the small table next to the bed. She held up her middle finger and examined the crumbs clinging to it. 'What were you eating before you went to sleep?'

Lena blinked as she tried to recall, her thoughts still hazy from the poison in her blood. 'It was a cake that Matilda gave me before she went to her sister's. I told her I had a headache, I've had a few lately but this one was the worst and she said to go and lie down and she gave me a piece of pound cake to have in bed as she knows I like it.'

Amber sniffed her finger. 'It smells like almonds,' she said. 'I'd wager that's cyanide, drawn from apricot kernels most probably.'

I thought of the bowl of dried apricots that Arthur had been eating in the kitchen.

Lena clung to my hand. 'Why would she try and poison me?' she said. 'I did everything she said. I never told no one what I saw.'

'What did Matilda tell you, Lena?' I asked her, gently pushing the hair back off her face. 'What did you see?'

Lena leaned into me and started crying and I feared we'd get no more out of her, but she calmed herself enough to speak after a while and we were grateful for that.

'I saw Lady Aston and Matilda having a great row that afternoon when I took the tea tray up to the drawing room. Lady Aston had found the bottle, you see, the one that Matilda had hidden up the chimney. I saw her reaching up into the chimney when I came in and it was such a surprise to see her doing that – Lady Aston never usually went near the hearth, none of the family did – that I put my tray down on the hall table and slipped back behind the door to watch and see what would happen next. I saw Lady Aston frown and tut when she found the bottle hidden up there. I didn't know what it was then, but Lady Aston must have realised it was one of them witch's bottles straight away because she rang the kitchen bell for Matilda with a furious look on her face. She knew that bottle was something to do with Matilda because Tilda was the one who feared witches the most in this house.

'She was always chattering on about how Gwen Foley was a witch and would come into the Hall down one of the chimneys and kill us all in our beds. Lady Aston had warned her before about keeping her lips closed on the matter but Matilda had gone on telling her tales all the same. I stayed hidden in the shadows behind the door and I saw everything that happened when Matilda came up. It was clearly a shock to her to see the bottle in Lady Aston's hands but she didn't deny it was hers and she went on about the White and witchcraft and all her usual stories and said that the bottle was the only way to protect us from Gwen Foley.

'Lady Aston wouldn't listen to any of it. She shouted at Matilda that she was a wicked, dangerous woman full of hateful beliefs and that she would have to leave the family's service. Matilda went wild when she said that. She loves it here, near her sister and all, and she lunged at Lady Aston to try and get the bottle off of her, but Lady Aston wouldn't let it go. Then Matilda grabbed one of the marble horseheads on the mantelpiece and bashed it down on madam's head with all her might and Lady Aston fell backwards.'

I imagined the scene as Lena spoke and could clearly picture Matilda, who was a good six inches taller than the diminutive Lady Aston and a great deal broader in the shoulder, being able to bring a heavy object down onto poor Loella's head with force enough to kill her.

'Then what happened?' I asked. Amber passed Lena the water glass, and she took another sip before continuing.

'When Lady Aston fell, she hit her head on the hearth stone. A horrible thud it made. I'll never forget that sound. She never got up again. Matilda just stood there staring at her and I came out of my hidden place and stood next to her. "What have you done?" I said to Matilda. "The lady's dead."

'Matilda turned to me with a fearful look on her face. "Don't you dare tell a soul what you've seen, girl," she said to me. "Or I will tell Lord Aston about your passions with Herbert and you will be dead too for he will kill you in a rage." Matilda told me to go back downstairs to the kitchen and turn the egg timer, and when all the sand was through to come up again and pretend that I found Lady Aston then and raise the alarm.

'I was so afraid of what would happen if Lord Aston found out about me and Herbert that I did what she said. But it's been hard, keeping it a secret. I told Matilda last week that I couldn't sleep at night for worry about Gwen Foley taking the blame for killing the Lady and that I was of a mind to tell your nice husband the magistrate what had really happened, but she begged me not to and said we could be such friends instead as we both knew something about the other that we didn't want telling, so we was the same. She made it sound right, although I knew it wasn't really and that lying is wrong. She started making me special pies and cakes and being so kind to me and I let her because it was easier, I suppose. And then when these headaches started I didn't have the strength to get into town to speak to Mr Albright, even if I'd had a mind to.'

Lena grabbed my hand again, her eyes full of woe. 'Have I been very wicked, Mistress Albright? Will I go straight to hell when I die?'

'No dear,' I soothed her. 'You have done wrong, but Matilda has done much the worse and thankfully there is still time to put it right, some of it at least. It is too late for poor Lady Aston of course, more's the pity.'

'I'll assist in whatever way I can,' said Lena bravely, although she quivered some when Amber told her what we would need her to say at Gwen's trial. She agreed in the end and I reassured her she would be safe at the Hall until then as, regrettably, we would be taking Matilda to the Guildhall Gaol forthwith and Lord Aston wouldn't need to know of her and Herbert's dalliance until it was stated in court.

'Did Herbert know that it was an argument between Matilda and his mother that led to her death?' I asked her as we readied ourselves to leave.

Lena nodded and bit her lip. 'Herbert did know, ma'am. He knew straight away because Matilda said to him what had happened – he came into the drawing room only a short time after I came out from behind the door – and she told Herbert that he was to say it was Gwen who had done his mother in or else she would tell Lord Aston about his fancies with me. Herbert stared at Matilda for an age looking so very angry, like he couldn't believe a servant could have such a power over him, but then he agreed. Matilda was still holding the marble statue in her hand that she'd hit madam with and Herbert grabbed it off her. It was all bloody. And he got the other one off the mantelshelf as well so it didn't look uneven and he took them both away with him somewhere to hide. He came back looking all surprised when I pretended to discover the lady dead and that's when he called out for Lord Aston and the Reverend Mr Brown.'

Amber let out a low whistle. 'What a formidable woman Matilda Syms is,' she said. 'She murdered Lady Aston and then had the gall to blackmail a lord's son, allow an innocent woman to die and try to kill another to cover up her own guilt. And Herbert knew the truth all along yet felt so little grief for his mother and was so in fear of his father, that he was willing to be an accomplice in Matilda's deceptions. What must be done about him?'

'Herbert can wait,' I told her. 'Matilda Syms must be dealt with first.'

We left Lena to rest and recover from the harm beset on her by Matilda's 'treats' and made our way down to the carriage to tell Matthew and Sarah what had happened.

'It was her books,' Sarah said, putting her hand over her mouth. 'Lady Aston hid her books in an alcove hidden behind the brickwork in the drawing room hearth. She told Michael that when he was helping her choose which scientific books to buy. She didn't want her husband to know she had them. That's how she found that witch's bottle. That's why it was in her hand when she died.'

'Samuel always says that knowledge can be dangerous,' said Amber. 'What a shame Lady Aston had to die for it.'

We sat for a moment in respectful silence, the revelations of the day weighing heavy on us all.

'Come,' I said to Matthew, 'you must find the strength to accompany us to Lizzy Syms's cottage. I have no authority to apprehend Matilda on my own.'

'Neither do I,' said Matthew, reaching for his stick. 'But it needs to be done.'

We found the cottage empty of occupants. A large ginger cat lay on the rag rug in front of the hearth where the fire was still blazing, but Matilda and Lizzy were nowhere to be seen. I looked upstairs in the bed chamber and Amber ran back out the door and searched for them up and down the lane and in the gardens behind but there was no sign of them.

The three of us sat in the parlour contemplating what course of action to take when a faint creak came from the room above. Matthew put his finger to his lips and we listened carefully. There it was again, a distinct creaking from upstairs. Amber was up there before Matthew had had a chance to stand, and I wasn't far behind. She knelt down to look underneath the brass ended bed and I dragged open the doors of the big oak wardrobe beside the window. It was there that I found the sisters huddled together behind Lizzy's dresses like a couple of errant children. I shook my head sadly and they crept out, meek as lambs.

'You must tell us what's been going on, the truth of it this time so we can get to the nub of this dreadful business once and for all,' I told them, and they followed me and Amber down to the parlour their heads hung in shame.

There was no more fight left in Matilda once I told her what Lena had said, and that we knew she had been trying to poison the poor girl. She put her face in her hands and sobbed with a good dose of drama and I felt sorry for her, though I could see Amber didn't much.

'I couldn't sleep at night could I, Liz?' Matilda said at last. 'So fearful I was of that ghostly woman. She is a witch all right, make no mistake about that. Father taught us how to spot them and she is one of them, a creature sent from the devil himself with no human skin on her body and the eyes of a demon. As soon as I saw her scuttling around the village, I knew what she was. I told old Mrs Hardwick and the servants at the Hall. I had to make them believe me. I tried to tell Lady Aston, to get her to understand the danger we were all in, but she wouldn't listen to any of it. She refused to let me chalk pentacles onto the door posts and hearthstones of the house to stop the White getting in and eating us alive, so I had no choice but to make witch's bottles like in the old days – Lizzy helped me – and I set them behind bricks in the chimneys the way Father had shown us. I put them in all the fireplaces in Little Aston Hall and I felt comforted. I could sleep peacefully again in my bed.

'Even though Gwen Foley was conjuring up misery amongst those down in the village, I knew we in the Hall were protected from her so long as those bottles were in place.' She looked around the room seeking out sympathy and found it only in Lizzy's eyes.

'What happened between you and Lady Aston that led to her death?' Matthew asked her.

Matilda frowned. 'She found one of them. She found the witch's bottle I had concealed up the drawing room chimney and she fair lost her senses that angry was she. "I will not have this superstitious nonsense in my house," she shouted and "How dare you go against my orders?" She realised then that there were most probably bottles all over the house and she said she was going to have them all found and destroyed and I nearly crumpled onto the floor in fear. "Please, madam," I begged her. "Please let the bottles stay. They do no harm to you and they are protecting us all from the witch in the village. I have filled them with pins and brimstone and rosemary. No dark forces will dare to enter the house with those bottles up every chimney. They are the only defence we have. Do you not place any value on the safety of your children?"

'But Lady Aston wouldn't listen to any of my pleas. She told me that I was to leave her house and the service of her family. I tried to grab the bottle from her, that's all I was trying to do. As my fingers touched it, she took a step away from me and tripped backwards on the edge of the rug. She hit her head on the hearthstone and I knew she was dead right away as her eyes rolled back and blood gushed out around her hair. She still had that bottle held tight in her hand and I went to get it from her when Lena ran forward with her hand over her mouth. "Don't you scream," I told her. "Don't make a sound; and if you tell anyone about the words between the lady and me, I will tell Lord Aston about you fornicating with his son. We will tell everyone it was the witch that killed her." Lena stared at me, her eyes wide with fright but she agreed to what I said, so afraid was she of Lord Aston's temper. Lena waited until I went downstairs and then she pretended to find the body. I got Lizzy to place some of Lady Aston's personal effects in Gwen's cottage to cause her to look guilty too in case there should be any doubt, but no one ever seemed to find them, useless duffles. Didn't need them in the end anyway. Everyone was so sure it was the White who had killed her.'

Matilda sat back in her chair, her story finished and blew her nose noisily on a handkerchief.

'You see, it was an accident,' Lizzy said. 'My sister wouldn't hurt a fly on purpose.'

'That is not the whole truth, though, is it, Matilda?' I said, pinning her with a stony stare. 'You must tell my husband how Lady Aston really died. We know the weapon that was used to murder her.'

Matilda's eyes shifted back and forth between Matthew and myself as Matthew lent down to his bag and pulled out one of the marble horses that I had sent Amber to collect after we had left Lena. Her mouth opened in horror as Matthew held the statue aloft.

'It was Herbert,' Matilda declared. 'Evil he is. He killed his own mother with that marble horse from the drawing room and then he forced me to keep quiet about it. He said he would murder Lizzy and all her cats if I didn't.'

Lizzy let out a whimper and pulled the kitten on her knee into a tight embrace.

'Enough of these lies,' said Amber. 'What reason would Herbert have to kill his own mother?'

'Lady Aston had found out about him and Lena,' Matilda said with a nod. 'She was going to tell Lord Aston.'

'If that is the case can you explain to us why Lady Aston was holding your witch's bottle when she died?' Matthew asked mildly.

Matilda took a gulp of air and then another. Unable to think of an answer to Matthew's question she closed her eyes and began reciting the Lord's Prayer.

'Tilda,' Lizzy interrupted her. 'You must tell them. We have come to the end of this now. To the end of everything.'

Matilda stopped praying and slowly nodded. She proceeded to give her confession quietly with her eyes still closed, as if the fight had been leeched out of her and all that was left was the ugly tale of what she had done.

'It was me. I killed Lady Aston,' she said. 'I hit her over the head with the marble horse because she wouldn't give me back my bottle and she was going to find the others and take them away too. Herbert hid both the marble horses so I wouldn't tell Lord Aston about him and Lena. We agreed to put the blame on Gwen.'

Amber nodded to me and I knew she was as satisfied as I that we had come to the heart of the matter at last.

Matthew cleared his throat. 'Matilda Syms, these are very serious matters,' he said in his most austere voice. 'You are responsible for the untimely, brutal death of your master's wife and therefore you have committed petty treason, a crime of the highest magnitude. Additionally, you have concealed the truth and allowed an innocent woman to take the blame for her murder. Furthermore, you have blackmailed Lena Harris and attempted to kill her through poisoning. Therefore you must accompany me to the Guildhall Gaol forthwith and await trial.'

'No, not my sister, you can't take her away,' Lizzy shouted in a panic. 'Don't let them take her away, she's all I have in the world,' she pleaded to me, her palms pressed together in appeal.

I shook my head. 'I'm sorry,' I said, deeply regretful of the fate that now surely awaited Matilda, but unsure how else the noose could be removed from around Gwen's innocent neck.

'Keep them here. I will fetch George and the carriage. He is waiting up on the lane,' said Amber, taking her leave out the door.

'Let me make my sister a last cup of tea,' Lizzy said tearfully. 'A final comfort before she leaves my warm home for the coldness of a cell.'

'Of course,' said Matthew, lowering his head in sympathy.

After seeing to the formalities of Matilda's statement Matthew left the sisters to say their goodbyes in private and joined me by the gate as I waited for the carriage. It came bumping down the muddy track in front of the cottage a few minutes later with Sarah leaning triumphantly out the window.

'Justice for Gwen Foley,' she called. 'Well done, Hester and Matthew.'

I tried to smile but I felt no joy at the prospect of another woman being sent to her death, even one as cruel and cunning as Matilda Syms.

I helped Matthew into the carriage and went back into the cottage to fetch Matilda. I was greeted by the sight of the sisters sitting in their armchairs by the fire, their heads drooping forward onto their chests. There was a cat on each of their laps and their teacups were empty on the low table between them. I wondered how they could find the lull to doze off at such a harrowing time before it struck me that they were completely still. I shouted for Amber, although I knew we were already too late.

'They're dead,' she said bluntly after a cursory examination. She picked up one of the teacups. 'Cyanide again, a much bigger dose this time from the strength of the smell.' She held it out to me but I shook my head, not needing to verify her judgement.

'We shouldn't have left them alone, not for a moment,' I said, feeling misery and regret rise within me. 'It's clear as day now that this is what they would do. Matilda and Lizzy couldn't face the punishment that they crowed over for other women. They were weak as kittens underneath it all.'

Amber wasn't of a mind to feel sorry for the Syms sisters, though, as her thoughts were focused on the fate of Gwen Foley.

'What does this mean for Gwen?' Amber asked Matthew as he steadied himself against the doorway, taking in the gruesome scene. 'Will she still have to stand trial for murder if Matilda can't now tell her story to the judges?'

'I doubt Matilda would have found the courage to do that anyway,' Matthew said, his voice trembling. 'I wrote her account and confession down as she spoke, though, and she signed it so we must hope that it will be evidence enough to exonerate Gwen.'

'Look,' said Amber, picking up a box of small bottles from the floor beside Lizzy's chair. 'There are all manner of toxins in here; cyanide, hemlock, arsenic. This must be where Robby got the arsenic for his mother.'

'What a sad pair they were,' I said, looking at Matilda and Lizzy's lumpen feet clad in matching woollen slippers.

'A dangerous pair, more like it.' Amber snapped shut the box of poisons. 'At least they can cause no more misery.'

'They will have to be buried at a crossroads as they have taken their own lives,' Matthew said sadly. 'And the coroner must put stakes through their hearts.'

Amber shook her head, the colour draining from her face. 'That is one duty that Dr Crouch will have to undertake on his own,' she said, stepping backwards. 'The thought of such an act makes me retch.'

I placed my hand on her arm to steady her, surprised to see Amber react in such a way, so steadfastly stoic was she in most situations that would make others gasp.

'Perhaps our Amber is more like you than we thought,' I said to Matthew as I led her gently out of the room, away from the deceased sisters and the cats who had begun sniffing at their motionless feet.

21

OIL

The next morning I was sitting in a pool of weak sun from the kitchen window, braiding Liberty's hair when there was a tentative rap on the door. Tam leapt up from his warm slumber beside the hearth and walked with me across the room. I was pleased to have him standing by my side as I turned the key in the heavy lock of the street door and slid the bolts open, not knowing who to expect on the other side and still shaken up from the extraordinary events of the previous day.

There stood a richly dressed man, his face covered with a black silk scarf. My stomach lurched as at first I thought it might be Gideon Fitchett come to demand his ownership of Gwen, but my angst was even greater when the man pulled the material aside and it was Herbert Aston. My legs went weak as water at the sight of him, especially as Matthew and Amber were both out and I was alone in the house with Liberty.

I placed my hand on Tam's back as the dog had begun a low, menacing growl and pushed the door nearly closed so I could speak to Herbert through only a crack.

'What is it you want?' I asked, fearful that he had come to

threaten us for what we now knew about his involvement in the events following his mother's death.

'I mean you no harm, Mistress Albright. Please let me enter and say my piece.' His cultured voice rang out in the quiet street and the shutters opened on the house opposite, curiosity stirred by the presence of such a refined stranger. Tamworth jumped up at the door, his claws scratching the wood and he started to bark.

'I will let you in, Master Aston,' I said, trying to pull Tam back down, 'but be warned, I have Gwen Foley's dog here with me. A big beast he is, and he seems to have taken a dislike to you already. Perhaps he remembers you from that night at the cottage when you manhandled his mistress and your father struck him down? I cannot promise to be able to control him. Only Gwen can do that.'

'I am not afraid of a dog,' Herbert said dismissively. 'I have a natural authority over animals. We have hounds with our hunt and they obey me absolutely.'

I threw the door open wide, piqued at his arrogance and watched with wicked glee as Tam leapt at him, his paws reaching Herbert's shoulders, and knocked him flat on his back on the cobbles. Herbert was winded and struggled to hold off Tam who was snarling and slobbering, trying to get a bite of Herbert's pink neck.

'Get it off me,' Herbert screamed as Tam drew his lips back to display his sharp yellow teeth. I began to panic that this was no game and that Tam was going to rip Herbert Aston's throat out, right there in front of our house, but I had no way of getting the huge dog to desist.

Liberty ran past me before I could stop her and put her hands on Tam's back. She let out a loud whistle, a sound I didn't know she could make, and Tam stopped stock-still. She held out a titbit of bacon and led him away from Herbert and back into the house, where she sat on the floor and hugged him as he ate his meat.

I marvelled at my daughter's calm assurance in handling Tam, before turning my attention back to Herbert who had picked himself up and was attempting to recover some composure.

I told him to wait while I put Tamworth in the garden and he acquiesced with no argument this time, knowing that the dog was far beyond his regulation.

'Come in,' I said once Liberty and Tam were outside happily engaged in a game of fetch the ball. I was secure in the knowledge that I could let Tam back in if Herbert's intentions towards me took an aggressive turn.

Herbert took off his hat and lowered his head to enter our parlour. He looked around the room with undisguised surprise. 'It's quite pleasant in here,' he said, taking in the Welsh dresser, the upholstered chairs and the yellow and green patterned wallpaper.

'Do you think all who don't live in a grand hall live like paupers, Master Aston?' I asked.

He shrugged. 'I've never given it any thought,' he said. 'I've never had cause to enter an ordinary house like this before.'

'Except Gwen Foley's cottage,' I reminded him. 'You entered there.'

'I did,' he said, pursing his lips. 'That was... ill-advised. I admit that now.'

We stood in awkward silence while we both recalled the shameful scene.

'Is your husband at home?' he asked. 'I would like to speak with him about yesterday's events in Little Aston.'

I shook my head. 'Matthew left early this morning to discuss the affair with his brother Philip and with the Mayor. There are many legal and practical matters to attend to in light of Matilda's confession and her sudden death.'

'Her suicide,' Herbert said bluntly.

'Yes, and that of her sister.'

'It is quite a drama that has unfolded is it not? Worthy almost of the Stratford bard.'

His attempt at humour met with a cold silence from me and I waited for him to announce the reason for his visit.

'May I sit down?' Herbert asked. 'I have a favour to ask of you.'

'You may sit down, Master Aston,' I indicated one of the hard chairs at the table, 'but you should know that I am not inclined to do you any favours. I see you still have the scabs from where Lena scratched you,' I said as his face became fully illuminated in the light from the window.

His hand went to his cheek and he sighed. 'Yes, I behaved badly with Lena. She wants no more to do with me.'

'You made her lie with you and you made her lie for you.' I tutted. 'What a disgrace.'

Herbert reddened and stared at the floor. 'In my defence, Mistress Albright, Lena was a willing bed partner. I am not a complete brute.'

'Willing bed partners do not scratch their lover's face,' I challenged him.

'No, they don't. That was a mistake. I thought we could carry on as we had before Mother's death. But Lena loathed me by then.' He swallowed and had the decency to look a little ashamed.

'Do you feel pity only for yourself? Not for Gwen? Not for your own mother?' I asked him.

'I do, of course,' Herbert said. 'My poor mother was dead, though, when I found her. There was nothing to be done to save her and so I saved myself from Father's wrath by helping

Matilda. He would have cut me out off if he knew about me and Lena so strongly does he abhor such unnatural relations between those of the higher and lower levels of society.'

He stood up, his chest puffed out like a peacock. 'I am to be the next Lord Aston and inherit Little Aston Hall,' he announced. 'It is my birthright. It is the correct order of things. Patrimony is the oil that keeps the cogs of civilised society turning. Gwen Foley is not part of that order, she doesn't belong to any decent class of people. She is a peculiarity, a quirk of humankind. She was a thorn in the side of Little Aston village. It was a noble and necessary deed for us to have her removed.'

I considered unlatching the back door and calling Tamworth in to finish what he had started in the street, but had to suffice with giving Herbert a withering look and a lashing from my tongue.

'How dare you speak of Gwen like that,' I said. 'Know this, Herbert Aston. Matthew is at this very moment sharing the statements of both Lena and Matilda that attest to the fact that you knew that your mother's murderer was Matilda Syms and that you took the weapon she used in her deadly crime, washed it and then hid it in plain view. Even worse than this, you convinced your father to believe that the culprit was an innocent woman and provoked him to make false accusations against her.'

'None of that can be proved,' replied Herbert. 'If you care to visit the Hall again you will see that the marble horses are back in their places on the mantel in the drawing room where Mother was found.'

'I never said the murder weapon was a marble horse,' I said, shaking my finger at him. 'How could you know such a thing unless what I said is the truth? If you had bothered to check you would see that only one marble horse remains on the mantel as we took the other to prompt Matilda into her confession.'

He narrowed his eyes at me. 'What of it? Mother's murderer is dead now. Do you truly think father is going to pay to pursue a prosecution of his own son?'

'No I don't,' I agreed, familiar as I had become with the sorry confines of the processes of justice. 'But I do think that much damage could be done to your reputation as the next Lord Aston if word gets out around Lichfield and beyond about your brutish behaviour towards Lena and your persecution of Gwen. Times are moving on, Herbert, especially among cultured people of the type whom you wish to spend your life mixing with. You should think on that.'

'Are you threatening me?' he asked, moving forward.

'No,' I said quickly. 'But there is a way for you to begin to make amends which would reflect well on yourself, and would be an apt tribute to your mother.'

'Go on,' he said, rubbing his chin.

'Claudia.'

'What of her?'

'Your sister is a bright, sensitive young woman who can hardly breathe in that Hall surrounded by you oafish men. She dreams of going to Italy and staying with your mother's sister in Milan and in due course attending the University in Padua to study science. It is what your mother wanted for her. Indeed, Lady Aston was helping Claudia learn Italian and buying her scientific books in the months leading up to her death.'

'Italy? University?' Herbert scoffed. 'That would never be acceptable to Father as a course of action for his daughter. He has in mind for Claudia to marry his brother's son in London. He has made a fortune in shipping; she'd want for nothing.'

'Claudia wants what I have described,' I said slowly. 'And Lady Aston wanted that for her too.'

'Father will never agree,' Herbert exploded in frustration.

'Then you must make him agree,' I said, banging my palm

227

on the table. 'I know you have sway over your father's thinking. Look how you got him to believe Gwen was responsible for your mother's death.'

Herbert sighed and tutted but seeing I would not back down, he finally nodded. 'Very well, I will make it so.'

'And, one more thing,' I said.

Herbert's eyes flashed with anger but he kept his temper. 'Which is?' he asked tightly.

'That Lena go to Italy with Claudia as her ladies maid, if she so wishes.'

'Fine,' Herbert said, pulling on his hat. 'Good riddance to bad rubbish.'

'That's just what I was going to say,' I said as I threw the front door open for him.

22

RED WINE

The Lunar Society met as planned in the bookshop on Saturday afternoon and we had much news to share. Sarah had told Samuel as best she could about the events at Little Aston Hall that led to Matilda's confession and the suicide of the Syms sisters, but there were still more details he wanted to know from myself and Amber.

'I can see why Herbert would go along with blaming Gwen Foley for the murder of his mother,' said Samuel carefully, 'as he didn't want Matilda telling his father about his liaisons with Lena. However, what I can't comprehend is why a man as educated and committed to the learnings of science as Lord Aston would be so easily persuaded that his wife's death was the consequence of witchcraft.'

'I can't answer that, Sam,' I told him, shaking my head. 'Amber and I and Matthew, we have gone through it many times and we are still none the wiser. Matthew went to speak to Lord Aston yesterday evening to explain what had happened with Matilda and he meekly agreed to drop all charges against Gwen Foley. He put up no fight.'

'Perhaps his commitment to rational philosophy wasn't as robust as Lady Aston thought?' suggested Sarah. 'Perhaps it was a false front so he could fit in with the group of intelligent fellows he respected and enjoyed the company of?'

'I don't think so,' said Amber bitterly. 'Some people just enjoy a hunt, especially one they know they are going to succeed in. Lord Aston is a man whose mind is fading from years of drinking strong liquor. He lost what little reason he had left when he saw his wife dead. He must have heard the rumours about Gwen, everyone in Little Aston had, and no doubt Herbert egged him on for his own selfish reasons. In his rage Lord Aston needed to hunt and hurt another to feel he was avenging Loella's death in the only way that made sense to him. It was that which drove him to behave as he did, in my opinion. Gwen was the quarry and Lord Aston and his son led the village hounds to her door to rip her apart, and they would have done had Mama and I not stopped them.'

Sam nodded. 'I agree with Amber. The tyranny of human nature can only be controlled through the law. Without it, mankind falls into a formless jungle, a state of dark chaos.'

'What a miserable way to view the world, Samuel,' said Sarah in surprise. 'Surely we can hope for better than that?'

'The law is an important tool to assist in the fight against evil, there's no denying that,' Sam replied. 'But human nature being so twisted it is not enough. We need other ways to fight evil too. Why, look at us gathered together here. Are we not also engaged in the struggle against the darkness and chaos that emanates from the base nature of man, and, alas, woman too? Is that not the aim of the Lunar Society?'

I felt saddened by Sam's words, that he should hold such pessimistic views at such a tender age. 'The aim of the Lunar Society is to show folk that there are ways to live together in peace based on rational thinking and considered action, not to fight against them or beat them down. There is more goodness in people than you allow for, young Samuel,' I told him. 'It's best you hold on to that or else you may find your way through this life beset with miseries of your own making.'

Sarah frowned at that, no doubt thinking of her husband's crippling gloom, but Sam wasn't to be persuaded that easily. 'Tell me, Hester, why did Matilda and her sister act as they did if there was any goodness in them?' he asked, holding his palms open. 'They had no reason to be so cruel; they chose to give in to the very worst aspects of their nature.'

'You have to understand that the Syms were caught in a wrong way of thinking that they were taught as children,' I explained to him. 'It was a different time then and a different place where they grew up. Their minds were twisted by their father. Matilda and Lizzy didn't have the capacity or the wits to move beyond that viewpoint and see that Gwen Foley was simply a harmless woman who was no threat to them or anyone else.'

'To take evil action is a choice. To do nothing is in everyone's power,' Sam said with finality, and we had to agree to differ on the subject for the time being.

'Have Philip and Mayor Robinson agreed to release Gwen?' Sarah asked, changing the subject to more practical matters.

Amber snorted with disgust. 'Pa has been petitioning them all morning, but they remain steadfast in their decision that Gwen must stand before the court and that the trial will go ahead.'

'Even with Matilda Syms' signed confession?' Sarah exclaimed.

'Yes, even with that,' Amber replied. 'Uncle Philip is of the opinion that the correct course of action is to present all the evidence to the Justices of the Peace and allow them to make the final decision.'

'It won't be a full public trial, though,' I said. 'It will hopefully be little more than a formality and then Gwen will be released without charge. She must remain in the gaol until Monday though which is a pity as she is weakening every day she sits in that foul place. Amber went at first light this morning to tell Gwen all that has happened and how her prospects look bright. She said Gwen could hardly believe the turn of her fortunes. She was fair overcome by it all.'

Amber smiled. 'I told Gwen that Tamworth and I will be waiting outside the courtroom for her on Monday and she said that the thought of it gives her the fortitude to hold on for a couple more days.

'I don't know where she'll go if she is released, though,' Amber said with a sigh. 'Robby tells me that her cottage in Little Aston has been burnt to the ground.'

'She can stay with us,' I said. 'I will be happy to have her and Tamworth under our roof until her strength returns.'

'Let us pray for her safe deliverance,' said Sarah, pressing her palms together and beginning a lengthy religious entreaty. I bowed my head out of respect for her beliefs, but instead of praying to a God I had no faith in, I spent the time willing the Mayor and the sheriff to see sense in their reckoning of Gwen's case.

We made quite a little band waiting outside the Guildhall on Monday afternoon, us four of the Lunar Society, as well as Liberty, Robby Baker and Tamworth. We had to stamp on the frosty ground to keep warm, but we were full of hope and good spirits awaiting her release.

Matthew was inside speaking in Gwen's defence and presenting Matilda's confession. Lord Aston had refused to attend, saying he had no more interest in the matter, and instead sent a written retraction of his charges against Gwen Foley.

It was over within minutes. Matthew came out first, leaning heavily on his stick and I caught his arm as he almost slipped on the icy cobbles. He nodded to us all and we cheered. Philip came out next, ordering us to be quiet and disperse or he would have us charged with public disarray. We booed him and he had the decency to slink back inside the Guildhall, knowing he had been defeated. We cheered again when Lena stepped out from behind him. She was flushed with her own bravery at speaking out to the assembled court about Matilda's actions, although she had chosen to keep Herbert's involvement to herself in return for the chance to travel to Italy with Claudia.

Gwen's tiny figure appeared at last in the doorway, wrapped in a frayed shawl. Her hands searched for Tamworth and he was by her side in seconds, nuzzling into her belly and reaching up to lick her face as she bent down to him. A merry sight it was and our hearts were warmed by their safe reunion.

Amber took Gwen's hand and we made our way back to our house in Dam Street to rest and get warm, before we shared a celebratory meal that evening.

When Gwen was settled in Esme's old bed upstairs with Tam curled up beside her, I sat down with Amber by the hearth and we smiled at each other in relief.

'The truth saved her, Mama,' Amber said. 'Gwen has her life because we found out what really happened on that fateful day at Little Aston Hall.'

I nodded. 'Tis a pity, though, that she has no family of her own to look after her. Family is everything, Amber, you know that, don't you? A person's family is their truth and the centre of their being. We can only understand ourselves when we understand where we came from.'

Amber glanced at me. 'Yes, I know,' she said.

I took a deep breath, intending to ask Amber one last time if she would read the account of her birth and the truth about Nell that I had written down for her. But before the words could form, Amber nodded and reached over to squeeze my hand. 'I'll read it tonight, Mama,' she said. 'After we have celebrated Gwen's release.'

'A toast,' said Samuel, holding up a glass of wine, his cheeks flushed with the pleasures of the day. 'To our friend Gwen Foley and to the triumph of logic over hysteria.'

'Hear hear,' we agreed, and went to sup, but Samuel wasn't finished. 'And a toast to our generous hosts Matthew and Hester Albright, without whom justice would not have been arrived at.'

'We couldn't have done it without you all,' I said, reddening at his kind words.

'In which case, I adjust my toast,' he said solemnly. He raised his glass again. 'To the Lunar Society. Long may it continue to shine light in the darkness.'

'The Lunar Society,' we repeated and there was much cheer, even squashed up as we were round the parlour table.

'Would you like to say something, Gwen?' I asked her, noticing she had been quiet as a mouse throughout the meal.

'Just thank you,' she said, her thin voice hoarse with emotion. 'You are good people.'

'You're so very welcome, Gwen,' I said. 'We were happy to help you in your time of need.'

Robby nodded vigorously from her other side. 'We wasn't gonna let what happened to my ma happen to you,' he said, his little face tight with resolve. 'That Lizzy Syms, she's the one who sold me that poison for Ma to put on my pa's eyes at night. It cost Ma all her savings it did, but she were desperate and Lizzy told me to tell her it would make him tender and kind, take the rage out of him and stop his fists flying. Lizzy never told us it could kill him. Ma wouldn't have put it on him if she'd of known that. She'd never have done something that would leave us as orphans.'

Gwen put her arm around the boy's shoulders.

'We know that, Robby,' I told him. 'Your ma loved you and it is a sore shame she is gone. She would be proud of you and how you've helped us defend Gwen.'

'I like helping people,' Robby said, 'and I'm not scared of nothing no more.'

Amber nodded towards him. 'And that is why I have asked Robby to be my apprentice when I take the surgery over from Dr Crouch in the summer.'

'That's happy news if ever I heard it,' I said, delighted that the boy would learn a trade and have a proper place to live.

'Will you have a strong enough stomach for such work, Robby?' asked Sarah with concern.

'There's a lot of blood and guts involved in surgery,' Samuel added.

Robby nodded. 'I'll just help Miss Amber,' he said. 'If she says it must be done then I'll help her to do it. Sometimes folk have to get bloody to get better, that's what she says and it sounds right to me.'

'Good for you,' said Matthew, raising his glass once again. 'You will have a marvellous teacher in Amber and she will have a loyal student in you.'

Gwen smiled at Robby as she heard his plans. 'I am so pleased he has found a path and somewhere to belong,' she said to me. 'It is a terrible thing to be lost in life.'

'And you, Gwen dear, what will you do? What path will you take now?' I asked her.

'I am free from that gaol,' she said, 'I have my Tam.' She stroked his head which was resting across her knees. 'I believe a path will rise to find me and take us to greater freedoms still.'

I patted her arm. 'You are welcome to stay here as long as you like while you wait for it to arrive,' I told her.

23

STEEL

We arrived in the city of Lichfield five days after we had left Walberswick and went directly to Matthew's family home on Collins Hill. Matthew introduced me to his father Lucien and his brother Philip as his wife, and you, Amber, as our child. Lucien was perplexed as to why his youngest son hadn't written to tell of these significant events but Matthew insisted that he had sent a letter that must have gone astray. As Lucien knew his youngest son to be a person of truth he accepted this, although Matthew told me that Philip questioned him about it when they were alone, persisting with the suggestion that we had married because I was already with child.

It didn't matter to me what Philip thought, I never took to him from the beginning, sensing a coldness in his heart that he covered up with geniality. All that mattered to me was that we had arrived somewhere we could start anew as a respectable family and that you, Amber, were safe.

Matthew had given up a well-paid tutoring position with a family of the highest social standing in Suffolk to take me and you away, and he used their letter of recommendation to find a good amount of work in the Lichfield locality teaching the children of the

gentry. We were set up quite nicely within a few weeks of our arrival
in the city and with help from Lucien we rented the house on Dam
Street where we reside still. After such turmoil Matthew and I were
glad to find a peaceful place to begin our lives together and have the
chance at last to get to know each other properly as husband and
wife.

I wrote to my mother several times once we were settled asking
her to reconsider and to come and reside with us, but she wouldn't be
persuaded. She repeated always that it was her duty to stay with
Father and, although her heart ached with longing to be away from
him, she couldn't find the strength to leave.

'Unhappiness is my lot in life' she wrote to me. 'God chose me to
be Seth's wife and now that is all I have. Without that position I am
of less import than a worm in the ground. A woman with no
husband is nothing but a parasite on another family and I will not
be that to you and Matthew in Staffordshire.'

How she could bear to be near Father after he let Nell suffer like
he did I don't know, but I had little choice but to respect her wishes
and in the end I stopped asking her to come and she stopped writing
to me at all. I found out from her friend Edna that Mother had died
of pneumonia in 1717. I would have gone to look after her if I had
known she was ill, but Edna wrote in her letter that Mother had
forbidden her to tell me that she was dying, and that I was only to
know after she was dead and buried.

I don't know if my father, your grandfather, is still alive and I
don't rightly care. I think he is probably dead, though, as I can't
imagine him being frail and elderly with only his memories to keep
him company. How haunted he would be if that were the case – I
wouldn't wish that even on him.

I think of the years since Nell's death when the fear instilled in
me by my father made me certain that my most important duty in
life was to protect those I hold dear, and I wonder if I have not been
that different from Matilda Syms clinging on to the false security of

her witch's bottles. Being part of the Lunar Society and striving for Gwen's release has made me see that nothing can stop the darkness from coming, but that standing together to bring forth light is the only and best path to safety that we have.

Be reassured, Amber, that from fire comes steel. Take heart, my dear, as it is my conviction that the tempest of anger and fear that surrounded your arrival into the world crossed over into your blood and bestowed upon you an uncommon character for a woman. I hope you come to understand that that is the greatest gift your parents could have given you, even though they were but children themselves.

I see that character in you every day in your work healing the sick, and now as one of the Lunar Society. It fills me with pride that my Nell's daughter is a force for good who wants only to help alleviate suffering and bring forth hope in those around her.

You truly are precious, Amber, to me and to all who know you.

With love always,

Mama

24

FLOWERS

I came down early the next morning to set the fire so it would be warm for the family when they got up, but I found Liberty already awake and standing in the kitchen eating a leftover pie from our dinner the night before.

'Hungry again?' I laughed, rubbing my belly and she smiled.

'I'd have thought that dog would be down here too, looking for food,' I said to myself, as I poured a scoopful of coal into the grate.

Once we were warmed up, I made Liberty a proper breakfast of porridge and butter and made a cup of tea to take up to Gwen. I went to climb the stairs when Liberty jumped up from the table and pulled me back.

She pointed upstairs and made the sign of a bird flying with her thumbs intertwined which we used to mean 'gone'.

Alarmed, I said out loud, 'They can't have gone. Surely I would have heard them come down? Or was I sleeping too soundly?'

I rushed upstairs and into the room that Liberty used to share with Esme. Esme's old bed by the window where Gwen and Tamworth had slept was empty and all trace of Gwen, the dog and her scant belongings were gone. I threw open the window and looked up and down the empty street but there was no sign of either of them.

'Where did they go?' I asked Liberty, holding my palms open with the question so she would understand me, but she shook her head in bewilderment.

We went back down to the kitchen and I sat at the table and tried to make sense of it. Liberty pointed to the back door and I nodded that as she was already dressed she could go out and play as she usually did after breakfast. She pulled on her shoes and ran outside, the sharpness of the cold breeze making me shiver in my night clothes, before she pulled the door closed behind her.

'Where are you, Gwen?' I asked out loud, pulling my shawl around me, although I knew she couldn't hear me wherever she was by now. 'I hope you are safe,' I added, fretting over her frailty and her strangeness in the eyes of others, comforted by the thought that at least she had Tamworth.

I was startled from my thoughts by the back door being thrown open and Liberty running in, her face aglow. She held out to me a single white flower of the type Mother used to call Candlemas bells, but which most folk knew as snowdrops, and I frowned at her in confusion.

I took it from her with a questioning gesture and let her lead me outside.

The sight that met my eyes made me drop the flower in astonishment. From the raised herb beds to the back wall our garden was full of snowdrops, their milky bells making a carpet of purest white across the stony ground where nothing I had planted before had ever grown.

The pale outline of the full moon was still visible in the morning sky between the spires of the cathedral and I felt Liberty's hand in mine as we took in the beautiful scene.

The thought occurred to me that this was Gwen's way of saying goodbye, that perhaps she did have a gift and could enchant the natural world around her after all, even though I knew such a thing was impossible. I chided myself, thinking what Samuel's response would be to such a preposterous notion, but for a few moments I could come up with no other reason for the charming sight before me, and my breath quickened in excited wonder.

I turned when I heard Matthew coming out the door to join us, his stick clacking as he supported himself down the step.

'Do you like your surprise, Hettie?' he asked with a smile. 'I know how you've always been irked by the stubbornness of this ground and snowdrops grow where nothing else will – Samuel looked it up for me in one of his horticultural books. I had a barrel of bulbs planted in the spring while you and Liberty were in Wales visiting John. Although I have to say, I didn't expect them this early or for there to be quite such a number of them,' he exclaimed, looking around. 'They surround us!'

I laughed and came back to my senses, even as I felt a pang of loss for the fanciful notion of magical happenings in our garden.

'Thank you, Matthew, they are glorious,' I said, kissing his cheek. 'You are as kind a man today as the first day we met. Now let us go inside where it's warm. I have to tell you about dear Gwen. She could wait no longer I'm afraid, she has left our home already.'

Matthew sighed. 'That is regrettable. I had hoped she would stay awhile and let us help her further. Gwen will let us know when she is safe after all we, and especially you, my dear, have done for her, I am sure of that.'

'This is the very morn she would have been hanged,' I said quietly. 'Gwen would more than likely be dead by now were it not for you and I, and Amber and Sam and Sarah. The Lunar Society.'

'It is a sobering thought,' Matthew agreed. 'We must be thankful for the outcome of our efforts, although I think it may be some time before Philip forgives us for making him look a fool.'

'Your brother does that well enough by himself,' I said with a small laugh, remembering his St Clement's Day dinner.

Matthew looked around the garden and frowned. 'Has Gwen taken Tamworth too?'

'She has,' I said as we watched Liberty pick up the dog's ball and pass it sadly from one hand to the other. 'But I think we should see about getting Liberty a pup of her own. Tam made a good friend for her.'

Matthew nodded and I was grateful as ever for his generosity and warm heart.

Nell came into my mind then, running along the beach with her long hair streaming behind her, and I found with relief that I was able to welcome the memory. Even though I hadn't been able to save my sister, there was solace to be had in the knowledge that I had tried and that I had kept my promise to her about Amber. I would always remember Nell, and now so would her daughter, who was also our daughter. Amber had read my letter alone in her room after our dinner with Gwen. She had come down when she was finished and put her arms around me, and we had held each other for a long time in the warm glow of the fire.

'I think Nell and your mother would have liked our Lunar Society and what it stands for,' Amber said, and I had nodded in agreement.

I looked up as I turned to go indoors but could see the moon no more. I knew she was there, though, behind the blueness of the sky, waiting for the night to come so she could shine her light in the darkness, just as we of the Lunar Society would do when we were needed again.

~

As we sat down to breakfast there was a tentative rap on the front door which filled me with hope that dear Gwen might have decided to return and stay with us a little longer after all. I rushed to open it to find instead Agnes standing on the step, and my heart sank in anticipation of her usual harsh words against me.

'I saw what you did for Gwen Foley yesterday,' she began.

'I am sorry we could not have done the same for Joanna, but...'

Agnes held up her hand. 'I'm not here to berate you, Mistress Albright, and I seek no more apologies.'

I was relieved by her assurance but perplexed as to the reason for her visit. I waited for her to continue with some apprehension.

'I've come to ask if I can join your Lunar Society,' she said tentatively. 'If you'll have me that is?'

I saw the look of humble determination in her eyes and gave a welcoming smile conveying my pleasure at her request.

'We'd be honoured to have you, Agnes,' I said, holding the door wide open. 'Come in and get warm by the fire and I will tell you about what we do.'

THE END

AFTERWORD

HISTORICAL NOTES

Although the Lunar Society in this novel is fictional, there was a real Lunar Society in the Midlands later in the eighteenth century. This was a dinner and social club of prominent industrialists, philosophers and intellectuals including Erasmus Darwin and Josiah Wedgwood, who met regularly between 1765 and 1813 in Birmingham and Lichfield. I have re-imagined the origins of the Lunar Society in *The Trial of Gwen Foley* as being several decades earlier, instigated by women and dedicated to bringing justice to the powerless.

The character of Samuel in the book is a fictional teenage version of the real Samuel Johnson (1709–1784), the great man of letters who famously wrote the first English dictionary. He was born and raised in the bookshop in Lichfield which still stands in the centre of the city, and which now houses the Samuel Johnson Birthplace Museum. Many of the words Samuel speaks in the novel are taken or adapted from his extensive published writings. The books Samuel draws on for his defence of Gwen Foley are also (mostly) real.

Some of the other characters in the book are based on real people too, including Sarah and Michael Johnson, Dame Oliver and Theophilius Levett. Key places in the book are still standing in the historic city of Lichfield including the magnificent cathedral, the Johnson's bookshop, the market square, Dam Street, the King's Head and the Guildhall. Little Aston Hall, which was built a little later than the novel is set, can be found several miles outside Lichfield and has been converted into luxury flats.

Each chapter in the book is named after an item or substance that has been found in one of the many witch's bottles that have been discovered in the brickwork of old houses in America and England, especially in Suffolk where some of the most infamous witch trials took place in Bury St Edmunds in the 17th century. Hecatolite, the title of chapter 8, is another word for moonstone.

ACKNOWLEDGEMENTS

Thank-you to Betsy, Tara, Clare and the rest of the team at Bloodhound Books for making me so welcome and for their wonderful support throughout the whole journey to publication. I am delighted to be in the kennels!

I would like to thank Joanne Wilson at the Samuel Johnson Birthplace Museum in Lichfield for sharing with me her in-depth knowledge of the Johnson family, and to her and her team for their wonderful curation of the artefacts in the museum. Thanks also to David Titley for taking the time to give me a historical tour of Lichfield and for helping me see the city as it would have been 300 years ago. Thanks to The Johnson Society for welcoming me as a member and for keeping the work and words of Samuel Johnson alive. Any historical, literary or geographical errors are, of course, my own.

Thanks and love to Graham and Mum for reading early drafts of the book and for their constant enthusiasm and support for my writing. Thanks always to Toby and Billy for being my best boys.

My final thanks goes to those who read *The Trial of Gwen Foley*. In the words of the great Samuel Johnson himself:

'A writer only begins a book. A reader finishes it.'

A NOTE FROM THE PUBLISHER

Thank you for reading this book. If you enjoyed it please do consider leaving a review on Amazon to help others find it too.

We hate typos. All of our books have been rigorously edited and proofread, but sometimes mistakes do slip through. If you have spotted a typo, please do let us know and we can get it amended within hours.

info@bloodhoundbooks.com

9 781913 942984